MACKENZY FOX

KNOX

BARREN RIDGE REBELS MC
BOOK 10

DEDICATION

For my readers, always x

AUTHOR NOTE

CONTENT WARNING: Knox is a steamy romance for readers 18+ it contains mature themes that may make some readers uncomfortable. It includes violence, mentions of domestic violence, religion and religious cults, stalking, coarse language…basically what the Bracken Ridge boys do best! And as always….LOTS of very spicy love scenes!

BLURB

KNOX

A new town.
A motorcycle club.
A brother and a sister I never knew about.
I thought I had a handle on my life, it turns out, I don't.
I came here to learn the truth. To start anew.
I didn't expect the red-headed woman at the bar with
the beautiful blue eyes.
Rebekah.
It was supposed to be one night.
A night of lust and passion with a stranger.
Then she turns up in Bracken Ridge.
And everything I thought I knew, turns upside down.
She moves me any which way she chooses.
I'm under her spell.
Powerless to stop it.
She's mine.
And I ain't running.

REBEKAH

I ran from my past.
From a religion I never chose.
From everything I thought I knew.
But my past caught up with me and I ran out of hiding places.
I didn't think I'd ever feel safe with anyone, much less a stranger.
We spent a drunken night together and now he's here.
My new boss.
And I can't stop looking at him.
He's tall. Broad. Masculine.
Everything a man should be.
But I have dark secrets.
If they came out, I risk losing the one thing that's good in my life.
The one man who listens, who cares about what I say, about me.
I've never had that.
And now I've had a taste, I want more.
Of him.
I want it all.

BRACKEN RIDGE
REBELS
ARIZONA
M · C

CHAPTER 1

KNOX

I stare at the man they call Steel.

My brother.

We share the same father, but the dead-beat died. And I've only just learned this information myself, finding out by chance when sorting through my father's things.

In truth, I wondered why he owned a small business in Bracken Ridge, left to my mom after his passing. I came here wanting answers and came up with a whole bunch of questions instead.

Jayson Steelman's a big, intimidating guy. He's tall as me, but wider. He has a strong face with a tense jaw and deep blue eyes. Eyes that give nothing away. Except he may want to kill me. That part I got loud and clear.

"Who the fuck are you?"

He might be hard of hearing, though, since I've already told him exactly who I am. I get this is weird.

"I'm your brother, Knox."

He frowns, his stance rigid, like he's getting ready for a fight. I didn't think it would come to this, but after finding out Jayson Steelman was the muscle for the local motorcycle club, I may just have to make a run for it. Somehow, my feet stay planted on the ground. I came here for answers, and I'm going to get them.

Before he can respond, a girl's voice calls out behind him. Then she comes running out of the clubhouse toward us.

"Steel?" she calls. "Sienna just told me…"

He gives me a distasteful look before turning to her. "Get the fuck back inside, Lil. I'm dealing with this!"

"Is it true?" she asks, halting when she reaches him, peering over his shoulder on her tiptoes.

"He's our brother?"

This is my sister?

"No, he isn't. Now listen for once in your life and do as I say."

She frowns, trying to push past him to get a better view, but he holds her shoulders so she can't move.

He's protective. Nothing wrong with that. I admire it, even.

"Steel! Let me go!"

A tanned, blonde-haired dude comes sauntering out and gives Steel a chin lift. "What's going on?"

"Will you take your woman back inside, Gunner. I've

had enough of her lip and not listenin'."

"I want to talk to him!" she explains. "It's not fair I get kept out of these things!"

"Fuck's sake," Steel mutters.

"Lily, let's go." Gunner eyes me cautiously, but steers her back toward the clubhouse, unwillingly.

Steel finally turns back to me.

"Fuckin' women," he grumbles. "Now, get to your point and do it fuckin' quickly 'cause the only dead-beat man I know as a 'father' was a no-good son of a bitch who's been dead for years."

I swallow hard. "Hank Steelman is my father. We lived in Phoenix. He came and went a lot for work. I never heard of Bracken Ridge, or knew about you. It was just me and my mom."

I reach into my inside jacket pocket and pull out a picture of me when I was about ten and hand it to him. "That's me and my pop."

Steel takes the photo and stares at it. It could just be me, but he seems to pale just a little bit. "All right, you've got my attention." He turns to the guy called Gears and the prospect on the gate and says, "Fuck off."

Gears shakes his head, and maybe I should've heeded his warning and left while I had the chance. Then again, I didn't come all the way out here to run away without any answers.

Yeah... this guy has a few traits that remind me of

Hank; they've got the same build, and he was a grumpy ass with a sharp tongue. Nothing pleased him. I don't know how my brother's temperament is, but hot tempers run in the family.

Steel looks back up at me. "Hank had a secret family?" I'm sure he's doing the math in his head. "How old are you?"

"Thirty." I'm guessing Steel is older than me, maybe thirty-five or six. "What about your sister?" Our sister.

"She's twenty-four." Steel palms the back of his head. "Fuck's sake."

"I'm sorry, man, for what it's worth."

"So, your mom only liked married men?"

My eyes go wide, and my blood starts to boil. "My mom had no idea Hank lived a double life." I stare at him and don't back down.

I can hold my own. Not that I'd want to start a fight with Steel, since that would be crazy. But if it comes down to it, I won't go down without giving it my best shot.

"How the fuck is that even possible?"

"I don't know, but he mastered it. I'm guessing your mom had no idea…"

"You'd guess right." Steel doesn't take his eyes off me. "He left when I was a teenager. Lily had just been born. The bastard didn't even stick around, not that we would've wanted that. He'd done enough irreparable damage to my mom and me. By then, I was old enough to knock him on his ass."

"Steel?" a man calls, walking up behind us.

We both turn.

"What's goin' on?"

The man's older, with long grey hair tied back. He's tall, solidly built, and probably in his mid-fifties. I can tell right away that he's somebody important. If not by the way two other men flank him, but by the way he holds himself and his eyes cut me like glass.

He must be their President.

"Nothin' I can't handle, Hutch."

Richie Hutchinson. I asked around about him. The people who told me where to find Jayson said that Hutch was a good man, but not a man to double cross.

The two other men hang back, eyeing me cautiously.

"Really? Because Gunner just came and told me this guy's saying he's your long-lost brother. Is that true?" The whole time this guy speaks, he looks right at me.

Steel palms the back of his head. "I don't know. He has a picture." Steel hands it to him.

"I'm Knox," I say, holding my hand out to shake his.

Hutch looks down at my hand and seems as unimpressed as Steel. "What the fuck?"

I take my hand away.

Clearly, they mean business.

"It seems Hank may have been living two lives," Steel mutters. "Would explain why he wasn't around much."

"I have a paternity test," I say, just in case there was any misunderstanding. "Maybe I can come back tomorrow. I didn't want to intrude…"

"Son, if this is some kinda hoax," Hutch says. "It won't go down well for you."

"It's no hoax. I came here because my mom recently…" I stop talking. My world spins.

My mom was my entire life. And now she's gone. I try to breathe. "She left something to me in her will. That's why I'm here."

"What did she leave?" Steel frowns.

"The Bracken Ridge Motel."

Everything goes quiet.

Then Hutch speaks. "How the fuck did she own that?" he barks. "I've been tryin' to buy that property for years."

"Must've put it in her name so we didn't get shit," Steel mutters.

I frown. I never looked at it like that.

"Hank never had a dime to rub together," Hutch says.

I fill them in. "My mom got an inheritance. Right before he passed away, he used her money to buy the business."

"No wonder it turned to shit," Steel says under his breath.

"So let me get this straight, you own the Bracken

Ridge Motel?"

I look him square in the eye. "Yep, that's what I'm saying."

"All that fucker left us was a mountain of debts and a bad name. My mom had to live with that for years," Steel barks, pointing at me like it's my fault. "And here he was, makin' money on the side, keepin' his new family in the life of luxury while we practically starved? I had three jobs by the time I was fifteen."

"It was hardly the lap of luxury. My mom worked as a cleaner. The motel income barely paid the overheads, much less our bills." Keep calm, I tell myself.

I'm not used to people pointing in my face and barking at me, and while I don't usually settle disagreements with my fists, I could easily be swayed otherwise.

"Lily was barely out of the womb when he split. She never knew him. Then he died and did us all a favor." I can see and feel the pain in his words.

I know. I've been there. Oh fuck, have I been there.

"He wasn't a nice person," I agree. "A bastard, if I'm being honest, but when I learned about you, I had to come and check it out. I had to see for myself. I never knew about our sister, though. It seems Hank kept us all in the dark."

"No big surprise there," Steel says.

Hutch places a hand on Steel's shoulder. Steel looks sideways at him. They share an unspoken understanding.

I don't know what happens in that moment, but Steel backs up, just for a fraction of a second.

I ran with a biker club many years ago; I know how it all works, but I haven't set foot inside an MC for a long time. Even though I've only been standing here for about five minutes, I can tell the club members have a lot of respect for their Prez.

That says something.

I don't know a lot about this club, only that Hutch has been here since the beginning, and that they aren't a one percenter club. All the bikers I've ever known were criminals, the pits of society who knew how to do very bad shit and do it well.

I never really cared for living life on the fly, always looking over my shoulder and being the shit kicker. It was no life. Neither was my stint in prison, which was something I probably needed when I was younger. It set me on the straight and narrow to do better, be better.

I never wanted to end up like my father, which is why I haven't touched the bottle since I got out of prison.

If I ended up like him, I may as well end it all then.

"If it makes you feel any better, my mom would've been horrified if she'd known."

Steel frowns. "If she'd known?"

I clear my throat. Shit. Why the fuck do I open my big mouth? I've been told I'm too fucking honest, too fucking nice. I didn't come here for a pity party. I came here to find out who the fuck these people are, and why my dead-beat dad never mentioned any of them?

I feel the bile rise in my throat.

Should I feel lucky that my mom never knew? It would have only caused her more heartache and she'd suffered enough.

I've made peace with it long ago. I let the demons out during my adolescence, and for my mom's sake, I'm sorry. It wasn't her fault she fell in love with a man who enjoyed inflicting misery on everybody he came into contact with. It also wasn't her fault that I took my rage out on everybody else.

"She died," I say. "About three months ago."

"I'm sorry," says Hutch. "That must have been very hard for you."

"It was," I reply. "And that's when I learned about the motel and, subsequently, my brother."

Steel clears his throat. "We'll set up a meetin' after the weekend, so we can talk more privately."

I guess it's the best I can hope for.

"All right."

Hutch hands me a card. Glancing down at it, it reads:

Richie Hutchinson

President - Bracken Ridge Rebels MC

I flip it over; his cell is on the back.

My lips twitch.

Old school, gotta respect that.

"Give me a call Sunday," he says.

"Yes, Sir."

He turns to Steel. "We good?"

Steel keeps a watch of me, like I may jump him any moment, and he wants to be ready for it. "Yes."

I give him a chin lift and he narrows his eyes.

I don't think he likes me.

I'd be suspicious too, I get it. Rocking up to someone's clubhouse and dropping a bombshell like this. I don't even know where to fucking begin. But at least Hutch didn't tell me to fuck off, not that I would have. I've nothing to lose, and at least he listened and didn't chew my head off. I know how bikers can get being on their turf. And it seems, my presence wasn't exactly good news.

I give them a chin lift and then turn to leave, walking back to my truck, which is parked by the sidewalk.

The gates shut firmly behind me.

I take a few deep breaths, run both hands through my hair, and start my truck. Driving away down the deserted road, I head back toward town.

I don't know what kind of reception I was hoping for, but I'm sure that wasn't it.

Maybe I've watched too many 'find my family' videos, but I'm sure as fuck there ain't gonna be a happy ending where Jayson Steelman is concerned. He's cautious, and I get that, but I'm the result of our father's cheating and lying. It's not like I had a choice in the matter.

In my heart, I suppose I hoped he'd be glad when he got over the initial shock. That maybe he'd show me around the clubhouse and talk for a while.

Nope.

Steel doesn't seem to want to get to know me, but maybe Lily might.

I drive back to the motel, unsure what to do next and how I break the news to my new 'brother' and 'sister' that I'm here to stay. I got nowhere else to go.

When I sold my mom's house to clear the medical debts she had, it only left me with the motel, and zero left to do any repairs.

I count my lucky stars; I've got a place to live and a very small income.

When I got here, I admit, I thought it would be in better shape.

Everything has seen better days. I dread to think what I'd find if I look a little closer. It's a shame, as it's in a prime location near the local pub—also owned by the biker club— which sits on the same street.

If I had a little bit of cash, it could clean up really nice. With twenty-five rooms and a pool, broken but a decent size, plus a dilapidated tennis court, it has potential.

If only.

I just need a spare fifty grand to get started. I snort to myself.

Fuck, if I had that much spare cash, I doubt I'd plunge it into the Bracken Ridge Motel. Even the sign is hanging on by a thread.

"I've been tryin' to buy that property for years."

It gives me an idea. I mean, the club would have the cash, but it would mean selling a hefty share. Then again, I can't do much with a broken motel. I'm surprised it hasn't been shut down before now, and selling rooms for thirty bucks a night isn't exactly raking in the coin. It'll keep my head above water, but there are still staff to pay.

The office manager seems very lazy. We've already had a run-in, and I doubt she's gonna stick around. For some reason, actually working isn't in her vocabulary. I guess having nobody come check on you, aside from my lazy ass dad who died years ago, makes you complacent. I need to put an advert in the paper.

The cleaners seem decent enough; they can only work with what they got. Can polish as much as they like, but a turd ain't gonna get any shinier. It's still a fuckin' turd.

I need to make a decision, and fast.

Walk away now, before the ship goes down. Or take a chance and go ahead with my crazy plans.

I know it's prime real estate. I could sell it and keep the

cash, set up some place else.

Where I would go, I've no idea. I'm glad to see the back end of the city though.

I came here knowing that my sibling, or should I say siblings, may not want to get to know me, and that would be awkward in a small town. But until I get some scratch together, I ain't going nowhere.

BRACKEN RIDGE
REBELS
ARIZONA
M · C
M · C

CHPATER 2

REBEKAH
TWO MONTHS AGO – PHOENIX

I sit at the bar, not intending to get completely shit-faced, but it is happy hour after all, and I've had a long, crappy day.

My boss was riding my ass all day at the tire place I work. It's like he has it in for me, all because he's a jerk who likes to leer and make crude jokes loud enough for me to hear. Men. I am done.

I run a hand through my hair and take another sip of my cocktail of the day. I don't even remember what it's called, just that it tastes like raspberry lemonade and has a lot of vodka in it.

"Can I buy you a drink?" I hear a voice as a man sidles up to my right.

He looks a little worse for wear, his suit jacket wrinkled, his shirt open at the neck and his tie loose.

"Uh, no, thank you. I'm good."

He sits down on the stool next to me as I turn away.

"Haven't seen you around here," he goes on. "I would've remembered."

Oh God, no.

What part about no do some of these douchebags not understand?

I know engaging with him will only encourage him, so I take a sip of my drink and try to ignore him. Surely, he'll go away and find someone else to slobber over.

It's the hair.

It's flame red and hangs long down my back.

Yes, I dye it. I wasn't born this way.

Growing up Amish, I never dyed my hair when I was younger, not until I ran away from home and never went back. I never wanted to be reminded of the person I used to be back then and how much I kept inside because I couldn't express myself.

My father was very abusive, something he told us was for our own good; he called it discipline. If you call being whipped when you misbehaved 'discipline,' and my mother couldn't do a thing about it. She suffered the worst.

I think about my life back then, and it feels like it was some distant dream. Did that really happen?

The douchebag I'm trying to ignore orders me another cocktail, even though I've already turned him down, and he proceeds to try to talk to me again.

I happen to be a black belt in taekwondo, so if he keeps

it up, I'm gonna kick his ass.

Why do men do this? Why do I have to pretend to be nice just so he'll fuck off and leave me alone? Can he not take a hint?

Strike one.

"…Texas?" he says, as I frown.

"What?" I realize I've missed what the hell he was even saying.

"I said I'm good at predicting where people are from, and I think you're from Texas."

Strike two.

"Let me guess?" I say, not even bothering to hide the smirk on my face. "It's the hair?"

He claps his hands together. "You got it! What part of Texas are you from?"

"I'm not from Texas, I'm from Ohio."

He frowns, then looks me up and down. "For real?"

Strike fucking three.

"Dear God, get me out of here," I mutter.

The bartender eyes him warily. I know exactly how he feels because I'm two seconds away from punching his lights out.

I look over his shoulder, and I see a guy sitting at the end of the bar, quietly nursing a beer.

The first thing I notice is his brilliant blue eyes as our gazes meet. He's got short, brownish hair and a slightly cropped beard. He has a warm, handsome face. The black shirt he's wearing is open at the neck and his sleeves are rolled up to the elbows.

I guess you could say I like the quiet, brooding type, not like the man sitting next to me. I look away.

The annoying man whips out his credit card to pay for my unwanted drink when I say, "I already have a drink, and I said no to the first one."

"A pretty woman like you shouldn't be drinking alone," he tells me, his eyes wandering down to linger on my chest. I'm sure he's got a tiny dick.

I snort. "Maybe I want to be drinking alone. Maybe I'm sick of douchebags like you who don't fucking listen when a woman says no. No means no, asshole."

He holds his palms up. "Jesus, sorry for trying to be a nice guy."

I roll my eyes. "Right."

This is the type of guy I used to attract. No good losers.

I just don't get jerks like this who think leering at you and staring at your breasts is going to somehow win you over.

"Probably can't fuck anyway," he mutters. "Probably frigid."

Charming.

"Is he giving you some trouble?"

I look up, and the dude from the end of the bar is

towering over me, glaring down at the man.

"It's okay," I say, waving the jerk off with one hand. "I was about to leave anyway."

It's then I see the logo on his shirt. What's the name of this bar again?

He nods to the bartender. "He's had enough."

"Hey!" the man protests. "You can't do that!"

He gets right up in his face. "I'm security here, and I can do any-fucking-thing I like." He hauls him by the shirt and yanks him out of his chair. "Now get out of here quietly, or I'll take you outside, and you don't wanna know what happens after that."

The size difference between the two is evident now the jerk is off his stool. Security guy is huge, solid with large biceps, and he didn't have a menacing face until he came over here. He went from beautiful to brute in all of two seconds.

The guy holds up his hands. "I don't want any trouble."

"Then fuck off and don't come back," Security guy snarls.

He heads to the exit swiftly and disappears out the door.

I'm still staring at the hot security guy. "Thanks," I say. "But I did kinda have it under control."

He looks down at me sceptically. He must be at least six-five... and that broad chest... those beautiful blue eyes...

Holy hell.

"You can never have it fully under control with drunk perverts like that."

I purse my lips with a smile. "That's true. Long gone are the days where a woman can have a quiet drink at a bar without some dick thinking they're out looking to pick up."

"None of my business what people do, but a woman also has a right to feel safe, even at a bar."

My heart does a little leap in my chest. Who is this freaking saint?

I nod over to his half-drunk beer. "You drink on the job?"

One corner of his mouth turns up, assuming that's the best smile I'm gonna get.

"I just clocked off." He gives me another chin lift and starts to walk off.

"Hey?" I call after him, and he turns around. "What's your name?"

His lips part, and I swear I almost see God. This man is gorgeous.

"Knox."

"I'm Rebekah, but my friends call me Bekah."

His lips twitch. "We're friends now?"

"Well, we're not complete strangers. I know your name and where you work." I shrug. "And I know you're not married."

"Why do I look not married?"

I glance down at his hand. "No wedding ring."

"Maybe I don't wear it to work."

I shake my head. "There's no white ring around the skin, dead giveaway."

His eyes dance with amusement. "You're a cheeky little thing, Rebekah."

"It's just Bekah. We're friends, remember?" I have no idea why the blood is pounding in my ears. Maybe because this is a man I am attracted to and would actually want to pick me up, if I were that way inclined.

I'm sure it was only this morning I told myself I was done with men and I'm never dating anyone again. Still, a girl's head can be turned. I wish I could stop staring at him. He's a bouncer, but he shouldn't be this gorgeous. All the bouncers I've ever seen are brutes; they don't look like this. And they certainly don't come to a woman's aid when she may be in trouble.

"What's a nice girl like you doing in a bar like this?" Knox asks. Oh, he's got that one eyebrow arch going on that makes my stomach do little flips.

"You work here." I laugh. "And it's not that bad."

"Weekdays are fairly tame," he agrees. "But on weekends, it's like the Wild West."

He leans his hand on the bar, and I cannot take my eyes off him.

"So do you rescue women from unpleasant situations very often?"

"More often than you'd think. Where men and alcohol are concerned. Then again, even some of the women get a little rowdy when they've had too much to drink."

"Sounds like you've seen it all."

"I've been out on the town for a while," he says. "I've seen the good, the bad, and the ugly."

He's warm, I realize. There's something about him that's captivating. Not just sexually or that he has a nice face and perfect lips that I wouldn't mind testing how soft they are, but he just seems so sweet. Something radiates off him that I've not seen in a long time. I feel instantly safe with him.

I've not felt that since I was back home with my cousin Daniel. He left the Amish just before I did, right after his brother Elijah committed suicide. He couldn't deal with it, none of us could. When I felt like I couldn't take any more, I ran away and got involved with the wrong crowd. I guess you could say that's the story of my life.

Trouble always seems to find me.

I wonder if Knox is trouble…

"I'm sure you have. Alcohol does bring out the worst in people, which is why I limit myself. That jerk asked me if I wanted a drink and I said no, but he still decided to buy me one anyway." I push the cocktail away. I don't want it.

"Which is why I kicked him out. Like I said, you have a right to feel safe, no matter where you are. It was nice to meet you, Reb…" I hold up a finger, and he smirks. "Bekah."

I smile back. "It was nice to meet you too." I don't want him to go, but I don't want to be desperate. "Have you eaten yet?" I blurt out.

He stops in his tracks, for the second time tonight. The look he gives me is mixed with confusion and, if I'm not mistaken, a little bit of intrigue. "Nope, I usually pick up something on the way home."

"There's a great little diner around the corner," I say. "Serves food till late. It has the best…"

"Chili dogs and curly fries in town?"

A smile erupts on my face. "Yes, actually."

"I know the place, Francine's."

So, we eat the same food at the same restaurant, that's gotta mean something. Or maybe he just has good tastebuds, like me. "I'm not picking you up," I say, my cheeks flushing. "Just so we're clear."

"Right, because we're friends. And friends can't cross that line."

I pick up my coat from the back of my chair. "Unless I'm a bad friend." I smile, strutting past him to the door, making sure I rock my hips when I walk.

I don't wait for him to catch up. I only hope I haven't

made an idiot of myself.

A few moments later, the door opens again, and he appears, shrugging his arms into his leather jacket. "Not safe for a lady to be out here at this time of night."

"You're big on safety." With my back to him, I smile. Relieved.

He comes to stand by my side. I'm tall myself, five-ten, but he literally looks larger than life now that we're alone. He doesn't give off creeper vibes, I feel at ease with him.

My instincts are something I trust wholeheartedly.

"My mama taught me well," he replies, looking down at me, giving me a crooked smile.

"What are you, six-four? Five?"

"Five."

"I can see why they get you to work security."

We start walking in the direction of Francine's. "Because of my rugged good looks?" he jokes.

"Aside from that, obviously, you are kinda intimidating."

"It's just because I'm big. Underneath, I'm really a big pussycat."

All I can picture is how big he is somewhere else.

My mouth feels dry.

"Well, you're very convincing." I turn to look up at him, his hands shoved in his jacket pockets. We're on the cusp of the end of fall and the beginning of winter.

The winters here aren't all that bad. We rarely get snowfall, and if we do, it's never very heavy.

"So, you don't usually ask strange men to dine with you?"

"Never. But you look like you might need a good meal."

He balks. "Are you trying to say I look underfed?"

I shake my head. "No, but when you said you usually pick something up on the way home, I figured that you don't cook."

"It's true, I don't."

"I love cooking," I say. I don't add that back when I was Amish, I had no choice but to be glued to the kitchen. All I wanted to do was go out into the field, and do what my brothers and cousins were doing. I wanted to work outside, amongst the machinery and the crop. But women aren't allowed to do that in our community. They're in the kitchen, cleaning, doing the washing, taking care of the day-to-day chores, and without electricity and running water.

I hug myself with both arms.

I don't like thinking back to those times. It makes me miss Daniel way too much.

"You do?"

"Yes, I've always been good at it… we… I had a big family, so I learned young. My grandma had a lot of amazing recipes that had been passed down through the years." No way I'm telling him about my awkward upbringing, but he can read between the lines.

"Can't say the same. I'm an only child, and I don't have any cousins I'm close to."

"You're not missing out on much," I tell him. "Though I did have a cousin I was close to, but he moved away. He was like a big brother, really. He looked out for me and made sure I was okay. I miss him."

"You don't see him at all?"

I'm about to blurt out that I ran away, but I barely know this guy. Why do I feel compelled to tell him my life story?

"No, we lost touch, and he doesn't have social media that I can gather," I reply. "So, I've not been able to track him down."

"That's a shame, especially if you got along so well."

The pain hurts my heart. I was closer to Elijah and Daniel than my own brothers. They were different. Their father was also strict, but not cruel, not like my father. I often dreamed I was a part of their family and not my own.

"I still look for him everywhere I go, but it's been years," I admit, surprised at how easy it is to say. Normally when I think of Daniel, I tear up easily, and I don't want to talk about him to total strangers. Again, the feeling that we've met before or that he's familiar just washes over me and I feel lighter than I have in a long time.

He's nice to be around.

"That's too bad. Maybe one day, you'll just run into him."

"I doubt it. I come from Ohio."

"Nice, I went there once on a school trip."

"You did?"

He laughs. "Yep. It's old country out in the sticks. Sometimes you forget how people live out in the country. Everything in the city is so fast-paced, and the people are… kinda rude, most of the time, anyway. They walk around with their heads down, typing on their phones and being disconnected from everyone. Having a conversation is a luxury these days. Now you don't even have to talk to someone to order food or pay for your groceries."

This boy is old school, and my little Amish girl likes it.

"Who'd have thought we'd be shopping on mobile phones fifteen years ago?" I agree.

"Watch your step," he says as we round the corner, and I trip over an uneven paver under my feet. He grabs me by the elbow so I don't fall. Even though my arm is covered by my coat, I feel a jolt of electricity where he touches me. Holy shit.

His eyes meet mine and, for a fraction of a second, I get lost in his depths. Swept away to another world. His warmth, his charm, his politeness. He's the whole freaking package.

I think I have a crush on my rescuer.

"Crap, I'm a klutz," I swear, steadying myself before he lets go of my elbow.

He glances down at my shoes. I'm wearing high-heeled boots; not practical, but they're sexy as hell. I paired my shoes with a black leather skirt and a fitted warm top, now covered by my parka.

"How do you walk in those?" He frowns, looking down at my feet.

"Easy, you should try dancing in them."

He chuckles. "I don't think I'd be good at either of those things."

"No?"

"Two left feet."

"Ah."

We stop outside Francine's.

It's a sweet little bistro with white and red tablecloths and booths that remind me of a forgotten era. I guess deep down I do like old things and it's a little nostalgic.

He pushes the door open and says, "Ladies first."

I smile, ducking under in his arm as we make our way inside.

It's late, so it's not crowded, and we take a seat in a nearby booth.

"I can't believe you know about the chili dog and curly fries," I say, shrugging out of my jacket as I make myself comfortable. "I've told a dozen people about this place, and not one of them has ever heard of it."

"City people," he says. "They probably pass it every day

on the way to work, but they're too busy on social media to bother with looking at the world going on around them."

"I take it you have no social media?" I bite my lip.

"Absolutely not…" He stops midway, his eyes glancing down at my mouth as that feeling washes through me again. I'm turned on completely by this man.

He's fucking gorgeous, and he likes to talk. I didn't think men like this existed.

Play it cool, bozo, or you'll blow it.

I know what I'd like to be blowing, but I don't want him to think that I just pick guys up in bars. Even if I did tell jerk face to take a hike.

He clears his throat. "I hate fake news. None of that shit on Facebook is real. People only show you what they want you to see."

He does have a point. "Tell me about it. The amount of people I know who are unhappy with their relationships, but continue to post cuddly selfies together where life seems perfect, just astounds me."

Jane, a server I know too well, comes over to take our order.

"Hello, Bekah." She turns to me. "Oh, hi… Knox."

I roll my lips and feel like face palming myself.

Knox smiles, and I'm almost blown away. Suddenly, I feel a surge of jealousy.

I want to be the one to make him smile like that, to

make his eyes light up. Not Jane.

Poor Jane. I don't even know the girl well, and I went from thinking she was really sweet to wanting to stab her with her pencil for something trivial like taking Knox's order.

"Hi, Jane," we both chorus at the same time.

She looks from him to me and starts to chuckle. "Aww, is this a first date? Because if it is, you're already speaking at the same time. Next, you'll be finishing each other's sentences."

My eyes go wide.

"Yes, we are actually," Knox says. "She suggested this cute little bistro that serves the best chili dogs and curly fries in town, and what do you know, we both found out we love the same food."

She giggles. "Too cute, so two chili dogs with curly fries. A Diet Coke for Bekah and a mineral water for you."

"Got it in one."

"Thanks, Jane," I say as she takes our menus and skips back to the kitchen.

When mine and Knox's eyes meet, we can't help but laugh.

"A bit of a coincidence?" I say, trying not to let my pounding heart get the better of me. "That we both know Jane, our favorite server."

"There are no such things as coincidences."

I don't know if he feels the electricity between us, but I feel it right between my legs.

His lips part, and my eyes dart down instinctively.

I can't even blame the damn alcohol. Nope, this is all on me.

BRACKEN RIDGE
REBELS
ARIZONA
M. C.

CHAPTER 3

KNOX

She's fucking beautiful.

I can't stop staring at her. Each time I think I can get away with it, she flicks her hazel eyes toward me, and I just about have a heart attack.

"There isn't?"

I shake my head. "Nope."

"Then tell me something?"

I lean forward instinctively, my elbows on the table. "Okay."

"How come you've been eating here for all this time, and we've never met?"

"I confess, I usually only eat here during the day," I say. "So our paths would never have crossed at this time of night."

I nod, like I'm taking in every word when the reality is, she's got me spellbound.

Her hair, that's the first thing I noticed at the bar, because it's not like you can miss it. Bright red, it hangs just below her shoulders and makes her pale skin and hazel eyes pop. Her face… she's fucking beautiful. High cheekbones, minimal makeup with flushed cheeks. I don't know if it's from the cold or if it's from our back-and-forth flirting. I'd like to think the latter, but it's been a while since I've been with a woman.

Since I've been taking care of my mom until she passed away last month, I haven't had the time or energy for women. Having an adult conversation was a stretch, so getting naked was definitely not on the cards.

But she's got me hard, and that's a problem, because I didn't bring her here to fuck her after, not that it wouldn't be nice. But I'm not that guy. I was serious when I said that I was looking out for her. As stupid as it sounds, I am the kind of guy who puts a drunk girl in the back of cab to make sure she gets home safely.

My mom suffered at the hands of a bad man, and I never want any woman to be subjected to that if I can see it happening. Even when I don't know the person.

It's caused some issues at work because there are some real fucking jerks out there. I like to think of it as my own private mission to keep women safe on my watch. That makes me feel a little better about the shitty world we live in.

"It's a shame," I say, though I don't know why. I could

slap myself.

Her eyes dart to mine, and her lips part. "Are you flirting with me, Knox?"

I grin. "If I were, Red, then you'd fucking know."

She swallows hard, and I sit back in my seat, satisfied.

"Red?" she coos. "I already have a nickname; we're creeping up to that 'just friends' line again."

I laugh. "It's not like I can help it, Bekah. You're a beautiful woman, I'm not blind."

Okay, so I'm flirting. I didn't come here with the intention of sex on my brain, but now it's all I can think about. To lose myself for the night with someone like Bekah. Fuck me.

I need some cold water…

Reaching for the pitcher, my fingers brush hers, and I realize we did the same thing at the same time.

She laughs again. "Coincidence?"

I shake my head. "Nope, but it is kinda hot in here." She can take that any which way she wants.

I start to pour her glass first.

"Maybe you should start taking some clothes off," she says, biting her lip again. Yep, she's feeling it too.

My eyes flick to hers. She has a cheeky look on her face, like she knows she's playing with fire, but she enjoys stoking the flames. Oh, sweetheart, I can poke all fucking night.

"Now who's flirting with who?" I pour my own glass,

set the jug down, and down half a glass in a few seconds.

"Touché, but you started it, coming over to kick that asshole out. That was kinda hot."

I want to reach under the table and adjust my dick, but that would be too obvious. It's straining for room in my pants.

"Well, I didn't do it to be hot, I did it because he was harassing you when you'd said no." My face is serious. I don't joke about this kind of thing.

"But still, chicks must hit on you all the time."

That's a whole can of worms.

I deflect and say, "You think you can walk into a bar looking like that and not draw a man's attention."

"I like certain men looking," she says, tucking a lock of hair behind her ear. "Just not assholes."

"Glad I don't fall into that category, then."

"You definitely don't."

Our drinks arrive.

"On the heavy stuff?" Bekah notes, nodding to my mineral water.

"I don't drink very often, and I don't like soda. Too much sugar."

She groans. "Are you one of those health nuts?"

I balk, almost choking on my drink. "Health nuts?"

"Yeah, like that type who drinks green smoothies and only eats organically grown food."

I laugh. I don't think a woman has made me laugh as much as she has in this short space of time. "I'm definitely not one of those."

"But you work out?"

Working out is my life. "You noticed?"

She gives me a look that tells me she wants me in bed. "Oh, I noticed."

I lean closer to her. "You gotta stop that, Red."

"Stop what?"

"Flirting with me."

"Why would I stop? Don't you like it?"

This fucking woman. "Didn't say that, but you know where this is headed if you keep looking at me like that."

"Like what?" She gives me that look again.

"Like that."

"I can't help it." She shrugs. "I like you."

My throat thickens. I don't know how I'm going to sit through this meal and not push everything off the table and drag her across it into my lap. Her riding me… fuck yeah.

I want to do the right thing; walk her home and tell her goodnight, not because I'm a saint, but because I don't presume anything. But she's the one coming onto me, flirting, making me smile, and even fucking laugh—which I've not done a lot of lately—and she's so easy to be around. We'd have fun for sure.

Her body is as divine as the rest of her.

She's got a nice round ass, curvy hips, and legs that go on for days.

I'd love to have them wrapped around me while I fuck her up against the wall. Or on my kitchen bench. Or the stairs. Or my bed. Everywhere, I want to fuck her everywhere.

"I like you too, but I didn't come here expecting…" I palm the back of my neck.

"Sex?" she finishes.

"Yes, sex."

She leans across and puts her hand over mine. "You're a really sweet guy, Knox, I can tell. I know that's not your style, just as I know that you're not an asshole or a womanizer."

"You know a lot."

She shrugs. "I have good instincts. Besides, I'm a black belt."

There goes my shit-eating grin again. "You are? In what?"

She nods. "Yup, taekwondo So, I bet I'd be pretty good at kicking your ass if you didn't behave."

"I won't tell you now that I'm a champion kickboxer," I say as her eyes go round, and I laugh. "Imagining you kicking my ass, though, that is a sight I'd like to see."

She doesn't take her hand away. Her thumb strokes mine as I almost shoot my load in my jeans like a fucking teenager.

"I'm not usually like this," she whispers, looking around. "And I don't want to seem like I'm being forward…"

Wait, what is she doing?

"Do you want to get the check?" I finish for her.

She smiles again, and her whole face lights up. She nods. "Yes, if you do."

"Is that a trick question?" I don't wait for her reply.

I stand to go find Jane and get her to make our meals to go. A few minutes later, I return with our dinner in a paper bag. I throw money in the middle of the table and move to stand as she slides out of the booth. Holding out my hand, she slips her hand in mine.

This is so fucking hot.

Without any more words, we leave the diner and go back out into the cold.

My heart is racing when I ask, "Your place or mine?"

"Which is closer?" she pants.

"I'm on Fifth and Elm."

"I'm on 22nd and Fischer."

"Mine's closer," I say, just as she tells me the same thing.

I grin again. "We really are finishing each other's sentences already."

She shakes her head, smiling as we take off up the street. We're only a few minutes' walk away from my apartment. Kicking myself that I didn't tidy up and I've got boxes everywhere because I'm moving, I push that thought aside. None of it matters because soon she'll be wrapped around me.

The minute we get to my apartment building, I turn to face her. "Are you sure about this? I mean, you can back out if you want to."

She frowns. "Are you changing your mind?"

My heart thuds in my chest. "Not a chance."

She presses her free hand into my chest. "Take me to bed, Knox. Hurry."

Fuck.

I key in the wrong pin three times to get into the apartment building. Finally getting it right, I yank her behind me as I stab at the elevator button repeatedly, impatiently waiting for the doors to open.

The minute they do, we get inside, the doors close, and I drop the food bag. I back her up against the elevator wall. "Last chance, Red. You're a beautiful woman, and I want to put my mouth, my hands, and my cock over every inch of your body, so tell me now if you're still good with that."

I must have her consent. Fuck, I hope she still says yes.

Caging her in, I don't touch her until she says what I need to hear.

She runs her hands up my abs, around my ribs, and grabs my ass, pulling me closer to her so my cock presses into her stomach. "I want all of what you just said," she murmurs. "Kiss me, Knox. I need your mouth on me."

I grin, cupping her face with both hands as my lips meet hers, and there's a whole new world waiting for me there.

We're hot and heavy from the get-go. My tongue is in her mouth, and she reciprocates, moaning as I push my cock farther into her stomach, relishing in the noises she's making. I move one hand down to cup her breast as I nip her bottom lip with my teeth.

She bucks under my touch as I squeeze a good handful of one breast, eager to get all her clothes off.

I turn around to check the floor numbers. It's so fucking slow.

"This thing better hurry up," I grunt, turning back to her. "Or I'm gonna fuck you in this damn elevator."

She wraps her arms around my neck as I lift her, her legs circling my waist, and her skirt rucks up around her hips. I want to devour this woman, give her the best night of her life. Take her body and give her pleasure in return. I want her so fucking bad. I can't remember the last time I felt like this. I'm so desperate to be inside her.

If this elevator doesn't get to my floor soon, I'm definitely gonna pull my dick out right here and screw away the consequences.

Luckily, my floor dings and, with her still attached, I exit, grabbing the bag of food from the floor as I pass.

We kiss all the way to my door. I awkwardly fiddle with the key jammed in my back pocket as I press her up against my door, trying desperately to get inside so I don't give my neighbors dinner and a show.

Once inside, I drop the poor food again and push her up against the door. Pressing my cock against her pussy. I bet it's fucking dripping wet.

Out of nowhere, my dog, who hasn't even bothered to greet me or see who the stranger in the apartment is, yawns loudly and Bekah's eyes go wide.

I laugh. "It's just my dog, Evie."

She peers over my shoulder but Evie is buried in a large, squishy pillow on the floor. It's like a giant marshmallow. "She's not much of a guard dog."

I turn back to face her. "Do I need protecting?"

She smirks and pulls me to her as our lips crash once more.

"You're a very sexy woman, Red," I tell her. "Look what you've done to me."

I grab her wrist and place her hand on my cock as she gasps. She fondles me, and I close my eyes. Fuck. Fuck. Fuck.

"You're so hard," she groans as I move my mouth down her neck, biting and nipping as she groans. "And so big."

"I need your clothes off. Now," I grunt as she unwraps her legs and slides down my body until her feet are on the floor.

"You first," she breathes, struggling to get the words out.

I keep my eyes on her as I kick my boots off, wrestle out of my jeans, and pull my t-shirt off. I leave my boxer briefs till last.

She glances down my body. "My God, you're beautiful," she whispers. "Your cock…"

"Touch it," I demand. If she doesn't touch it soon, I might have a heart attack.

She reaches for me, slipping her hand under the elastic as she squeezes me and frees my cock from its enclosure, but it isn't enough, so she yanks my boxers down to my thighs. Grabbing my cock, she starts to stroke me.

I move and tug her jacket off, then I pull her top out from the waistband of her skirt and slide it over her head. Reaching to cup her breasts I glance down and a groan leaves my throat. Her tits are perfect. I can see her erect nipples peeking out through the black lace as I rub both thumbs over them.

"Knox!" she cries. "Oh…"

I cup the back of her head as our lips crash together again. One hand kneading her breast as she continues to fondle my dick.

"You're fucking beautiful," I growl, our tongues colliding as I pull the cup of her bra down so I can feel her skin. I push her back against the door and drop my head to her exposed breast, covering her nipple with my mouth as

I release the other. I suck as one hand reaches into my hair, tugging at my roots as she still fists me with the other, and I think I'm going to die from need.

What is this woman doing to me?

We're insatiable with each other as I play with her nipples, my mouth moving to the other one as she closes her eyes and groans out, "Fuuuuuck."

I need to taste her. I stand suddenly, holding out my hand as she folds hers into mine. My apartment isn't big, and I'm at least glad I made my bed this morning.

I pad naked as she follows behind, still in her boots and skirt with her tits hanging out of her bra, and I push her down on the bed.

"Spread your legs," I tell her.

I kneel down on the carpet as she does what I say, moving my hands to her boots and unzipping them, then pull them off one at a time and throw them behind me.

I shove her skirt up, my eyes meeting hers as I start kissing the inside of her thighs, working my way upward. I haven't even touched her pussy yet, and judging by the way her breathing is becoming all the more rapid, I know she's dying for me to do just that.

Reaching between her legs, I touch her lightly. Feeling how damp she is there makes me want to rip her panties off with my teeth. Fucking goddess that she is.

"Yes," she whispers, throwing her head back as I swipe

my tongue over the lace. She shudders under my touch.

"Watch me, Red," I mutter. "Watch me eat your pussy."

"You're really gonna…"

I slide her panties down her legs carefully. It'd be rude to rip them in half.

"Yeah, I'm really gonna…"

Something tells me she's not used to this, which is such a shame. Being between her legs is an absolute privilege, and I won't take it for granted.

Keeping her skirt on, I shove it higher, pushing her legs wider as I see her in all her glory. She's bare, and fucking soaked. I groan, moving my mouth to her slit as I tongue her all the way from her hole to her clit.

She cries out, trying to close her legs, but I push them open and hold her at the knees as she tries to move her hips. I know she needs friction, and it fucking turns me on that I'm denying her that. She tastes like fucking paradise.

I do it again, swirling around her clit as she grips my head harder, my tongue working her over and over, teasing her. Parting her with one hand, I suck her clit into my mouth, and she almost bucks off the bed. I want her first pleasure on my tongue. I want it all.

I insert a finger inside her hot, swollen pussy, and she whimpers, her short pants coming in faster. As I suck and finger her at the same time, she lets go, crying out as she flutters her release against my tongue. I've never heard such a sweet sound as her body shudders beneath me.

I lap her up as she squirms, her back arching off the bed as I ride her through it.

"Fuck me," she cries. "Knox, I need you inside me. Please."

How can I deny the cries of a sexy woman splayed out on my bed with her legs spread wide. I grin, taking off her skirt as I toss it aside.

I lay down on top of her, pressing a kiss to her lips so she can taste herself. "You've got me so damn hard, Red; my whole body is on fire for you."

"Give it to me," she whispers softly. "I need you."

I swallow hard, pushing off her as I get up and go to the nightstand. Taking out a rubber, ripping the foil off with my teeth, I give my dick several slow pulls as I roll it on. She watches me, lying back on her elbows, her eyes all over my body as they finally settle on my dick.

I pull her to me, flipping her over and onto her knees. I smack her ass lightly as she jumps.

"Such a beautiful body, Bekah," I grunt, still sheathing myself. "Your pussy is so fucking sweet. I can't wait to bury myself inside you."

She releases a guttural groan as I line up my cock and run it through her folds, making her gasp. I love how responsive she is to my touch. She wants this as much as I do.

"Knox…" she cries. "Oh…yes, yes, that's it."

"You're a bad girl," I tell her. "Flirting with me, wearing fuck-me boots, and inviting me out for my favorite food while acting all innocent. What are you doing to me?"

"Hurry, I need your cock…"

Those words. Those fucking words.

"Impatient." I chuckle, shifting so I'm lined up with her entrance. As I slide in, we both groan. I slide out and do it again, slowly, even I'm surprised at my level of control. It's a battle between fucking her stupid and taking my sweet time. I can't have both.

"For you, I am," she whispers.

Fuck, she's so hot.

I squeeze one ass cheek, and she groans again. Sliding out and moving back in, I thrust a little faster this time. Running one hand up her back, I grip her hair as she calls my name. It's like an angel calling to me. Making me wicked. Making me want to lose all self-control.

Around her, it seems I don't have much left.

I speed up as she pushes back against me. Watching my cock disappear inside her pussy is such a sweet sight.

I don't want to come fast, but I can't help it. It's been a while, and I'm so turned on that I know I'm gonna keep her up all night.

Our skin starts to slap as I thrust harder, resting my hands by the side of her arms as I give it to her full tilt. My balls slap against her as she makes sounds that make me wanna spank that ass till it's raw.

"I'm… oh God… I'm coming… Knox…" She lets go as I pump with everything I have, riding her through it as she curses and pushes against me until I'm shouting my own release.

Knox

BRACKEN RIDGE
REBELS
ARIZONA
M · C

CHPATER 4

AEBEHAH

He pulls out, discards the condom, and rolls me over, looming over the top of me as I reach up to hold his face.

His eyes, they're so beautiful that I just stare at him, dumbfounded.

"You all right?" he asks, looking down at me.

"Perfect," I whisper.

"I wasn't too rough?"

"You have a big cock, Knox," I say, reaching between his legs. "I'm gonna feel the repercussions of that tomorrow, but right now, I want you so fucking much. Your body should be illegal."

"Yours should be," he scoffs. "But I spanked you without asking."

"You don't have to ask. I liked it."

"Still." His face looks grave.

"You're big on consent, aren't you?"

"Any decent man should be."

My heart skips a beat. Again, I'm reminded how sweet he is, and it warms my heart and makes me melt in his arms.

It makes me wonder why most men aren't like this, and they certainly don't make sure your needs are cared for before theirs. Very rarely, in fact. Sometimes in the past, I've felt like drawing them a road map to my clit. I mean, it's not that hard, for pity's sake.

Knox doesn't need a map. Oh, he knows a way around a woman's body just fine, and he just fine-tuned me like a fucking guitar.

"You're very sweet," I tell him.

"Even when my head is between your legs?"

I find myself flushing and I thank God it's dark in here. "Especially then."

He dips down and kisses me. It's wet and hot and he has me fired up all over again.

Round two? Like for real?

He already made me come with his mouth and once with his giant cock, and now we're gonna do it again?

"It's been a while for me," he says, surprising me. "That's why I have to apologize for being so quick. I couldn't help myself."

I'm stunned. A man like him? Surely, he'd have chicks all over him left, right, and center.

"We've got all night," I whisper. "And for the record,

you don't need my consent to spank me. Just making sure that's clear."

His lips twitch. "You're an incredibly sexy woman, Rebekah," he tells me. "Gorgeous. Any man would be lucky to have you in his bed."

"Is that your way of asking me if it's been a while for me, too?"

He chuckles. "No, it wasn't."

I run my hands down his back as he hovers over me, holding his weight off me. "Well, I admit that it has. I sort of had a no guys policy for a little while after my ex."

He frowns. I don't want to talk about exes, but I don't want him to think that I'm someone who just jumps into bed with any guy that comes along. I'm extremely choosy, so he should take that as a compliment.

"Most exes are bad news, that's why they're exes."

"Well, he was a special kind of asshole, not that I want to talk about that while we're in bed together."

He chuckles. "You're a very rare breed, Red, very rare indeed."

"I hope that's a good thing?" I mutter.

"Of course it is. I'm sure you have men hitting on you all the time," he says. "Exhibit A, tonight. Every man in the bar was looking at you the minute you walked in."

I know that's not true. Maybe the drunk guy who hit on me, but that's nothing to write home about.

"Even you?"

"Oh yeah, I couldn't keep my eyes in my head."

"Me either. Your eyes are what did it for me. I'm a sucker for blue eyes," I say.

"So, you wanted me to come over? Something tells me you're not the shy type," he muses.

"I never would have approached you."

He frowns. "Why not?"

"I told you; I wasn't looking to hook up. I know it seems a little coy to say it now, but I don't randomly hook up with strange men."

"No judgment from me. And what's this strange men business? I thought we were friends."

"Friends with benefits?"

He snickers. "I'm coming up in the world. This is good."

"So did you know we'd end up in bed together?" I ask, gesturing between us.

He kisses me on the nose softly. "No, I didn't, but I'm glad that you asked me to join you at Francine's."

"I was hungry." I can't help but throw that one in.

"Uh huh."

I screw up my nose. "But we didn't get to eat, and now I'm starving."

"We will after."

"After what?" I tease, gripping his ass again with my

hands, digging my nails in this time.

"After I hear you scream my name again."

Jesus, he's got the face of an angel but the mouth of a dirty devil, and I can't get enough of it.

"Are you the type of guy who can go all night?" I chuckle, knowing already that this guy has stamina. We're going at it again and he's still hard.

"Only when it comes to you."

"Bet you say that to all the girls."

He looks at me earnestly. "I've never lied to a woman. If anything, I'm too honest and that lands me in trouble sometimes. My mama raised me right. I respect women."

"She must be so proud of you. You're a good guy, Knox."

His gaze shifts away, and I immediately know I've said something wrong.

"She was."

Uh oh. Was?

"Knox… I…" I begin.

"She passed away… last month, actually."

My eyes go wide. "I'm so sorry." My heart thuds in my chest as his face falls. "I didn't mean to…"

"I know. It's not your fault; it's a perfectly true comment. She was proud of me. Fuck knows I put her through some heavy shit over the years. It's all still pretty raw."

"I'm sure it is. I really didn't mean to upset you…"

He brushes a strand of hair behind my ear. "You didn't,

it's all right. She wouldn't want me to wallow and waste my life away. She was a good woman. She worked hard to give me everything. I turned my life around because of her faith in me. I miss her every fucking day."

I swallow hard. I know I haven't lost Daniel entirely. He's still out there somewhere, but it almost feels like a death without him in my life. Still, there is no way I could compare that to this situation. I can't even imagine… I think about my own mom and that makes me sad. She'll never get out of the bad marriage she's in, she'll stay with my father forever. I can only hope that my brothers step in and keep her safe, I know when they're around, my father isn't such a monster. Not that any of that makes me abandoning her any good. But I can't go back now. I never can. I'm shunned.

Disgraced. None of my family would be allowed to talk to me, and if they did, they'd be punished.

His beard scratches my skin as he starts to kiss my neck, distracting me from my thoughts. His mouth moves to my décolletage, then lower to the top of my breasts as I wriggle underneath him. God, this man, he's so damn hot.

"I love your body, Red," he mutters in between kisses. "It's like it was put on this earth just for me to devour."

I feel the tingle between my legs. I feel it all the way down to my toes.

I push on his chest, rolling him over as I straddle across his lap.

"I think it's time I reciprocated by showing you my skills."

He places both hands behind his head, his biceps bulging. "Yeah?"

"Oh yeah."

I lean down and kiss him quickly, then move my mouth down to his neck, then his chest, sucking each nipple as I pass by, working my way down the length of his body. Slowly kissing and laving my tongue at the hair around his navel. His cock is hard and heavy as I bypass it and kiss his thighs, teasing him like he did to me. Then I move my mouth to his inner thigh, again, avoiding his cock until he groans.

"You teasing me, Red?"

I look up at him, his blue eyes so bright they may just be the prettiest eyes I've ever seen. "No, but I think this cock needs attention."

"Fuck," he hisses when I use my tongue to lick the underside of his length, cupping his balls lightly as I groan at the feel of him.

I lick his tip, coating my tongue with his precum, savoring his taste as I try not to rush it. I want this to be good for him after what he just did for me.

"Do you like your dick being played with, Knox?" I drawl.

"Fuck yeah." He moves his hands to grip the sheets beside him as I take him a little farther into my mouth.

I start to suck on the end, gripping his length with one hand as I move him deeper and deeper. He spreads his legs wider, letting me have full access, and I take advantage, cupping his balls harder and giving them a tug.

He swears again, gripping the sheets harder as I hollow my cheeks and go to town on him, bobbing my head as I slide him farther until he hits the back of my throat.

I half expect him to grab my head and start pumping—Lord knows most guys do that—but even in bed, Knox is a gentleman. Though he doesn't have to be. He can be rough with me, spank me, flip me over, pound into me, I don't care. I want all of him. I want it to be good for him.

"Baby," he murmurs as I suck harder, bobbing faster, taking him down my throat so I almost gag, and I feel his cock get even harder, like he's almost there. "Stop, Bekah, I'm gonna come…"

I smile around his cock and shake my head. I glance up and he stares down at me, his face glowing with ecstasy as he watches me with pure lust in his eyes. All of a sudden, he yanks me from between his legs and he pulls me on top of his body so I'm straddling his hips. "Nearly came down your throat." He's breathing hard.

"I wanted it."

He grips my ass. "Bad girls get spankings when they don't listen."

What was I just saying about him being a gentleman?

I don't know which side of him I prefer in bed. Both equally, I think.

"I'm very bad at taking orders," I admit. "So, I may need to be taught a lesson."

He reaches between us, running his fingers through my wet center as he hisses. "You're so fucking wet from sucking me off," he growls. "That turns you on?"

"I told you; I like doing it."

He sits up, spinning me around so I'm sideways, and pushes my head down onto the duvet. My ass is on full display across his knee.

"Did you think I was a good boy, Red?" His voice husky, his breathing rapid, I can feel the urgency as I lie across his knee. "Did you think I would go easy on you?"

I bite my lip, unable to answer.

He chuckles. "Cat got your tongue?"

"I never thought you were a good boy," I say, my breathing coming in hard and fast. "But this is something else."

He starts to stroke my ass cheeks. I can feel his cock digging into my stomach, and I'm needy for it. I want to chase my orgasm again and again while he tells me what a bad girl I am.

"Do you like hearing that I think you're bad?" he whispers close to my ear.

I nod.

"Tell me why you think that," he goes on. "Why am I gonna spank you?"

"Because," I stammer. "Because I like your cock so damn much, and I didn't want to stop sucking it."

I hear a low growl in his chest. "Very good. Any other reasons?"

"I wore fuck-me boots with a short skirt and I wanted you to take me on the bar when I saw your pretty eyes."

He grips my ass harder, then gives it a playful tap. I know he's working me up to it and I'm salivating at the strength of my feeling. I need this. I need it right now.

I could combust with anticipation.

"That is very bad, Rebekah."

Hearing him call me by my proper name does things to me. God, I'm so damn wet.

I wiggle my ass and he gives me another playful tap.

"I also wanted you to fuck me in the elevator." Oh, I can play along if this is what he likes.

"Bad girl behavior," he tells me. "Whatever will I do with this perky, hot as fuck ass?"

"Spank it, I deserve it."

"You do deserve it, tempting me like this when all I wanted to do was see you got home safe."

I almost come just from his words. I need friction, and fast.

"Do it," I beg. "Spank my ass, Knox."

He chuckles again, and out of nowhere… whap! He spanks my left cheek.

"Oh!" I cry out.

He spanks my other cheek, the sting instantly burning my skin. Oh yes.

"You should see how fucking sexy you look right now," he grits out. It sounds like he's having trouble even getting the words out, and that makes me smile.

"But I've not learned my lesson," I cry. "I need more!"

"Greedy little girl," he admonishes, then whap, whap… he spanks each cheek again. "Spread your legs wider," he demands. I comply quickly, spreading out before him as he yanks me up so I'm on my elbows, my ass sticking in the air. I feel his mouth at the side of my hip, and he soothes the cheek he can reach with soft, slow kisses. "Fucking beautiful."

He spanks my pussy gently as I gasp and buck forward, gripping the sheets under my fingers as I cry out. Oh God, yes!

"That feels… so good," I groan. "So, so good."

He does it again, then immediately runs his fingers through my slick folds, avoiding my clit as I moan in equal amounts of pleasure and frustration.

Whap, he spanks harder on one cheek, then the other. "Are you sure you've learned how to behave?"

I nod. "Yes! I have. I'll be good from now on. Just make me come."

He chuckles again, then spanks my pussy once more and keeps tapping my folds and my clit in rapid succession as I move my hips to gain some friction. I'm squirming, and when he grabs a handful of my ass hard and whispers, "Come for me, Red, scream my name," I do.

My orgasm is long and drawn out because of the pace and the fact he's hitting all of my pussy in all the right places. My skin is flushed as I cry out his name over and over, tingles running through my body as I jerk back and forward until it's over.

I'm not even done recovering when he pulls me up and says, "Straddle me. Sit on my dick, baby. Ride me while I fuck you."

My mouth is dry as I flip my legs around his hips. Our lips crash as he stays upright, but one hand reaches out to knock the box of condoms off the side table where they scatter and he curses.

Laughing, I reach down and fumble around until I find one. Pulling one out, I rip the foil off, and he watches as I roll it on his thick length, his eyes devouring me as I complete my task.

Holding his cock at the base as he grips my ass, I ease myself down onto him. We both groan at the same time. He dips his head down to my breasts, sucking one nipple, then the other, as I start to ride him, back and forth, rubbing my sensitive clit over his pubic bone as I unravel quickly, groaning again as his cock fills my tight pussy. I feel so damn full.

"That's it, Red, ride my cock, baby. Ride it good." As he settles back on the pillows, his eyes move down to my tits and he cups them, pushing them together. I gasp and begin to bounce, but it isn't enough. Realizing what we both need, his hands move to my hips, and he begins to bounce me up and down. "Eyes on me," he growls when I close them. They snap open again, meeting his as I grip his biceps, holding myself up.

He sits up, thrusting into me as I ride him harder, my orgasm building. When he takes my nipple into his mouth again, I cry out, calling his name as I come. He follows behind, grunting his release as he stills, emptying inside me.

"God, that was good," I pant, wrapping my arms around his neck. "I like when a man on his back puts in half the effort."

"Worked up an appetite yet?" He smiles against my lips, his breathing ragged.

"Starved."

He smacks my ass lightly. "Good. Let's eat."

After we chow down on our chili dogs and fries, I need to find my clothes and locate my underwear.

"Where are you going?" he asks as I pick up my clothes strewn across his apartment.

"I have to get home," I say. "But this was fun." Back to reality.

"So soon?"

I can't help but smile. "It's pumpkin time."

He frowns. "If you really have to?"

This man…

"I should. I mean, I have work tomorrow."

"You're not far from here. I could walk you back."

"I'll be fine."

He frowns even more. "I didn't mean tonight. I meant in the morning."

My heart couldn't melt any more than it already is.

"You want me to stay over?"

"If you want to? But don't look so horrified." He palms the back of his neck and fights a smile.

"I'm sorry," I stammer. "It's just usually… uh, I mean, the guy—not that there's been that many—is happy to sleep alone, basically."

A soft smile spreads across his face, and I think he could be the most handsome man I've ever seen.

"Well, I'm not like most guys."

We stare at one another. Him clad only in his boxer briefs and me in his Guns N' Roses t-shirt.

"I can see that."

"So, do you want to stay? To sleep, I mean."

Good Lord, I want to stuff this man and take him home.

"I wouldn't want to put you out."

He gives me a lopsided smile. "I wouldn't have asked if you were putting me out."

I try not to skip to his bedroom, but it's a little hard to wipe the smile off my face.

"I never thought I'd ever be glad to have some dick hit on me," I say, walking toward him.

He takes my hand in his, and drags me back to bed.

"And I never thought for a second that you couldn't handle yourself, I just wanted an excuse to talk to you."

Be still my beating heart.

Give yourself tonight, I tell myself. You deserve this.

So I do what I've never done before; I stay with him, in his arms, all night long.

BRACKEN RIDGE
REBELS
ARIZONA
M · C

CHAPTER 5

KNOX

She's amazing.

We spend the rest of the night talking, laughing, and making out. I feel like a teenager again.

Admittedly, it was a little unorthodox asking her to stay. I don't know what came over me. I was enjoying myself, and she was too, and I didn't want her to go.

I haven't felt this way before, and that makes me even more curious to find out why.

What is it about this woman? We have off-the-charts chemistry. Together, we're sizzling hot, and I start to wonder what the catch is.

Nobody is this perfect.

Aside from being gorgeous, she's also intelligent, articulate, can take a joke, has just the right amount of attitude and sass and, of course, she's sexy as fuck.

We talk about work, the city, places we like to eat and

what we do on the weekend.

It's all light banter and it sucks I have to drop the bombshell that I'm leaving. I'd love to see her again.

"I kinda figured from all the packing boxes around the house," she muses. "You know we have a lot in common because I'm moving too. I just don't know when."

I feel a sudden pang of regret that I may never see her again. "Are you moving out of state?" I ask suddenly. She shrugs. "I've got a few offers, I just don't know yet. I guess if I can find a job easily enough, then I'll move to another state. I like Phoenix, though."

"But your family's in Ohio, right?"

"You pay attention."

I draw small circles on her shoulder with my finger. She's lying with her head on my chest; it seems neither of us actually want to get any sleep.

"Old habits die hard," I say.

"What about you? Are you staying in Phoenix?"

"I'm gonna couch surf for a few weeks before I head south. I've no set plans yet. I guess I'll see what happens. I've got family there, but it's complicated."

"Aren't all families?"

"You got that right." I laugh. "It sucks, though."

"That we're both moving?"

"Yeah."

"Would you take me out on a date?" She laughs.

"Of course I would. But it could be a real date; a movie followed by dinner, then I'd drive you home safely at a reasonable hour. Maybe I'd get a kiss goodnight if I behaved myself."

"And what if you didn't behave yourself?"

"True. I'd have a hard time keeping my hands to myself when it comes to you."

"You are good with your hands," she says, stifling a yawn.

I chuckle. "Am I keeping you up, Red?"

"You wore me out," she admits. "I feel like I just did a spin class fifteen times."

"That's a nice way to boost my ego."

She turns to look at me. "In case I forget to tell you when I leave, I had a really great time tonight."

I smile down at her. I wish I didn't have to leave. I want to see her again.

"Me too," I reply. "Now get some sleep. What time do you have to wake up?"

"I set my alarm for seven o'clock." She lays her head back down and her eyes are already closed.

I kiss her hair. I want to remember this. Her smell. Her soft breathing. The way her body is wrapped around me, comforting and warm.

"I won't forget this night either, Rebekah," I say softly. "I promise."

The sun streams through the curtains, blinding me. I'm on my side, spooning the beautiful woman who laid in my arms all night. Her bright red hair is strewn across the pillows like some kind of goddess who doesn't belong in my bed.

I can't help touching her. My arm tightens around her waist, and I feel her stir. Then she sticks her ass into my cock, which I can't keep restrained when she's around, and I let out a low groan.

"Morning, sunshine," she sing-songs, moving her ass deliberately over my cock.

"If this is how you greet a man first thing, I might not want to let you go," I mumble in her ear, kissing her neck.

I run my hand over her stomach and find my way up the inside of her shirt to her nipple. I give it a gentle squeeze, and she groans in response.

"I've never had much morning sex," she says on a sigh as I continue to play with her body. "I think it's seriously underrated, though."

"Definitely," I agree, nuzzling her neck and peppering her with kisses.

Before long, I reach down and tug off the t-shirt, delighted to find she's still not wearing panties. Then I tug down my boxers, letting my cock spring free.

To be honest, I wasn't expecting morning sex either, but I want to feel how good it feels to be inside her just one more time.

She groans again as I pinch her nipple harder, squeezing her breast as I move my hand south over her stomach and ribs, down to the apex of her thighs. She spreads her top leg wide automatically, giving me full access to her pussy.

I groan when I feel how wet she is. "Always so ready for me," I muse, biting her shoulder gently.

"You seem to bring out the vixen in me. I want to be a very bad girl when you touch me like that."

"You know what bad girls get," I remind her. "Your ass knows anyway."

She wiggles it against me again, and I almost shoot my load. I reach down and tug on my dick, once, twice. Fuck yeah. She's got me so damn hard.

I want to slide into her bare, with nothing between us, but I know that's impossible. I don't fucking know why that thought even occurs to me. I don't know this woman, really. But I know that my feelings are going haywire, and it needs to stop. I'm made of stronger stuff than this. I survived prison. I can survive Rebekah.

I stroke my fingers through her slick heat as she makes delicious noises, then to my surprise, she reaches around toward my dick as I help her, placing her hand over my hard length.

"That feels so good," I tell her as she grips me.

We fondle each other.

I play with her pussy, pulling gently on her lips, swirling my thumb over her clit as she murmurs incoherently. I spread her slickness all around, inserting a finger slowly inside her as she pushes her ass back against me. She grips my cock harder, pulling me off as I glance down to watch her, precum leaking from my tip.

I've never gone this many times in such a short space of time. I guess I've learned something new about myself in the last twelve hours.

"Need to be inside you," I growl in her ear. I move my hand, inserting another finger as I fuck her with them slowly, in out, in out, the heel of my hand rubbing against her clit as I watch her beautiful breasts heave and her nipples darken and harden. I want to drive her into the mattress. But I also want her just like this.

"Oh, Knox… Oh… Oh… that's it, right there… yes!" She comes on a long, dick hardening groan as I keep the slow rhythm going so it'll last longer for her.

When she's done, I turn quickly to grab a rubber, rip the packet, and roll it on.

"Hurry!" she whispers.

I squeeze her ass, making her yelp. Grabbing my cock, I slide it down through her ass crease, wishing I could take that too, until I'm lined up with her entrance. I push into her wet, swollen pussy full tilt, and she gasps.

This isn't gonna be no gentlemanly fuck. Oh no. She's got me worked up so damn easily. Teasing me and being a bad girl who wants to be punished, just how I like it.

I pull out and immediately push back in, my cock so hard and swollen that I'm sure she feels every inch of it as her tight hole grips me like a vice.

"Fuck, you're beautiful," I mutter, reaching around to cup her breast, squeezing it as she pushes her ass against me as I slide in and out of her, hard. "So fucking beautiful, Rebekah."

We fuck. She squirms, moaning as I rock back and forth, kissing and gently biting her shoulder as she tells me she's close. I need to really thrust, and this position isn't gonna give me that, so I ride her through her orgasm, playing with her clit as our bodies slap together and she cries out.

I pull out, roll her onto her stomach, climb behind her, and say, "Get on your knees, hold on to the headboard."

She does as she's told. Good girl.

I hold my cock and thrust it inside her again, her slick heat making me groan as I pull out and do it again, and again, and again. My balls slap against her pussy as I fuck her harder, thrusting deep inside, giving her everything.

"Yes, Knox! Oh yes, oh you're good, so damn good.

I love that big cock filling me. I'm so tight, and you're so big…"

I smack her ass, loving the sight and the sound as her cheek reddens. Her dirty talk almost knocks me over the edge.

"You've been a bad girl again, Red," I grit, trying not to come, though I'm close. "Good girls don't wear my t-shirt to bed without underwear on."

"I was hoping you'd wake up and fuck me," she pants. "Easy access…"

I smack her other cheek. "Doesn't sound like a very good girl to me. You sound like a cock tease. Rubbing that beautiful, sexy ass over my cock before I've even woken up."

"You wanted it," she breathes.

"Damn straight I did."

I pull out and move up behind her, on my knees, my chest pressed against her back as I join my hands right next to hers on the headboard.

She turns her head, and we kiss, my tongue in her mouth as she rubs against me, begging me silently for my cock.

I chuckle, spreading her legs wider with my knees, and line up again. As I shove into her tight pussy, she watches me over her shoulder.

"You like the feel of this big cock, Red?"

"Yes!" she cries out.

"Your tight little hole can't get enough of me, can it?"

She shakes her head frantically. "Faster. Harder."

"You're a fucking Queen, Rebekah," I tell her. "Don't ever fucking forget it."

"Oh, Knox!"

I drive into her just as she asked me to, showing her no mercy. I fuck her so hard, the bed groans beneath us, hitting the wall as we both pant and moan at the same time. She unravels again as I cup her tits, pulling her nipples and biting her shoulder. It's so hot, so full of unbridled desire that I can't hold on any longer. I shoot my load violently, crying out as I call her name, stilling as she milks me of every fucking last drop.

She falls back against me, her head rolling to my shoulder. We're both covered in sweat, panting like lovesick teenagers who can't get enough of each other's bodies.

"God, Knox, this is so unfair."

"I know," I pant. "But I want your number. We can work something out…"

She reaches around to grasp my hair in her hands as I kiss her shoulder. I pull out as she lets me go and I discard the rubber. Holding out my hand, I help her turn around as she plops back down on the duvet.

I chuckle.

"What?" she says, frowning.

"You look like you've been thoroughly fucked."

A grin spreads across her face. "Ugh, I bet my hair looks…"

"Ravishing."

She shakes her head. "Now I know your lying."

I give her a grin, lean over, and grab my boxers. "I'll make us some coffee, then I'll run you a shower before you leave."

She slides under the duvet, pulling it up to cover herself as she sits up, her back against the pillows. "Are you sure you didn't just drop down from heaven?"

My fucking face hurts from all the grinning I've been doing. "Pretty sure." I make a circle around my head. "Oh wait, just gotta straighten that halo."

I move off the bed as she tries to slap my ass.

"Very funny."

"How do you take your coffee?"

"White with two sugars."

"Two sugars?" I make a face.

"What can I say, I need sweetening up."

I lean over to her, because I can't help it, and give her a quick kiss. "I seem to remember exactly how sweet you are, Rebekah, and if I get the chance to meet you again, I'll be sure to pay better attention to that peachy ass of yours, then you'll know the meaning of sweet."

Her cheeks flush. "I take it back," she calls as I push off

the bed. "You're a bad boy in disguise."

I fucking wish I wasn't moving.

"You found me out," I call over my shoulder.

My chest tingles. I know I should push the warm feelings down. I want to see her again, sure, but I doubt it's gonna happen. She might be going out of state and I'm moving fuck knows where; I can't even remember the name of the town. I just know I've got a lot to do. Since finding out my mom owned a business I never knew about, in a town that I apparently have a brother in I've never met, I've come to expect the unexpected.

There are so many unanswered questions. When my lease ran out a few months ago, and I put my mom's house on the market to pay for her medical bills, I figured it was time to make a change.

I just wish I could have met this girl at a different time, in a different place.

I go to make the coffee with a tinge of regret marring my mood.

Hours later, she's still on my mind. Even after I walked her home, and we exchanged numbers. For once in my godforsaken life, I had a spring in my step. Then I felt defeated the minute she left, and I realized that's all we'll ever have for the moment.

I'm not usually like this. I don't fall hard, in fact, I don't fall period. I've had a couple of serious relationships, but nothing stuck. I was committed and loyal to them, but we just weren't going anywhere. I want a family; it's all I've ever wanted. So random hook-ups are generally not my thing, and neither are women who just want casual sex. Something some of my friends just don't understand and have wondered if I'm gay. I'm not. I just know what I want. And I made an exception to the one-night stand rule with Rebekah because I felt that spark. That light inside me came alive, and I think she felt it too.

I don't understand how I can know this girl for less than twenty-four hours and I'm considering if I even wanna leave town just so I can take her to the movies and that dinner date I promised.

It's ridiculous.

Pull yourself together, I tell myself for the millionth time this morning.

But I can't. It doesn't help my clouded judgment on where my life is actually going, and now all I keep thinking about is her. Our magical night together, the time in bed this morning, and in the shower. She was surprised when I ran the water for her till it was hot enough, leaving her a fresh towel and some privacy, but she had shocked me by taking me by the hand and pulling me into the shower with her.

It was completely unexpected and so fucking hot.

Of course, I couldn't keep my hands off her and that time was on her. The other times, not so much. I didn't exactly make it a secret how much she turned me on.

I bent her over and gave it to her a little softer. She was okay with me pulling out, rather than wearing a condom, something I never do, either. Feeling her completely bare, with nothing between us, will live in my memory forever. So will spurting on her back while I jerked myself into oblivion.

I've never had sex that many times in one night. It's like my cock won't go down where she's concerned, and it doesn't want to.

She told me multiple times I was the best one-night stand she'd ever had. And while that sang to my ego, the one thing that stuck in my head was the 'one-night stand' part. I'm no fucking saint, and I'm definitely not an angel, but to take things to the next level, I've got to feel a connection. It's just how I am. If I don't actually like them, but they're sexy as fuck, it doesn't matter. Somehow, something in my brain wants the whole package.

Sexiness. Intelligence. A girl who can laugh, isn't afraid to eat a chili dog and isn't obsessed with taking selfies or texting on their phone, especially when you're trying to have a conversation.

Like I said, I like what I like. I'm a simple guy.

Rebekah.

She's a goddess.

Flaming red hair, a body made for sin, and a mind that could render a man to his knees.

And it may be the last time I ever see her.

Knox

BRACKEN RIDGE
REBELS
ARIZONA
M · C

CHAPTER 6

REBEKAH

I've thought about him every day. Especially at night. Night time is the worst for me. Everything is so still and quiet, and you have time to think and go over things in your mind. The other side of the bed is glaringly vacant, like he's missing.

Which is insane. I only knew the guy for a matter of hours, yet I catch myself smiling when I think about him calling me Red, or the way he spanked my ass when I was being a bad girl, biting down on my shoulder as he plucked my nipples, and most of all, making me laugh so hard, like I never have before.

It's safe to say, Knox will remain a vision in the back of my consciousness. Like a dream that I can cling onto at night when I crawl into bed alone and hope for something more than just the mundane.

Why this had to happen to me, just as I'm moving into a new phase in my life, is beyond me. It's like the universe is punishing me.

I try not to think of all the Amish beliefs that come flooding back. Going down that road won't get me anywhere except to more heartbreak. And that's something I've had more than enough of in my thirty years.

But Knox. There's something about him that I just can't get enough of. The way he made me feel safe. How he gallantly walked me home like he said he would. His pretty eyes, smile, face, body—everything—but most of all, how sweet he was.

It's the little things that most men just don't get. Yet Knox just knew without having to be told. Running a shower for me. Making coffee in the morning after giving me another orgasm. And going down on me like a man possessed. I fan myself just thinking about it.

"Mama!" Brayden yells, jolting me out of my reverie.

I clear my throat. "Yes, honey?"

"I can't find my other shoe," he whines.

I clutch my coffee cup, willing this headache to go away. They've become more regular, and I know it's stress related. As if moving isn't enough, changing neighborhoods, finding a good school for Brayden, my son, and getting a job, it's taken its toll and I'm ready to sleep for a week.

Brayden is ten going on twenty-five.

He's exactly like me in a lot of ways, including his impatience.

"I'm sure if you have a proper look where you last

kicked them off, you'll find them in no time," I holler back. "Retrace your steps."

He grumbles, and the search continues.

No, I didn't tell Knox about my kid that night. Not because I'm ashamed of him, or that I didn't want him to know I'm a mom, but the likelihood of us seeing one another again was slim. I didn't want to complicate things.

Brayden was having a sleepover the night Knox and I hooked up. I wonder what he'd think if we really were dating and he just found out I have a child. I find myself wondering if things would be different.

Fantasizing about what I would say to him if we ever meet again plagues my thoughts day and night. Even when he dropped me at my doorstep the morning we said goodbye, we'd hugged, exchanged numbers, and looked at one another with a tinge of regret. I'd like to say it's for the best, but I'm not so sure about that.

I like to torture myself when I also recreate our night together in my mind, because my life really is just that sad.

When a few more moments of silence ensues, I yell, "Did you find them?"

I hear his footsteps banging up the hallway as he runs into the kitchen.

"Found them!"

"Were they where you left them?"

"Yup."

I shake my head as he bounces down to sit at the table, grabbing a piece of cold toast as I lean over and try to comb down his hair.

"Mom!"

"Do you want to go to school looking like you just rolled out of bed?"

He ignores me, downing half a glass of orange juice like he's been out in the desert for two days. "Mom, it's not a school photo day or anything, jeez."

Silly me.

I smile to myself. "Fine, but make sure you don't forget your coat."

"You're driving me, Mom."

"Still, it's chilly out." I worry about him, even though he's a tough little nut.

"Mom?"

I look up at him. "You're making that face again."

"What face?" I argue.

"The one that says you're going to chew your nails off because you want to stay at school with me to make sure the other kids are nice." He knows me too well.

"That would be a very normal response. You are still my baby, after all."

He grabs the carton of milk and drowns his cocoa krispies with it. "I'm not a baby!"

"No, I said you're my baby, and you always will be,

even when I'm old and gray."

He laughs. "Mom, that's ages away."

I smile. "I'm glad you think so."

"Will you pick me up after school?" He munches down his cereal noisily.

"Of course. Once the weather warms up, we can ride our bikes instead."

He beams. He loves his bike. He loves anything outdoors.

"This town isn't so bad," he tells me. "They even have drag races and a motorcycle club."

I frown. "Where did you hear about that?"

He rolls his eyes. "It's a small town, people talk."

I shake my head.

My son. The super sleuth.

"Well, don't be listening to small town gossip. We'll make our own minds up about the people in it," I say, even though I don't like the idea of a motorcycle club in such a small place. Aren't those types of gangs filled with criminals?

All I can think about when I hear the name 'Bracken Ridge Rebels' is a scene from Sons of Anarchy.

I chose this town because there are more job opportunities and less competition than in the city. When I looked into how much it would cost to move states, I quickly canned the idea. I don't have that kind of money and I don't have a degree behind me. I never finished my education when I left the Amish. But most importantly, I wanted Brayden to grow up in a small town and go to a good school. I've never been a big city girl; the bright city lights lose their appeal after a while. Small town charm has always had a place in my heart, and Brayden loves being outdoors; something else we both find we do more of since being out of the city.

But, I do need to get a job, and fast. I wasn't too fazed about not finding work, as there seems to be a boom in this town and there are plenty of jobs. I have a couple of interviews lined up over the coming days.

I have a little money saved, but most of it disappeared to pay for the security deposit for the rental. It's only a one-bedroom, but we'll make do. Brayden has never been the kind of kid to complain about anything.

He's not spoiled. We may have our ups and downs, but he's a good kid. I love him more than life.

It's just been the two of us for a long time. Ever since I left his father.

I close my eyes to steady myself.

He'll never find us.

We moved states. I turned my world upside down to get away from him… even changing my name.

I took my son and I left a bad situation, and it was the best thing I could have done.

"I know," Brayden sighs. "I just hope I make some friends and people don't treat me like I have a disease."

I don't know where he comes up with these things. "All you have to do is be yourself, Bray," I tell him. "The kids will like you; you are pretty adorable."

"You have to say that; you gave birth to me."

"I don't have to say it. Who wouldn't like you? They'd have to be crazy."

He wriggles around in his seat. "You're right, I am pretty awesome."

"Ten out of ten."

He's always been a responsible kid, does his homework on time, packs his own lunch, and makes sure his schoolbag is ready. He also helps me around the house. He's a good kid.

"Are you just saying all that because you want me to do something?"

I laugh. "Why do I always have to have an ulterior motive?"

"Because it's usually true."

"I thought we could have a little treat tonight, and maybe try out the Burger Joint?"

His eyes light up. "Could we?"

The Burger Joint is the best burger place in town. It's not cheap, but I've heard from the locals that it's second to none and the burger sauce is legendary. We've only just settled in a week ago and haven't really had the time to check out any of the local haunts. It'll be nice for Brayden and it might take his mind off things if his first day is a little daunting.

"I think it'd be nice, and you can tell me all about your first day at school." Lord, please be nice to him.

It'll crush my soul if he comes home unhappy.

"Yes!" He fists pumps the air, spilling cereal off his spoon. "Mom, you're the best!"

"Well, hurry up and finish that and then go brush your teeth and we'll get going. You don't want to be late on your first day."

He discards his spoon noisily, slopping milk all over the table as he darts off to the bathroom.

I love being Brayden's mom. It's the only thing I'm truly good at, and sometimes I feel like I'm not the world's greatest expert on raising a kid, but he's happy. He's healthy and we're doing okay.

We've got each other. I can take on anything as long as my kid is all right.

My first interview is at a coffee shop aptly named, The Coffee Bean. I've done tons of waitressing before, even if office work is more my kinda thing and it's what I've been doing for the last few years, but beggars can't be choosers.

They have several shifts available and tell me I can start as soon as I like. At least I've got that to fall back on if the other interviews don't work out. I've got another interview at the Zee Bar tapas lounge in an hour, and tomorrow two receptionist positions, which I'm kinda hoping will pan out.

I said I'll get back to The Coffee Bean by the end of the day tomorrow.

At least things are looking hopeful. I'll have enough to pay for rent and food and a little left over for gas and utilities. Until I'm back on my feet, at least if the bills are paid and we're fed, it's better than nothing.

I take a walk around town after I leave The Coffee Bean. It's going to be strange having our first Christmas here, in this strange town, where we don't know anyone, but I hope that will change as soon as I start work and begin to meet new people. Surely, there will be some moms at school I could connect with and become friends with. At Braydon's school in Phoenix, some of the moms were very clicky. If you didn't fit into their little club, then you were out. I don't think I'm a hard person to get along with, but moving regularly meant I also never really planted down any roots.

My one real friend, Mallory, lives in Nevada and is a single mom too.

The night I met Knox, she had Brayden for a couple of nights before I joined them for a few days of R&R. I've wondered, over the last month or so, what he would've said if he learned I had a kid and perhaps we'd dated. Most men would run away; they don't want the excess baggage. But I'm genuinely curious what his reaction would've been.

I guess we'll never know. I'm one of those people that believes everything happens for a reason. That if things were meant to be, they would. The fact that we were both moving has to mean something. It just wasn't our time, that's what I have to keep believing… or maybe it's just something that gives me comfort because I had the best night of my life.

As I walk down the street, I pass Steelman's Autos, and I notice a whole bunch of motorcycles parked out front. So, this must be one of their hangouts, aside from the Stone Crow, the local pub and eatery also owned by the bikers, like most things in this town. I chuckle to myself. At least if the locals don't seem to have a problem with them, I shouldn't either. I will keep my thoughts about bikers to myself. Perhaps they're not criminals at all. Maybe they are just reasonable everyday people, and I'm just being narrow-minded, which I have no right to be. You can't tar everyone with the same brush. I, of all people, should know that.

As I glance their way, I see a man with dark hair, a big build, his back to me with his hands on his hips. His motorcycle club jacket bears the club's logo which reads: Bracken Ridge Rebels MC Arizona, with a large skull and crossbones patch. Subtle.

I don't know why, but my heart hammers in my chest for a moment, and I frown in confusion. Turning away, I keep walking and realize, as I pass, what it was; he reminded me of my cousin, Daniel. I shake my head, what a ridiculous thought to have. The last I heard, Daniel was in Idaho. He'd not been back home in years. He was never the same after Elijah… a cold shiver runs through me. I was close to both of them and Elijah's passing still shakes me to my core. He hung himself because the man he was in love with, and planned to leave the community with, ended up keeping the charade of marrying a good Amish girl. He betrayed Elijah and hurt him so deeply. When Daniel found him in the barn, his father made him cover up the suicide. Spreading the lie that Elijah was injured and died from an accident with the farming equipment. Suicide, much less being gay, would not be understood or tolerated in our religion.

I think something in all of us changed after that and it makes me so mad.

I still believe in God, I always will. But I can't live the way I was brought up. I just can't do it. In the end, even family wasn't enough to keep me there. I had to get out, and I knew once I did, there was no turning back. My family shunned me for running away. If I ever did return, which I'd almost been forced to do when I was sleeping on the street, I'd be ostracized, my family disgraced. Bringing that much shame on them after leaving our family, I can't say I regret it. I've always had a rebellious heart. I've always wanted to be free. I don't even know what I would say to any of my family if I saw them now. They have their way of living and I have mine.

I've just always wondered what happened to Daniel. We were so close, more like brother and sister. He was the only one who let me be me. He'd let me help in the field when he wasn't supposed to, often taking the brunt from my father when we got found out.

A woman's work is always in the house, not outside where the men work. I knew I was rebellious from an early age, but the truth is, I never saw myself leaving the Amish, or my way of life. It was all I knew.

Until him.

Until I met Brayden's father.

I ran to him because I believed a lie, one of many.

Falling madly in love with him, and having no prior experience with boys or knowledge of the outside world, I stuck to him like glue. I was so young, so naive, and so very innocent.

That all changed, of course. Being with him changed me, and some of it wasn't for the better.

Some of the lessons in life have been hard to learn. Leaving my family unit, venturing out into the world, it was meant to be fun. An adventure. But that all quickly turned sour.

I can't even bring myself to change the past. Without it, I wouldn't have my son.

I rub my arms with my hands, instantly feeling cold whenever I think about it and how far we've come. He'll never find you. I have to believe that. I've managed to escape him for this long, though we had a couple of close calls a few years back.

If he ever found me, he'd kill me. He's crazy.

Thinking about him and that time in my life makes me edgy, which is why I try hard not to think about it and bring up any feelings that threaten to throw me off course.

I'm in a good place now. I've been in a good place for a while.

I'm never going back there.

I make a quick stop at the grocery store and go home to unpack the last of the boxes in the garage. I need to keep busy until Brayden is out of school, as I'm anxious to know how his day was. When I arrive at school pick-up, I wait with the other parents near the gate.

"You new around here?" a woman to my left asks as I turn my head.

"Is it that obvious?"

She's got long, platinum hair, and she's wearing shiny jeans, knee-high boots, and a large, black parka. She's stunning. I rake my hand through my hair nervously, realizing that I could have run a brush through it before leaving the house.

She smiles. "Only to me. I'm Angel." She holds out her hand.

"I'm Rebekah." We shake hands. "Though you can call me Bekah, and yes, I just moved here. Today's my kid's first day."

"That's why you look like you may snap at any moment. Trust me, this school is pretty good compared to most. How old's your kid?"

"He's ten."

"So is mine. Well, one of mine," she goes on. "If he's new, Rawlings will take him under her wing. She's good like that. That's my daughter, by the way."

I like her, I decide. She's got a sense of humor and she had the guts to speak to me, something I would've never done.

"Sounds like he's in good hands," I reply. Make conversation… I remind myself. Meeting new friends is easy. "So, you have other kids?"

"Yep, a newborn boy and a two-year-old girl. They're both a handful. What about you?"

"Just the one," I say. "He's a good kid. It's just the two of us."

She nods. "Here she comes." She waves to a little girl who looks just like her with the exact same wheat blonde hair… and she's walking along with Brayden. "That your kid?"

I laugh. "Yep, that's him."

She laughs too. "Told ya."

Brayden waves when he sees me, and I wave back. He has a big grin spread across his face.

It makes my heart happy.

"Looks like he's had a good day," I muse, then add, "Thank God."

"Welcome to Bracken Ridge," she says. "This is the best part of my day."

"Thanks." I can't help the smile spreading across my face, too. "I think it's fast becoming the best part of mine as well."

BRACKEN RIDGE
REBELS
ARIZONA
M · C

CHAPTER 7

KNOX

The meeting I thought would be awkward turned out to be just that.

I accepted Richie Hutchinson's offer to meet up at the clubhouse, but he pushed it back to Monday.

I didn't know what to expect. I haven't been inside a biker clubhouse for a while, but when it came to the crunch, I had to talk to Steel. I wanted to get the awkwardness out of the way. Since I was going to be living here and all, we were bound to run into each other from time to time. It's a small town, and I didn't want to get off on the wrong foot.

The clubhouse isn't what I expected.

Aside from the subtle skull and crossbones emblem on the front door declaring: The Bracken Ridge Rebels MC, Arizona - Ride or Die, I have to admit, it's a pretty impressive door. This whole place is.

When I step inside, I don't know what I expect, but it's not this.

Instead of stripper poles and the mud wrestling pits I

imagined, the place is spotlessly clean and smells freshly painted.

First up is the bar facing the entry, with every liquor bottle known to man neatly stacked on the shelves. There's a long table that must seat twenty, and couches spread around the room with a huge flatscreen TV on one wall. There're also a couple of pool tables racked and ready to play.

To say I'm largely impressed would be an understatement.

I doubt they scrubbed this place clean just because I'm coming over, which leads me to think it's always like this. I've been around long enough to know that the women of the club have certain jobs to do and one of them is to cook and clean.

I wonder what Steel went home and told his mom. It had to be a blow, even if she washed her hands of my father years ago.

Still, that longing inside of me that's always wanted a family is screaming to be let free. To see where this goes and if Steel will accept me as his brother. Fuck knows he wasn't impressed with our first introduction, but one can hardly blame him. It did kinda come out of left field.

I try to remind myself that I'd probably react the same if some strange guy showed up on my doorstep, claiming to be a long-lost brother.

The fact I even got past the Rebels' gates is some kind of miracle.

As I'm staring around looking at everything, a moment later, Steel appears from an adjacent room to the left. He crosses the threshold, and it's only now, in the light of day, that I get to see just exactly how alike we actually are. Aside from the long hair.

He's a lot wider than me in the shoulders, but our muscle build is the same, as is our height. He'd love that he may just be a little taller than me.

"Knox," he says in a low, not entirely pleasant, voice.

"Jayson," I reply. "Thanks for seeing me."

He nods somewhere behind him. "We can talk in here. And call me Steel, only my Mother calls me by my real name."

He stares at me, as if trying to see if I have an ulterior motive that he can pick up on. The fact is, I got nothing.

I nod. "All right." I follow him across the floor, adding, "Nice digs you got here."

"Sounds like you were expectin' a dive."

He isn't far off. "Something like that."

We walk into what I can only assume is the meeting room. There's a long table, the club's logo carved into the middle, and Hutch sits at the head. He half stands when I enter.

"Knox," he says. "Good of you to come." At least

he's cordial.

Steel takes a seat to his left while I sit on the opposite side of the table, to his right.

"Likewise, we broke the ice, and that's the most important thing. These kinds of revelations are never easy." I glance at Steel.

I wonder suddenly if he's the mediator. Fuck.

"So, everything you said checks out," Steel says, his face unreadable. "I guess dear old Dad had more skeletons in the closet than we first thought."

I swallow hard. "Trust me, it's just as much a surprise to me as it is to you. My mom put up with a lot, but she never would've put up with him having another family that he lived with in secret. It would've devastated her."

Steel looks down at his hands folded in front of him momentarily, as if trying to gather his thoughts. "He was a special kind of bastard."

An awkward silence hangs between us.

Hutch stays silent until I give him a chin lift. "Just trying to get my shit sorted out. I didn't come here looking for trouble."

Hutch nods. "I get that, but you're here nonetheless."

"There's nothing for me in Phoenix. If there were, I'd be there and not here making an ass out of myself, trying to run a business I've no idea how to operate. I've got a lot to learn, but I'm willing to start at the bottom and make this work." I don't know why that sounds like a sales pitch. "I came with very few possessions because I wanted to start fresh, so I've got my truck, my dog, and my bike. The rest ain't worth shit anyway."

"Do you ride a motorcycle?" Hutch asks.

"I've been riding since as long as I can remember. I've always had a fascination when my fa-" I stop, closing my mouth, clearing my throat as I go on. "Well, I was always fascinated with his bike, so I guess it kinda rubbed off onto me."

"What do you ride?"

"I helped a friend restore an Indian, and my 1961 Harley is my baby."

"What model?" asks Steel, suddenly interested.

"Panhead."

He grunts. Eyeing me, he asks, "You restore motorcycles?"

"Not exactly. My friend did the majority of the work. I mainly scoured the parts and helped him put it back together. I got all the tedious, shitty jobs, but it paid off."

He rubs his chin.

I can't help but notice the change in his demeanor, and I don't know what it is.

Hutch also eyes me curiously. "You know Steel is a mechanic?"

"I did know that. I saw the garage when I first came

to town."

"And that he restores motorcycles and vintage cars?"

I swallow hard.

We have something else in common besides our genes.

"I didn't know that part," I admit, looking at Steel. "Just that you had the garage."

"It's a labor of love," he tells me, surprising me. "It's a project a long time in the makin'."

"Must be hard work, doing restorative work for a living."

"I only concentrate on custom jobs now," he says. "It's long, tedious, sure, but worth it when it's finished. There's no greater satisfaction than piecing back together an old car or vintage motorcycle."

I try not to smile. Clearly motorcycles, or wheels of any kind, are a passion of his. I make a mental note to bring that subject up if we ever hit a rocky patch.

So far, nobody's thrown me out, and we're having small talk. Surely, this is progress?

Still, it's a tough gig.

"What did you do before takin' over the motel?" Hutch gives me a chin lift.

"I'm a carpenter by trade. I completed my apprenticeship after I did time."

I don't think either of them were expecting that, but if we're being totally honest and transparent, then I'd rather be upfront now about it.

"What did you do time for?" Steel asks, his arms folded across his chest.

"I broke a man's jaw in three places and gave him massive internal bleeding because he disrespected my woman."

Silence.

Steel asks, "Did you kill him?"

I shake my head. "Unfortunately, no."

Hutch almost smiles. "I think you two are a lot more alike than I first thought," he mutters.

I glance at Steel. "I don't have to remind you what an asshole our father was or how he treated women. Because of that, I vowed I would never be like him. I keep my calm most of the time, but there are certain lines that can't be crossed. You cross them, you suffer the consequences."

"I knocked him down when I was fifteen when he hit my mom," Steel says as I wince. "He left after that, before Lily was even born. We were glad to see the back end of him. But what I wanna know is, how big was the guy you knocked down?"

I hide my smile. He thinks I beat on a small guy. I try not to laugh. "Big enough to take down. I competed in martial arts since I was five, so that kinda worked in my favor."

In all my years, wholeheartedly, I don't think I've ever seen a man as solid as Steel. Maybe a bodybuilder could come close, but he's one big motherfucker. I may be big myself and have the bonus of having martial arts up my sleeve, but I still wouldn't want to meet the end of his fists.

"I guess it does," Steel says. It's hard to say what he's really thinking. He's kinda hard to read.

"So, you're takin' over the motel?" Hutch interjects. "And your long-term plan is to stay in Bracken Ridge?"

"Yes," I say, turning my attention back to him. "This is all I've got. Like I said the other night, my mom left the business to me but, to be honest, I think I've taken on more than I can chew."

Hutch rubs his beard, watching me. "There's a shit ton of work to be done."

"Yep, and my office manager just quit."

Hutch chuckles. "You pissed off Vi enough to quit, and you've been here for how long?"

"She had it in for me," I say. "I don't know what else to say. The woman is completely crazy."

"Bitch ran that place into the ground," Steel goes on. "Everyone knows it. That's the trouble with havin' no one around to supervise. She's never done a day's work in her life."

"That's true," Hutch admits.

"I'm the last one to be finding this out," I say. "I've got some interviews lined up tomorrow for her replacement. Hopefully, someone will want to take it on. From what I can gather, there's a lot to fix, and I don't have a lot of spare cash to put into it.

I'll do what I can."

"Not lookin' for any investors?" Hutch pipes up. Steel looks at him sharply.

I meet his eye. "Maybe." I don't want to make it seem like I'm desperate, which I am. If the motel wasn't able to be salvaged, hands down, I'd walk away.

Even though I've only been in this town a short while, I know it's a potential goldmine. It's on the main fucking street. There is no competition as all the other hotels and motels are out of town.

I just know I can turn it into something if I can only get my ducks in a row.

"Have a think about it, about the club investing," Hutch says, surprising me once more. I don't even know this man and he's throwing money at me? What am I missing? Or is it just that he sees the potential too? "Do you have a business plan?"

I shake my head. "No, but I could write one up. A proposal and an estimate of how much the repairs would be."

"My daughter is an interior designer and decorator. She could completely overhaul the rooms, but what I'm worried about is structural and electrical."

"Had it all passed about two years ago, though I think there could be some rewiring needed in the office and the adjacent house, since it's probably the original electrics."

"Axton could do it," Steel mumbles to Hutch. "Deanna

could have a look at a couple of the rooms and see what's needed. As for the grounds, they need a complete overhaul. The pool doesn't work and hasn't for years."

"I've already got a quote for that," I say. "It's about five grand to reline and seal the entire pool. The concrete around the rim needs to be replaced, but it's only a small section. It needs new shade sails and brand-new filters, and the pump may need attention. Then there's the tennis court, which is a complete write-off."

"Easily fifty grand," Hutch says. "Maybe a hundred."

That's enough to put anyone off.

"But you yourself can see the potential it has," I say, before they change their minds. "There's a big mountain bike conference coming up in March. We'd have three months to get the majority of the work done just in time. It could be a big money spinner. At the moment, they're charging thirty-five a night, but we could easily get one twenty-five on a weekday and up to one seventy-five on weekends. For events like this, the price could go over two hundred a night. I've looked it up and there aren't many places to stay here for an event that big. People would have to commute from Mesa. If we could book out the entire weekend with all twenty-five rooms, that's fifteen grand just there." I'm getting excited now because I know we can make that money back fast. Bracken Ridge population has swelled in the last two years, and it's a popular tourist destination with Shothole Canyon, the wild gorges, botanical gardens, National Park, camping, scenic flights, 4WD tours, hiking, kayaking… the list is endless.

"You have done your homework," Hutch remarks.

"It was a big decision, uprooting my life to drive into the unknown, but something about this place spoke to me." I probably sound like a sentimental asswipe, but I don't care. I don't have to pretend to be anything other than what I am. Not for them, not for anybody. I'm protecting my peace this year; I vowed that when my mom passed away. I won't give anyone a piece of me this year without them earning it. Even with Steel and Lily. If they don't want to get to know me, that's fine, I'll live with it. But at the end of the day, I did nothing wrong. Hank did. And he's not here.

"They're also building the Skywalk at Shothole," Hutch pipes up. "It'll be open for the spring."

I read about this too. The lookout itself projects twenty-five meters beyond the gorge rim and is around a hundred meters from the river below. The views over the mountains, gorges, and desert below will be spectacular and will draw tourists from all over the country and the world.

"There is no reason why the motel couldn't be booked out for the grand opening," I say. "At the moment, we've no bookings in the system for that weekend."

I can see the wheels turning in their brains, but still, it is a lot of money to invest, and I'm not even 100% sure I want that. With investors, or in this instance, the Bracken Ridge Rebels motorcycle club, there'll be more than one person thinking they can boss me around and tell me what to do. That ain't happening.

Hutch is right. I do have to sit down and have a game plan and not just throw numbers around in the dark.

"Tourism is already up from last year," Hutch says, sitting back in his chair, his hands linked behind his head. "Don't see this year slowin' down anytime soon."

Steel nods in agreement.

I clear my throat. "How about I draw up a business plan, get some quotes, and you could do the same with Axton and Deanna, and then we'll know from both our standpoints if this is feasible or not," I say, hoping they'll give me a few days to get my shit together.

"Let's reconvene on Thursday," Hutch says. "I'll have Axton and Deanna come around to have a look around the property. We've got plenty of men that can hit hard and clean shit up, so that won't be a problem. The women can help Deanna set the rooms up, paint, decorate and shit, make it look all pretty."

"A pretty motel room," Steel mutters. "You feelin' all right, Prez?"

Hutch turns to look at him. "Never better."

I can't help the smile from spreading across my face. "Okay, well, in that case, I've got some homework to do."

Steel points at me. "Don't leave town, Lily wants to meet you."

In all the excitement, I'd kind of let that slip my mind. "That would be amazing."

"Yeah, well, Lily is impressionable, softer than the other members of the family," he says bluntly. "I don't want you gettin' her hopes up with any family reunion shit. I don't even know you. If she gets hurt…" He points at me.

"I'd never hurt her."

"I meant her feeling's, she's… emotional at the best of times. I'm layin' it on the table now. I'll throw fists and ask questions later if you do anything underhanded. I don't fuckin' care how many black belts you have, I'll still kick your ass, got me?"

Our eyes meet across the table. Now I see where I get my temper from, and it definitely wasn't my mom's side. She was the gentlest, kindest soul I've ever known.

"I got you, but like I said, I came here to make good. To get to know you and make a life here. I've no intention of hurting anyone. It's the last thing I would ever do."

He takes in my words for a few moments and gives me a chin lift. I think that means we're okay, but I'm still learning Steel grunt speech and what it all means.

Okay, we're definitely more alike than I gave him credit for. I'm fiercely protective of the women that have been in my life, and I'd protect my sister with all that I am. He needn't worry there. I have no intention of doing anything untoward. If anything, I should be suspicious of them. They're a biker club.

I run a hand through my hair, my emotions getting the best of me. I feel the anxiety creeping in and I know I have to get out of here.

"Get me those figures," Hutch says, wrapping the meeting up as he stands.

I follow suit. "I will, appreciate it."

Steel gives me another chin lift and I reciprocate, ideas and inspiration hitting me from all sides.

I know I want this. I know it feels right. I just have to weigh up if I want a biker club, with an estranged brother, who may or may not hate me, as my business partners.

A thought comes to mind as I leave the clubhouse; be careful what you wish for.

I just don't know if it's good or bad.

Knox

BRACKEN RIDGE
REBELS
ARIZONA
M · C

CHAPTER 8

REBEKAH

I'm ecstatic that Brayden had a great time at school today. He's spent all afternoon telling me all about his day and the new friends that he met. To say I'm relieved is an understatement. If my kid's happy; I'm happy.

As promised, we'll go to the Burger Joint for dinner, and I'll let Brayden order whatever he wants. This usually consists of the works burger and an extra-large order of fries, followed by an ice cream sundae.

The place is packed and it's a Monday night. I'm glad I rang ahead and booked us a table.

My kid is not usually nervous, but he has been for the last few days, so to see him with a happy heart and a spring in his step makes me feel like I've made the right decision by uprooting his life once again.

If only I could tell him it's for the best. Now that I'm sure we're safe, we can plant some roots and really settle down. I won't have to keep looking over my shoulder. Being in Phoenix was a steppingstone to this life, and I've done it. Finally.

Making it on my own is one of the biggest achievements I could ever ask for. I know I need to give myself a little more credit because I've worked hard. But seeing Brayden's happy face is all the reward I need.

With my two interviews lined up tomorrow, I'm hoping that I'll get offered one of the office jobs. Not that I'm opposed to serving coffee, but I'd much rather be in an office situation, which is where I excel.

At least the people here seem friendly. That's a bit of a relief. It really is a cliche that country people are just nicer.

I'm honestly not used to people looking me in the eye and saying "good morning" when you pass them down the street, or someone holding the door open for you rather than pushing past to get there before you. It's common decency, but not something that is prevailing in the city.

Everything just seems to be falling into place, and while I'm not a pessimist, I'm waiting for the punchline. I can't help it, it's just how I am. Can things really be this good? Even with talking to Angel this afternoon. She seemed really nice, and she's a working mom like me, although she has a husband, who I later learned is the Vice President of the Bracken Ridge Rebels. Not that I'm judging, but I never would've picked her for being the owner of the tattoo parlor in town. One of the greatest things in life is when women succeed, especially working moms, because we've got so much on our plates.

I would've liked to have more kids, but it just didn't work out for me. In some ways, I'm grateful because I wouldn't have wanted to have any more kids with my ex. Sometimes I dream about settling down with the right guy, a nice guy just to keep the dream alive, but it's not like I'm getting any younger. I would've loved to give Brayden a brother or sister, but a ten-year age gap is pretty big.

I don't know why my mind flicks to Knox the minute I start thinking about babies. The thought is preposterous. It was one night, so it's not like I know much about him, even if he had kids, which I don't think he did, but I never really got around to finding out. We texted a couple of times, but nothing really transpired because we were both so busy with moving and me trying to get my life together. It's not like I intended on our night together to be something more or to make it into something more than what it was. I don't wanna taint it, because it was just one really great night and I have to come to terms with that. Even if I do still fantasize about him and wonder what he's doing right this very minute. I should reach out, see if he's doing okay.

My hand reaches for my phone, and while Brayden is telling me all about Rawling's sticker collection, I decide to shoot him a text message.

Me: Hey Knox, how is everything? I hope you're
doing okay.

I hover after "okay," wondering whether to put a cross
after it, as that's what I automatically do in all my texts. But
I don't want that to seem too overzealous.

Then I realize I'm just overthinking it. I backspace over
the text. What good can come of torturing myself, even
though we agreed to just be friends? I laugh to myself, as if
me and Knox could just be friends. Not gonna happen. Nada.

I don't honestly think that two people who have had
sex before can be just friends. I think that's a load of horse
shit. And I don't also know what I would say to him if I
ever saw him again. Sometimes I fantasize about that too.
Would we hug? Would we kiss? I almost laugh again at
that. After what happened and the places he sent me that
night, I think a platonic kiss on the cheek would be safer,
but I'm probably incapable of keeping my hands off of
him. Lord knows I wasn't very good at it the first time, not
that he was complaining.

When Knox takes you to bed, he really does knock it
out of the park.

I don't know how Brayden fits in a strawberry sundae
after his meal, but then again, he's like me as a kid, with
hollow legs. I couldn't eat enough food, but I was working
all day when I wasn't in school, helping Daniel and Elijah

on the farm, milking the cows or sowing the seeds and gathering the crops. I miss being outside like I was back then. The fresh air. The smell of the earth. I'd love to one day have a veggie garden or a greenhouse to grow my own food. Some roots are deeply planted inside you and they'll be there forever, I've decided.

We head home after dinner, and I feel the heaviness in my heart lifting slightly as I tuck Brayden into bed after he brushes his teeth and puts on his pajamas.

"Mom?" he calls, when I go to leave his room. "Do you think we'll stay here a while?" His voice is sleepy as he battles to keep his eyes open.

We've moved a lot over the years, and I know it hasn't been easy.

I smile, turning out the light. "I think so, baby," I say. "Now go to sleep, you've had a big day."

"Night, Mom." He yawns while saying my name.

"Love you," I whisper as I leave his little makeshift bedroom.

I hope that I'm not lying to him inadvertently. He's a kid; he shouldn't have to worry about making friends and then packing up and leaving again. I haven't told him much about his real father, since I left before Brayden was born. But he can read between the lines, he's not dumb. But I won't put that burden on him. He needs to have a normal childhood where all he has to do is look forward to each day that we spend together, and he goes to school and makes new friends. I want that for him. I want it for me too.

After talking with Angel, I've realized how much I've missed having a real friend to talk to. I love my bestie Mallory.

But now that she's moved away, we don't get to see each other as much as we'd like to. She's the only person that knows about my previous life and I trust her with that information. To have someone to unload to when I needed it was a godsend, and the same for her. We've been there for each other in so many ways.

I turn off the TV, I'm beat. I check the locks on the doors before I switch off the lights and head to my room. I kick off my clothes and have a quick shower, pulling on my warm pajamas when I'm done. I crawl into bed with the intention of reading on my Kindle, but my mind wanders, like it always does, and I swipe open my phone.

> **Me:** hey Knox, how's it going? I'm sure between the two of us that we're expert packers by now. I hope you're well and things are working out for you
>
> x

This time, I don't hesitate. I press send before I can chicken out.

I don't know what's come over me. I mean, it isn't like we haven't texted before, but it's been almost a month.

I have no idea if he'll even give a shit, or reply, but I'm shocked when a reply comes back within a minute.

> **Knox:** hey, Red. I'm good. I would say my packing skills leave little to be desired. Paper plates are looking good here. How are you?

My heart skips a beat.

How am I?

God, it's a simple enough question, but my mind has an uncanny ability to go circling all the way back to him and our passionate night together. It's not my fault Knox is a fucking stud and he has the ability to fine tune my body in a way no other man has.

That's a goddamn gift.

My vibrator, thanks to him, has never been so overworked in its life.

Now I'm thinking about him, I start to panic, and then I don't know what to write back.

Be cool, I tell myself. For heaven's sake, he's probably living across the other side of America. The truth is, I haven't asked him where he moved because I really don't want to know. I don't want to know how long it would take me to get there from here, which is something I would totally do if I knew what town he was in.

I take a few deep breaths.

Me: Chinese takeout works wonders, and no dishes. I'm good, busy but good. I'm job hunting. I have an interview tomorrow.

The grey bubble starts to move as I wait for his reply, the butterflies in my stomach beginning to flutter.

Knox: I'll have to take note of that. Good luck with the job, though I'm sure you won't need it. How's your truck holding up?

I'm surprised he remembered. I told him in our last few texts my truck had broken down, but a Good Samaritan had helped me get it to the mechanic. It's running fine now, but I know I need a new car and soon. Another thing that I can't quite afford at the moment.

Me: It's holding up okay. It needs a lot of work so I'll be looking for a newer car before long. She's been good to me, but it's time.

And this is how it's been. No 'what are you wearing' questions or anything remotely sexy. It's like we've inadvertently moved into the friendzone.

Oh God. I don't know how to be his friend.

I want to be honest with him about how I can't stop thinking about him, but I don't know how he'll react, and I don't know if I'll just embarrass myself.

Knox: An upgrade is always good when a car reaches the point of you spending too much on it.
Me:I know but I love my truck. It's sentimental.
Knox: *laughing face emoji*
Me: why are you laughing at me?
Knox: I restored my Harley Davison. I get where you're coming from.

He rides a motorcycle?

Me: You did?
Knox: It's something I did in my spare time because the bike was beautiful… it just had no engine.

I snort a laugh.

Me: I can see how that would've been an issue.

I snuggle under the covers and turn off my lamp.

Knox: When I see something that tugs on my heartstrings, I'm a sucker until it's done. I can't rest, eat, or sleep.

Lucky fucking bike.

Me: I love that!

I don't know why I type that. I guess I have always loved restoring old to something new. Back when I was with the Amish, we learned early on the value of things and to make things ourselves. I appreciate what goes into a project like that.

Knox: I don't wanna sound like a weirdo…

My heart clunks in my chest at his words.

Me: But?
Knox: *laughing face emoji* but…I can't stop thinking about you. Is that wrong?

My eyes go wide. Holy crap!
Do I tell him the feeling's mutual? That all I seem to do is daydream about him.
Play it cool, I tell myself. He doesn't need to know everything.

Me: I can't stop thinking about you, either. That night we spent together was so damn hot.

Right between the fucking eyes. I slap my forehead.
What the fuck are you doing???

> **Knox:** I think about it all the time.
> **Me:** So do I.
> **Knox:** Want to know a secret?

I lean closer to my phone, like someone will overhear
us.

> **Me:** Yes. What?
> **Knox:** It's pretty shocking.
> **Me:** And here I was thinking you were such a nice
> guy.
> **Knox:** I am a nice guy, but around you, I've got a
> dirty mind.

Holy fucking crap!
My arm pits start to sweat. This man. This fucking man.
Is he… sexting me?
Am I down for that? I've never done anything like that
before…
I decide to play along.

> **Me:** What about when you're not around me?
> **Knox:** I've got an even dirtier mind.

I swallow hard. Before I can stop myself, I type,

Me: Do you touch yourself?

My heart is racing so hard, I can feel the blood pounding in my ears.

I wait anxiously for his reply, wondering if I've gone too far. But then…

Knox: Every fucking night.

I feel my nipples harden, and I clench my pussy. Jesus, he's so hot. The hottest fucking guy I've ever seen or been with, and he probably lives a million miles away. Life is so fucking unfair!

Me: I have no words.
Knox: Do you touch yourself, thinking about me?

My ears are hot as I sit up in bed and throw the duvet off. This is what this sex machine of a man does to me. He has me all hot and bothered over a few text messages and now I'm panting like a goddamn dog.

Sexting is so hot, and so much fun…

Me: Yes.

Knox: Battery operated, or manual?

I start to breathe in deeply so I don't combust.

Me: Both.

Knox: I bet you'd prefer my mouth on your pussy, wouldn't you, Red?

I almost reach for the nightstand. No! This is insanity. He shouldn't be able to undo me like this. Not over text.

Me: Jesus, Knox.

Knox: You're thinking about me right now, aren't you?

He likes the dirty, kinky shit, and I'm slowly realizing that I do too. I like being his good girl.

Me: I liked you spanking my ass.

Knox: Fuck.

Me: I felt you for days after.

Knox: You were a bad girl. You know what happens to bad girls who turn me on.

Me: I may need reminding.

I'm so wet. I slide my hand down into my pajama

bottoms and groan. My clit's sensitive as I run my fingers through my heat, picturing his tongue.

Knox: Fuck, I wish I could be there.

Me:I'm touching myself. You feel so good.

I'm unashamed around him, too. Something else I'm just beginning to realize.

Knox: Me too. My dick's so hard. I remember that hot little mouth.

Me: You started it. You went down on me first. No guys ever do that when you hook up.

Knox: That's because they're selfish bastards.

Me: I have to agree on that.

I ruck up my pajama top so I can see my breasts, settling my phone on my pillow pad. I start to play with my nipple, the other hand still rubbing myself. I know if I touch my clit, I'll come right this second. I want to draw it out.

Knox: Spanking your ass was a highlight.

Me: Yeah?

Knox: Yup.

Me: I wanted you to do more.

Knox: More? Like…fuck your ass?

I clench my legs together and stop rubbing. Shit. This is so damn hot.

Me: Maybe.

Knox: Maybe? Do you not like it?

Me: I don't know. I've never let anyone do that.

Why do I picture that smile spreading across his face?

Knox: Take your vibrator out. Hurry.

I reach to the side table and do as he says, starting the thing on a low setting.

Me: Got it.

Knox: How wet is your pussy?

Me: So wet.

Two seconds later, the phone rings. I panic…

I turn the speaker on and answer. "Hello?"

"Red?" Knox says. "I needed to hear your voice."

"You've got me squirming around here all alone in my bed."

He grunts. I know he's jerking himself off, his voice sounds strained. "Fuck, I wish I were there, baby. Touch yourself with it. Tell me how it feels."

I run the vibrator through my folds as it buzzes lightly on my clit. "Oh, God," I whisper. "Oh, Knox…"

"Fuck, that's it, Red, picture my tongue, lapping you up, eating you out, your fingers gripping into my hair as you grind your sweet pussy against my face."

I close my eyes, unable to think. I'm almost there. Shifting the vibrator back down my folds once more, I press it harder to my clit as my toes curl.

"Yes!" I whisper-shout. "Oh yes!"

"You're a bad girl, Rebekah. Bad girls get punished."

"Fuck me," I muffle, gripping the sheet beneath me as my whole body tightens.

"Don't come," he warns. "Don't come yet."

"I am… I'm coming… oh, Knox… oh yes!" I throw my head back and my release feels so intense. It's like I leave my body for a few moments.

This man. This fucking man.

I may never recover from my one-night stand and there isn't a damn fucking thing I can do about it.

BRACKEN RIDGE
REBELS
ARIZONA
M · C

CHAPTER 9

KNOX

I barely hold on to my sanity when I hear her come.

"Rebekah," I growl. "You came before I said you could." My cock grows even harder at the thought of her pleasing herself, calling my name when she did.

I had no fucking idea that we'd end up doing this after a few back-and-forth text messages, but I suppose I did instigate it.

"I couldn't hold it," she gasps. "You had me so turned on."

"Your ass is mine when I see you next," I tell her.

"I am bad. I need to be punished."

I grip my cock harder. I had to stop when she came so I didn't follow so quickly. I want to hear her over and over before I shoot my own release.

"How do you want me to punish you?" I grit out.

"Playing with my ass."

I snort a laugh. "Playing?"

"Well, to begin with. I liked you spanking my pussy."

"Jesus."

I spread my legs wider, cupping my balls and tugging them as I stroke myself, remembering her hot little mouth. I'm pissed that she's using a fucking vibrator and not my cock. I need to fucking see her. I haven't been with another woman since her. And I've already been accosted by a few of the local single ladies. I just can't bring myself to do it. There's something wrong with me, and it's all her fault.

"I'm gonna do a lot more than that when I see you again," I vow. "Touch your tits, Red. Pull on those nipples and put the vibrator inside your pussy. Fuck yourself slowly with it."

She sighs. "Oh…"

"How does that feel?"

"Good, but not as good as you."

I grin. My hand starts to speed up as I picture her tits bouncing like they did when she rode me. I also picture her over my knee when I spanked her ass red, then took her in the shower, bending her over and giving her my cock.

"You've got a dirty little mouth," I growl.

"You've got a nice big cock," she says back, her breathing shallow.

"What do you want that cock to do to you?"

"Tease me, rub the head against my clit, but don't let me come, making me wait for it. Making me needy for it. I'm so wet for you."

I bite down on my lip, my hand working faster as I

picture it. "That's it, baby, oh yeah. I wanna taste that sweet honey on my tongue. I wanna fuck you with it until your screaming my name and nobody else's. That pussy is mine, Red, that body is mine. Got me?"

"Yes… it's yours… oh, Knox, I can't hold on…"

"Fuck yeah. Come, baby, tell me how much you like my cock inside you."

"It's filling me," she cries in a soft whisper. "It's so big, oh yes, yes! Oh, Knox!"

Her groans send me over the edge. I start to come, fucking my fist, wishing more than anything it was her pussy I was thrusting into and not my own hand. Spurting hot sticky cum on myself, I close my eyes and try to regain control of my breathing.

"Red?" I pant, a second later. "You still with me?"

"Yes," she whispers. "That was so good."

"You like me talking dirty to you?"

"I think you already know the answer to that."

I grin. "I'd better get cleaned up."

I can imagine her biting her lip as she watches me, seducing me all over again with those deep hazel eyes.

"Yes, I'd better do the same."

"That was fun," I say, then feel like a fucking asshole.

"It was," she says quietly. "Goodnight, Knox."

I want to ask her when I can see her again, where she is, and how soon I could get there… but it's late, and she obviously wants to go.

"Goodnight, Bekah."

She hangs up and I'm left in my own wet puddle, wondering if this is how things are gonna be from now on and not feeling very good about any of that.

I need her.

And I can't fucking have her.

I've never felt so torn about anything in my whole life.

I wake up to my dog licking me on the face. "Evie," I groan when she does it again. "Lay off."

She makes a groaning noise and proceeds to circle around me, finally crashing down half on top of my legs and half on my torso, winding me in the process. My dog likes to think she's a human, and this human has no boundaries or cares about personal space.

She's a very large Boxer and has no idea that she's as big as she is.

One day, she showed up at my place, skinny and full of mange. I fed her and she kept coming back. One day, I'd gained her trust enough to let her inside so she could keep warm and have a safe place to sleep. After that, it was decided she had to bathe. She stank like a garbage truck. She never left.

I took her to the vet, and we learned she had a broken bone in her leg that was likely caused by being run over. It had never quite healed properly by itself.

She had no microchip, and she wasn't registered at any shelter or pound.

The day I took her home after being treated at the vet, I knew we'd found each other at the right time. My mom had just been diagnosed with cancer and I'd broken up with my girlfriend. Life was pretty shitty. Then Evie came along, and she put me through the ringer.

In a lot of ways, she saved me. I had to give her medication, look after her, feed her, walk her, teach her to go outside and not all over my rug, and it was the best thing that ever happened to me. That was almost three years ago. Now she runs the household.

"You weigh, like, sixty pounds," I say, trying to push her off. "And that's my bladder."

She groans when I slide out of bed, not moving one inch, as I go pee and turn the coffee machine on.

I don't even want to think about today and what it entails. My head may spin off.

I brew the coffee, waiting impatiently, and when I walk back to my bedroom, Evie is snoring on her back.

I chuckle, shaking my head as I head to the shower.

I don't stay in there for very long, and I definitely don't think about Rebekah. God, that was so hot last night. I don't even have words. Hearing her voice again was one thing, but hearing her moans down the line was quite another. I never expected this and it's all my fault. I shouldn't have initiated the dirty talk; I should've left things alone, but typical of me, I didn't. I decided what I wanted and I went for it.

She has absolutely no clue what she does to me, but I've never quite had a night like that before. Sexting isn't something high on my repertoire. I'm kind of old school. I don't even remember to text people back.

Remembering her soft lips, her flaming red hair, and that curvy, sexy body. I meant what I said, it should be illegal. It's not like I haven't thought about it, what it would be like to be with her if we lived in the same place.

I'll text her today and find out where she is. I need to see her. I don't even care if I have to fly to another state, it would be worth it. I dress quickly, leaving some biscuits out for Evie after she's been out and peed, and throw some toast down my neck.

I've got a couple of interviews today, and since my office manager refuses to come back, I get to conduct the interviews, which isn't something I've ever done before. I mean, how hard could it be? I even googled some interview questions, so at least I'll appear to not be quite as clueless as I look. Or at least that's what I hope. Judging from what some people have told me about some of the locals around here, I'll be lucky to find somebody competent enough on short notice.

The number of times that I have heard already that good workers are hard to find, it's almost now a mantra in my head. The least I can do is put positive vibes out there that I will get the right person. There is no way that I can do the office work myself and take bookings or align with all the repair work needed. It's just not possible. I don't even know how to work the computer system, and quite frankly, I don't want to. I'm not usually one to panic, but if I don't hire somebody soon, this whole business could go under, and I haven't even finished writing up my business plan yet.

I spent all night last night working on it until Rebekah texted me. But I need to get my head in the game if I'm gonna get through today, and that means no more thinking about her. Nothing can be gained by reliving last night. I can save that for later, anyway. She is fast becoming a woman I just cannot get out of my head. I've hardly told her anything about myself, but I feel like I could. There's just something about her voice. And she has a cute little laugh too. Those hazel eyes, they feel like they're looking right into my soul.

I guess I've always been a bit of a romantic at heart. I always hope for the best in any situation. Even the ones that seem fruitless, when I've been down on my luck, and nothing seems to go right, I always try to see the bigger picture. Things always work out one way or the other, and sometimes it's not the way you think, but I've learned to understand that everything really does happen for a reason.

I just can't work out what the reason is, why we are apart. More to the point where I don't have to slap myself. I've turned into a pussy overnight, but I've heard of it happening and it's happened to my friends. When you meet someone and just have that spark. And then out of nowhere you realize that gravity isn't holding you to the earth anymore, but it feels like she is.

I have to believe for whatever reason, I'm here in Bracken Ridge, and I'm doing the right thing, and if I'm not, well, I guess I'll find out soon enough.

I've decided that if Hutch and the club are on board, I will take them up on the offer. What have I honestly got to lose? I don't know for a fact that somebody like Hutch wouldn't put up money like that, serious money, if he didn't think it was a gold mine too. Like he said when we first met, he'd been trying to buy this place for years. That right there tells me everything I need to know and that's why this opportunity has presented itself, and I can't look a gift horse in the mouth.

I've got everything worked out on my end. I'll do a lot of the carpentry myself. I'm pretty good at landscaping too. What we really need are lots hands willing to do hard work.

Sure, we can get Axton to rewire the electrical, we can install new heating and cooling, we can realign the pool and fix the tennis court, and get Deanna to redecorate all the rooms, but it's impossible to do all the groundwork without a team. And since the motorcycle club has a lot of members, I'd be stupid to pass this up.

A part of me felt a bit pigheaded in the beginning, because I wanted to succeed and do this on my own, for my mom's sake. For some reason, I felt like I had to prove something to her, even though I already know she was proud of me, and how far I've come.

I just wish she told me about it sooner, and I wish that she lived a better life. Even though she never complained, and she always had a smile on her face, she didn't deserve what Hank put her through, and maybe that's what I'm doing, trying to wash away the sins of my father, which is ridiculous. The mistakes he made were his alone and not my burden to carry.

I'm fairly happy about how things went with Steel, even though I can't tell whether he actually likes me or not. I keep coming back to the part where he didn't kick my ass, so that's gotta be a good thing. And Lily wants to meet me properly, something I can't wait to do. I think I'll stop by the beauty salon this afternoon and say hi. It may be kinda awkward, but I've always loved the idea of having a sister. It actually makes me chuckle when I remember Lily trying to get to see me that night at the gate, and happy since she was a little fireball that reminds me of my younger self. I like how she was trying to see me. She's definitely got the Steelman genes. I'm fast learning that we've all got a bit of a temper. Maybe she'll be a little more accommodating, a little less suspicious, but I won't hold my breath.

And then there's Steel and Lily's mom. I honestly don't know what I'd say. "Hi, Mrs. Steelman, I'm your ex-husband's secret love child" doesn't exactly have a ring to it.

I guess I'll deal with that and cross that bridge when I come to it.

My first interview doesn't show up. We're off to a great start. My second interview is with a young woman who acts like she's been forced to come here by the unemployment office to say she's attended. I feel like today could be one of those days where I flip out.

After lunch, I have one more interview, and I'm rummaging around to find her application and resume, so I don't look like a complete asshole. I don't know what fucking Vi did in this place, but tidying up and keeping her space clutter free weren't high on her agenda.

I hunt high and low and then finally find it when the phone rings. Spilling my coffee all over the paperwork, I cuss and answer the phone at the same time. Maybe I should have let Evie just stay lying on top of me and not have gotten out of bed today. That would've been a better idea, in hindsight.

As I'm trying to get the computer on to check some dates, having no clue how I would even do that, the door chime sounds. I hold up a finger without looking at the customer, and tell them I'll just be a minute, while balancing the phone between my ear and my shoulder.

The computer makes a weird noise, which doesn't sound good. In the meantime, the customer on the phone decides to give me their life story and why they're visiting Bracken Ridge. Clearly, they must've seen some photos on the internet that do not resemble the motel. For one, we have no jacuzzi or a steam room. When I try to interject, they keep talking over me, wanting the best price possible because they're return guests.

Ain't no way these people have stayed here before, I think sagely.

"I think you have the wrong motel; we don't have those facilities, I'm afraid."

"But you have a pool, don't you?"

"Yes, but it's under repair at the moment."

"Will it be working by April?"

"I hope so." I scratch my head.

"Is it heated?"

"At the moment, it has more sand in it than the Sahara, so it wouldn't be fair to say it's heated as such." Are people always this difficult?

"And you have a restaurant?"

"No, we don't. The Stone Crow is a short walk on the same street in the heart of town. Our motel is currently under construction…"

"Do you have disabled facilities?"

"No, but we're…"

"Isn't that illegal?" This woman is doing my head in. Seriously. I may just bang my head against the desk from sheer exhaustion.

"Like I was about to say, we're fixing that."

"So, you've no steam room, jacuzzi, your pool is full of sand, there's no restaurant or disabled access, and you're charging over a hundred dollars per night? That's disgraceful. You should be ashamed of yourself! I need to speak to the manager."

"Too bad, she quit. And for the hundredth time, no, we're not charging over a hundred dollars per night. You have the wrong motel. Our rooms are thirty-five dollars per night. I don't know how many times I have to say that WE'RE UNDER CONSTRUCTION." My voice gets louder, and I want to fucking choke this woman.

"Do you do room service?"

I hang up the phone.

How do people deal with these kind of situations all day long? If someone is going to call up and abuse me, they could have the decency to get the right place when doing so.

I lean forward and bang my head against the desk.

Then a woman clears her throat.

My eyes spring open.

Shit.

In all the commotion, I forgot about the customer who walked in.

I scratch my head, feeling a little flustered, and stand at the same time.

"I'm so sorry about th-"

I stare at Rebekah.

What in the ever-living fuck is she doing here?

I squint like I may have just conjured her up in my mind because she's inadvertently now my 'happy place,' but that doesn't mean I want her showing up in the middle of my work day, while I'm arguing with a customer. I blink a few more times.

"Knox?"

"Rebekah?"

She nods. "Uh, hi."

I stand there like a bleating idiot. "What are you doing here?" I stammer.

Her eyes are wide, and her cheeks are flushed. "I, uh, I'm here for the interview."

Interview? I'm still clutching the paperwork, which is still wet from my coffee spilling episode earlier. Glancing down at it, I see her name at the top.

Rebekah Dove.

Granted, I didn't even know her last name. Trust it to be something pretty, just like the rest of her.

I run a hand through my hair. "Uh, hi."

My day from hell may have just turned a corner.

Things are finally looking up.

BRACKEN RIDGE
REBELS
ARIZONA
M · C

CHAPTER 10

REBEKAH

I stare at him, blinking, unable to fathom what he's doing here, behind the counter of the Bracken Ridge Motel. And then it hits me. Have we actually fucking moved to the same town? I try to stop the heart palpitations racing away in my chest as he stares back at me in complete bewilderment. Like I may disappear just as fast as I showed up.

"This is a surprise," I manage, suddenly feeling bashful. Especially after what we did last night. My poor vibrator got a hammering.

He looks lost for words. Then he says, "I wasn't expecting…"

"Me either." I pause for a moment. "So you moved to Bracken Ridge?"

I feel like an ass, it's obvious, but I just need to clarify that he's not just down here filling in or something.

He runs a hand through his hair, which he's done several times since I entered the reception area. This is a new side to Knox. I haven't seen him flustered before, but I think that last phone call just about did him in for real.

"Home sweet home." He drops the papers he's holding on the desk and walks around to my side, closing the gap. "Can I hug you?"

I'm taken aback that he has to even ask. I mean, after everything we've done together? Just the shock of seeing him, standing here in the flesh, has my feet planted to the ground, and I can't move.

I fucked myself with my dildo last night and called his name out several times while he jerked himself off, and he wants a hug? I almost see the irony in it and hold back a laugh, my happiness at seeing him again overshadowing all other emotions.

"Of course, you can hug me," I say. Everything about his sweet side comes flooding back. How he has to get consent. How attentive he was. How he took care of me.

As he gets closer, I remember how good he smelled. He has a deep, musky scent. It's very masculine, very Knox, and so damn sexy. Already my hormones go into overdrive. There is just something about this man, and now he's standing here right in front of me, and I have no idea what to say.

We embrace, and as I fold my arms around his back, they barely reach the whole way round. That's how wide he is.

When he lets go, I realize I've been holding my breath.

He stands back, and his hands reach to my shoulders as he stares down at me. "How have you been, Bekah?"

I nod, trying not to show how overwhelmed I am right now. "I've been good," I say. "Busy… I had no idea you moved here… to Bracken Ridge… we never said where we ended up."

"That's probably because I would have hunted you down even if you'd moved to Australia." He smiles. "I thought you were going east?" His eyes, his fucking eyes…

"I was, but when I took a drive down here one weekend, I instantly fell in love with the place. Moving out of state was just too expensive, and I had to get out of the city. I did some research and found the rentals were cheap, there were plenty of jobs… and I wanted somewhere quiet and safe." I almost let it slip about Brayden's school. He doesn't even know I have a kid, and now I need to tell him.

That's the truth of it. Sometimes I just get a feeling about a place. I can't describe it, it's like I get good and bad vibes, and for some unexplainable reason, Bracken Ridge just really sang to me. Brayden also loved it, and I could see us riding our bikes and having ice cream on the weekends, enjoying the amazing hiking trails and even camping, completely leaving the past behind us. It's country meets the desert out here, with that small town feel where everyone is close knit and looks out for one another, something else I crave.

"Wow." He still stands there, looking down at me with a

grin spread across his face. "Talk about a coincidence."

"Well, apparently, there are no such things as coincidences," I say, trying to keep the conversation light.

"I can't believe it's you." He shakes his head, rubbing his chin with one hand.

"You're probably the last person I expected to see," I admit, still dazed. "Working in reception?"

He laughs. "Don't even get me started. Clearly, you can see I have no skill at all when it comes to customer service or using a computer. Can I get you a coffee?" He turns back to the desk, and I check out his ass in the jeans he's wearing. Holy fuck. I cannot work with this man. I want to jump his bones right this very minute.

"That would be great," I find myself saying.

"Follow me."

I look around as I pass by the messy desk area and follow him into what looks like a makeshift break room, just as messy as the reception desk. Wow, this man needs help.

"You're working here now?" I find it hard to believe that this is his forte.

"Worse, I own the joint."

My eyebrows rise in surprise as he flicks the coffeemaker on and turns to me.

I remember him saying he had family south of the city, but that it was complicated.

"You do? Wow."

He nods. "My mom owned the motel, actually. I came out here to try to make a go of things, but it's been one disaster after another. He spreads his arms wide. "As you can see."

"What happened to the last person?" I try not to smile.

He puts his hands on his hips and gives me a grin. "You think I did something?"

"I guess I probably do assume that, considering the office looks like a bomb hit it, and you're answering the phone without knowing how to work your computer and ticking off customers, then hanging up on them." I give him a lopsided smile.

"I guess you found me out," he replies, leaning against the kitchen bench. "I can assure you I have no way of digging my way out of this hole, and to answer the question, the office manager quit the minute I got here when I had the audacity to ask her why this place was such a dump and why she didn't do any work. She walked out on me."

"Knox, I'm so sorry."

"I get that funds were limited, but still. Look around, this place is a shambles."

"It does need a little bit of TLC," I say, not wanting to be rude, but I also don't want to sugarcoat it. It looks terrible. "Or a lot."

He snorts a laugh, turning to take two mugs from the cabinet, his t-shirt rising up at the back so I see the muscles above his waistline. My mouth waters. He is one fine specimen of a man. "Yeah. A lot is more like it. So, how's everything going? When did you get to town?"

"It's going well. I got here about two weeks ago."

He shakes his head. "I can't believe I've been here for about the same amount of time, and I haven't run into you."

"I stay in a lot," I say. "I've been job hunting, unpacking, and trying to get the house in order."

He nods, completely engaged in what I'm saying. "Unpacking is the worst. I can't believe the amount of shit you accumulate, and I only had a small apartment."

I smile. "Tell me about it. Do you live onsite?"

He nods. "In the apartment just above. Convenient, but it also means I'm here every second of every day, and then I start fixing shit at weird times of the day and night when I can't sleep."

My whole body tingles thinking about us living in the same place and not even knowing.

Was he just saying all of that last night because it was the heat of the moment? And living far away, or so we thought, made it much more exciting than it would normally be?

One look at his face and his warm, strong body taking up so much room in this tiny space tells me I'm wrong.

Knox is just that; warm. It radiates off him. You can't help but feel that warmth in his presence and gravitate toward it. Not for the first time, I feel relaxed around him. I can't explain it.

"White with two sugars?" he asks, his back to me.

My eyebrows shoot up. He remembered how I take my coffee?

"You have a good memory."

He chuckles. "For some things."

My heart warms just a little bit.

I watch him diligently make my coffee like it's his mission in life, all the while I cannot get my head around any of this. Talk about fucking weird.

"So, do you think you'd be a good addition to the team?" he asks. Then I realize he's talking about the job.

"Is this the part where my interview starts?"

He turns and gives me a devilish grin. "Well, you told me you worked at a tire store running the office, so I kinda figure that makes you way more qualified than me right off the bat."

I look down at my feet, then back at him again. "This is a little more complicated, Knox."

"How come?"

I swallow hard. "Do I have to spell it out?"

"Because we slept together?"

"And last night." My cheeks flush.

His back goes rigid, and he does this thing where he stills, and then shakes it off. "That was fucking hot," I hear him mumble.

"See, right there. I can't work for you when we have a… history."

"History?" He chuckles, turning to hand me my coffee. I take it gratefully. "You're just saying that because you think all I want is sex."

I let out a slow breath, trying to calm myself. "See, that right there. Bosses and employees don't discuss… sex," I whisper. "It's not what you'd call ethical around the workplace."

He chuckles again. "Bekah, I'm in need of somebody to dig me out of this hole. If you're up for a challenge, the job's yours. It'll just be sorting the office out, filing shit, learning the booking program, and checking guests in—not that there are many of those. Once things pick up around here, I'll get someone else to fill in. I'm paying above the national average, and I'll be a good boss. I'll stay out of your way." The way he says that part indicates he has no intention of doing so.

Stay out of my way? Huh? That's the last thing I want.

"I just think… it could be a great opportunity, but also a little awkward."

"Do I make you uncomfortable?"

I shake my head. "It's not that…"

"Then what is it then?"

"Knox, that whole thing about people being friends

after they've… had sex… that's one thing, but working together?"

"Are you afraid I won't respect you?" His brow furrows.

My heart could fucking melt. Won't respect me? I want him to bend me over, pull my hair, and call me his dirty slut.

I take a deep breath.

Obviously, I can't say what I'm thinking out loud.

"No, but I'll be honest, this has all come right out of the blue." And also, the fact that I won't be able to take my eyes, hands, and mouth off you.

"Let me get this straight, you won't even let me give you the job description?" He looks at me without a trace of a smile, but I know he's being flirty as fuck. His eyes, like the crystal blue depths of the ocean, just about bring me to my knees. I think he knows the power he has over me, and my body.

"I think I'm well aware of exactly what you have in mind for a job description," I drawl.

One eyebrow quirks. "I can keep my personal life separate."

I laugh. "Really?"

He shrugs. "How hard could it be?"

"You clearly have been out of the game for longer than I first thought."

His lips twitch. "I guess I have. What if I got down on

my knees and begged?"

"I'd like to see that." I take a sip as he places his mug on the little table and starts to get down on his knees. My eyes go wide. "I was kidding!"

"I'm a desperate man."

"Knox!" I chastise, laughing. "Stop it, get up off the floor!"

"I'm just saying, if you leave me here, I could get lost under the mountain of paperwork and never resurface. Do you want that on your conscience?"

This man is incorrigible.

"You don't even know if you want to hire me yet. I could be useless."

He snorts. "Yeah, right."

I shake my head, blowing into my coffee as he rises from his knees, a dark, sexy look on his face. "Well, it's true. But you're welcome to call my references." Please stop looking at me like that.

"I don't need to do that, Rebekah. I know who you are."

I swallow hard.

The truth is, he hardly knows me at all, yet it feels like we've known each other forever. And as much as I try not to, I can't stop thinking about last night. Is he thinking it too?

"You do?" I quirk an eyebrow.

"If you want, I could walk you through the basics, and

you can decide if you want to climb aboard."

I look at him, startled.

He makes a face. "That wasn't meant to come out the way it did."

I try not to laugh. "Now everything we say is going to sound dirty, no matter how innocent it is, right?"

"Something like that. I'm just so happy to see you again. Am I allowed to say that?"

There goes my damn heart, thrumming harder in my chest. "I don't know what the rules are between a one-night stand and a potential boss, but it's something I'm willing to get to the bottom of."

The side of his mouth turns up. I press my legs together, remembering where he had that mouth is all too much to think about right now.

Taking a job here is not a good idea. NOT A GOOD IDEA!

Do I ever listen to my inner voice that tells me no? Nope.

"You're not like anybody I've ever met, Rebekah. Do you know that?" He moves closer.

"I just…"

My heart thuds again. "You just?"

"I said that if we ever met again, I'd take you on a proper date."

I want him to, so much. But I also know that if I'm

crazy enough to take the job where I've fucked my boss and we had phone sex, I'm asking for trouble. This won't end well.

A part of me knows that, not when we're attracted to one another.

"You really don't have to do that. Anyway, if I take the job, we probably should set some rules."

His lips do that twitch thing again. "Rules?"

"I'm not even sure if working for you, after what we did, is a good thing, so having rules means we both know exactly what's what, right?"

"Are you secretly turning me into a submissive?"

I almost choke on my coffee. After just seeing him on his knees, now I'm picturing him on his knees completely naked, his arms tied behind his back. Holy mother of God.

What the hell is wrong with me?

I blame him. In all fairness, he's the one talking about kinks.

"I wouldn't dream of it."

"Good, but I can't deny that I like a woman who takes over in the bedroom."

My mouth feels dry, and I'm wet between my legs. I contemplate going over to the door, locking it, and climbing aboard, but just as I think it, the bell over the door sounds as someone enters the office.

Knox doesn't take his eyes from mine. "I'll be right

back. Don't go anywhere."

I nod, but don't say anything.

Saved by the fucking bell.

I hear voices out front, and Knox greets the dude.

"Colt," the guy says, introducing himself. "Hutch sent me and the prospects over—who are late—to start haulin' shit out of the pool."

"Knox." It sounds like they shake hands. "Thankful for all the help I can get."

"I dread to think what's stuck in those filters."

It's weird. The man's voice seems familiar, and I don't know why, which is dumb. I don't know anybody else in this town aside from Knox, and I didn't know he lived here five minutes ago.

I'm reeling about these feelings for Knox that are surfacing and how this is going to work.

Me as his employee?

After we fucked?

I just don't see how any of this can be good in the long run. It's messy.

Then I remind myself I have bills to pay and the money here would be more than I'd be making at The Coffee Bean.

This isn't fucking high school anymore. We're sophisticated adults, so surely, we can work together and not let it affect whatever goes on outside of the office? People can do that, right?

My how I have changed my tune in a matter of minutes. Now I'm convincing myself that this arrangement could work.

If the man wasn't so goddamn attractive, then I might be able to keep a straight thought in my head.

A few moments later, he walks back into the break room.

"Would you like a grand tour?"

I bite my lip, unsure all over again. This is an intersection that could impact my life permanently. No, I definitely shouldn't follow him anywhere, yet I find myself nodding as I take him in, larger than life in the doorway. "It couldn't hurt."

He gives me a chin lift, clearly satisfied with that reply. "Perfect."

I down the rest of my coffee, noting how good he made it, just like he did that morning after we… No! No more illicit thoughts about Knox in the buff. It's too much.

I need to remember that money pays the bills, not daydreaming about a man who is now going to possibly be the one calling the shots. I feel uneasy, but it isn't his fault. He couldn't possibly know. Not every man is after something; there are some nice guys out there.

He's one of them. I'm sure of it. Still, my heart is wary.

Instead of letting him know my tiresome inner monologue, I smile instead and say, "Lead the way."

BRACKEN RIDGE
REBELS
ARIZONA
M · C

CHAPTER 11

KNOX

I let her walk in front of me as we leave the staff room. Showing her around the rest of the office, the grounds, and one of the rooms so she can see what they look like. She nods politely and smiles, and when every now and again her eyes meet mine, it's like I'm seeing her for the first time.

She's more beautiful in person than my memory could ever give her credit for. I didn't do her enough justice. The fact she's wearing business attire; a pencil skirt, a blouse, and a blazer, turns me the fuck on. Her long, fiery locks are tied back, barely kept in place by a loose bun. I keep imagining my hand wrapped around it, yanking her hair loose.

I don't know the fucking protocol here.

I'm in unfamiliar territory.

But the only thing that feels awkward is what I'm going to do with my hands. I don't know if I can keep from touching her, yet she isn't mine.

What if we did please ourselves last night over the phone because we knew that we couldn't see each other in real life, and that's why it was so fucking hot? I didn't know just how fucking close she was.

"The property is much bigger than it looks from the front," she says quietly. "I can see what you mean about it being rundown and looking old. So did your mom have someone looking after the place?"

"Yes, she did. She only came down here a couple of times, but it was years ago. They had a small budget to keep the grounds clean and tidy. The rooms were dirt cheap, needless to say, so was everything else. I'm guessing the photos they took and sent to my mom showing how everything was looking were completely fake."

"That's really shady," she says. "No wonder you fired the manager."

"Technically, I didn't fire her, she quit. I think she was hoping that I would fire her so she could sue me for unfair dismissal… she had it in for me ever since I set foot in the place."

"Because she was used to doing whatever the hell she wanted, which wasn't much."

"Exactly."

"So what do you plan on doing with the place? I guess there's a lot of maintenance to do in order to fix everything and get things how you want them."

I run a hand through my hair as we walk. For about the last ten minutes, I've had absolutely no tension at all, which is a first. Ever since I stepped foot in this place because all I've done is worry.

All I've been feeling is anxiety when wondering how I'm gonna get through paying the bills and keeping the place afloat without sinking. There is so much to do, so much, in fact, that the Bracken Ridge Rebels are lending a hand. I'm grateful for it.

"It's a money pit," I agree. "And I'm not exactly rolling in dough."

"It's a shame, it has potential. The location, for one."

"I've had offers to buy the place. It's prime real estate, but all they want to do is bulldoze it, and probably build some monstrosity in its place. I guess I'm kind of nostalgic about old buildings, even though this place is clearly a wreck. I feel like I can do something with it."

"Like all good things, you have to have the vision first," she says. "But I can see that there's a lot of work that's going to go into it to get it up to scratch. I'm starting to think that the office work is the easy part."

"Completely agree. Now you can see how daunting it all is."

"I don't envy you. Though have you thought about investors? I'm sure there would be no shortage of businesspeople wanting to keep the motel local, and not bought by some conglomerate or overseas buyer."

"I've had plenty of interest, but a part of me is stubborn.

Kinda like my mama in that way. If I see a challenge or something that scares me, instead of running away, I'll run toward it, at full speed, until it doesn't scare me any longer and it's just a blip."

She looks at me, her eyes soft, and we share a moment. It's soft and tender and catches me off guard.

We are technically complete strangers. I know small pieces of information about her life, but nothing concrete.

It's like I gravitate toward her so easily, and I shouldn't. I should keep my distance, especially since she's about to become my new employee, or so I hope.

"I've never really heard anyone say that before," she says, a little smile on her lips. "But I guess the only real way to overcome a fear, or an obstacle, is to go straight through it. That makes sense."

"Or maybe I'm just a glutton for punishment." I laugh.

"Maybe?" she agrees.

"So what do you think? Do you want to come and work for me?"

She hesitates, and my heart sinks. I know it's sure to be a little awkward, given our attraction, but it isn't a good enough reason for her to turn it down.

Suddenly, I want her to say yes. I want her to come and work for me, not just because a part of me wants to be close to her, to watch her every day, making sure she's safe, and above all else, ensuring she's around me and not some other guy. It's not right of me to feel this possessive of her. I barely know her. But that doesn't seem to stop me; it only makes things worse, and it only makes me want her even more. This is very dangerous territory. I know it, she knows it, yet here we are. She's standing in front of me, looking like some sort of angel, even if I'm fully aware that she's a bad girl underneath this whole prim persona she has going on.

I should really stop these lustful thoughts, especially because I want her to work here so bad and I don't want her to think I'm being a creep. I'm not.

"What, if you're just saying that you want me to work for you because you feel bad?"

I stare at her, bewildered. "What would I have to feel bad about?"

"The fact we slept together, and you now feel obliged to give me a job."

"I would never do something like that," I say earnestly. "I admit it would be a perk seeing you every day, and I'd be lying if I said otherwise. But there's something about you, Red. There is a warmth to you that makes the people around you feel relaxed and comfortable." I hope that doesn't sound too weird.

She stares at me, and hopefully she doesn't think I've lost my mind. I've always been a straight between the eyes kinda guy, and often it gets me into trouble, but I can't lie to her. I have no reason to. I've never lied in my entire life, and I don't plan on doing it now, just to save face. My ego isn't that big.

"It doesn't sound weird at all," she says. "I feel the exact same way about you, as it happens."

We slowly walk back toward the reception area, and I look down as she keeps her hands occupied by interlacing her fingers. Why is she nervous?

"Well, I'm glad I haven't freaked you the fuck out. Sometimes I just say things that fly out of my mouth, without thinking. Most things I should probably think through before I say them out loud."

This gets me a little laugh. And it's a lovely sound, so very sweet, just like her.

I don't know how the fuck I'm gonna work with her.

"I'd love to give it a shot," she says, surprising me. "But I have to go ahead and ask the question, what about… us? As in, do we just forget about what happened and continue on as… friends?"

I love the ways she says "us."

Shut this down.

This woman is maddening.

I definitely do not like the way she says friends.

In fact, just the thought of her being just my friend makes me feel uneasy. Then it means that she's on the market for any other guy to come along and sweep her up.

Again, that possessive urge comes over me. It's something I usually feel for the women I've had relationships with, including my mother. But certainly not for a woman I've only just met and spent a little time with. We have a connection. That's all there is to it.

"Do you really think it's possible that we just remain platonic?" I find myself asking, curious as to what she's going to say.

"Think about it, Knox. If we dated… or whatever, then when things didn't work out, or you found out something about me you didn't like, what then? It'd be super awkward at work. I wouldn't be able to stay, and we'd both be back at square one."

Maybe she's thinking we just had one hot night and that's all there is to it? What if she's letting me down gently, and I'm just not getting it? What if she just really needs this job, and I'm reading too much into it? Am I that much of an asshole?

"What wouldn't I like about you?"

She shrugs. "Plenty of things."

"Such as?"

"I can be annoying."

"I find that highly doubtful."

"I have one of those high, squeaky laughs like Minnie Mouse."

My lips twitch as I fight a smile. "You have a perfectly

normal, and slightly adorable laugh." Jesus, I wanna fuck her throat.

"I can be messy."

"I can tell you're not by the way you're dressed and how neat you have that unruly hair tied into that bun." A cock-teasing bun, no less.

I catch her eyes flicking down to my mouth. She can't look at me like that. It isn't fair.

I know she needs this job, and I certainly don't want her to feel obliged to take it, but to have her this close… it would be absolutely impossible. Keeping my hands to myself would be a fucking full-time job in and of itself.

"It's my interview hair. Sophisticated and boring, and the drabbest clothes I own to impress my future boss."

"It's working, and trust me, it's far from boring."

I go to open the door at the same time she does and our fingers touch. She gasps as she darts her hand away. The feel of her skin, even so slightly, has my dick hard in my pants.

This woman made me give myself a hand-job last night that just about gave me a fucking heart attack.

Her lips part as I hold the door open and motion for her to go inside.

"Thank you," she murmurs under her breath as I follow her inside.

"If you want to, why not come in tomorrow. I can show

you the booking system, which I barely know anything about, and we can go from there. That's if you want to."

"Are you hiring me, Mr..."

"Steelman."

"Your name is Knox Steelman?"

"In the flesh."

She giggles. I realize I like that sound, too. "That's a very strong name. It suits you."

"You don't get to call me Mr. Steelman, though."

She turns to face me, and I know I'm in her personal space, but I no longer care.

"How come?"

"Because I don't think I'd recover."

I don't mean to flirt, but it's so fucking hard. Maybe I should convince her to turn around and walk straight out and not come back, not that I want that, but she's right that we're playing with fire.

Her tongue darts out to lick her bottom lip for a split second, and that move alone is too fucking distracting.

I don't want her to work for me. Oh no, I want her to work under me. But now if we go back on it, it'll seem like I just wanna sleep with her and nothing more.

She doesn't seem to realize that I'm slightly in awe of her.

"And that's why I should take the job at Coffee Bean," she mutters, with a slight sigh, like it's the last thing she wants to do.

I frown. "Coffee Bean? They're not reliable enough and the pay is shit."

"They're not reliable enough?"

I fold my arms over my chest and shake my head. "Nope."

That adorable 'V' appears above the bridge of her nose. "The pay didn't seem too bad."

"We pay more, as well as medical."

Her eyes go round. "You include benefits?"

I nod. Well, it's news to me, but she's considering leaving already. I can't let that happen.

Rebekah Dove is mine. I don't fucking care how long I've known her.

I don't care if she thinks it's too hard or that we'll cross a line. If I have to stay away from her so she can work, then that's what I'll do, or at least I'll try.

"Yup."

She frowns some more. "That is… awfully generous."

I give her a lopsided smile. "We aim to please."

There go her eyes again, darting to my mouth.

"If it's okay, can I have until tomorrow to think about it."

I hide my smile. What's there to fucking think about?

"Of course, take all the time you need."

She glances around the mess. "All the time I need?"

I smirk. "Until this time tomorrow. Then I need an answer. Deal?"

She looks unsure again. I wonder if I bring out this nervous side in her. It has me puzzled.

It's a far cry from the sassy, dirty-talking woman that I spent the night with. She was so confident in her own skin, like nothing could stop her from doing anything. I get her reservations, but surely this has got to be better than The Coffee Bean?

"Okay, it's a deal. I'll let you know by this time tomorrow." She bites on her bottom lip, and I almost reach out and tug that lip away. "Listen, there is something you should—"

The door opens and Buzz and Mac, the two prospects, I'm assuming, from the labels on their motorcycle jackets, come barreling in. Looks like the cavalry has arrived.

"We're here to look at the pool," the one, I'm assuming is Buzz by his haircut, says, thumbing behind him somewhere.

"The pool's at the back. I can show you, if you like."

Buzz's eyes shift to Rebekah, and he looks her up and down.

Instantly, my hands ball into fists, and I have visions of me smacking his fat forehead into the metal handle on the door frame repeatedly. If she notices, she doesn't say anything.

"Call me tomorrow," I say to Rebekah.

She nods. "Bye, Knox."

I smile, watching her as she leaves the office.

"Fine piece of ass," Buzz says, watching her leave.

"I'd do her, for sure," Mac agrees.

"How about I bang your fucking heads together until no more words come out permanently?" I grit out, trying to control my temper.

I did warn Hutch. Protectiveness is my downfall. I will go all in.

Eyeballing a woman is never a good look, especially when she's not interested.

Buzz holds his hands toward me in surrender. "Just havin' a joke," he says, like we're old chums. "No need to get your panties in a twist."

Mac snickers.

I'm in front of him in two steps. "Move your smart mouth now, fuckface, or you'll be drinking out of a plastic straw for the rest of your miserable life."

"Fuck, man," Mac says, backing away. "Dude, he's sorry. Right, Buzz?"

Buzz looks like he might shit his pants. "Can tell you're Steel's brother," he mutters.

They turn to walk out the way they came in, and I can't help but shake my head and wonder what the fuck I've gotten myself into.

They can mess with me all they want, but don't fucking try it with her.

It'll be the last thing they do.

I want to text her, but I know I should stay away and let her think about it.

It's a lot.

Seeing her again, it was so damn good. We fell into that easy conversation where it's never awkward. Her laughter and her smile, two of the things I like about her the most, both took my breath away.

I know I've got to stop obsessing, but I can't.

I offered her fucking benefits. Fuck knows how I'm gonna pay for that, but it might just be the clincher I need to get her to come work for me.

We both know that this fire we're messing with could burn us both, but I like her, a lot. And why can't we keep things civil? I'm not a sex maniac, for Christ's sake, though admittedly temptation around her is strong.

I work on my business plan all night instead to try to distract me. Lord knows I need something to take my mind off her. Even worrying about the motel is better than how anxious I feel about the possibility that she won't come back.

It's not gonna happen.

This is fate, that's what it is.

If I have to back off to let her know I don't just want sex, that I care about her, then that's what I'll do.

It'll be like a truce.

I'll show her that I'm not like other guys, that I can treat a woman with respect.

Not that I relish the thought of keeping my hands off her, but she needs a job, and I'm not that guy. The one who's expecting anything. Just seeing her is enough.

Something today made her nervous. I don't think it was me directly, but I saw something in her eyes when she had to make a decision. She looked completely lost.

She never has to hide from me, I want her to know that, but I don't want to come off as being too intense.

It makes me wonder about some of the guys she's dated before, but I don't want to pry. The little I know about her tells me that the guys she may have been with before didn't appreciate her.

Especially after the comment she made about her ex being a special kind of asshole and she had a no-guys policy for a while after him.

All I wanted to do on that hot night we spent together was worship her. A woman like her deserves to have a man at her feet. And I want that man to be me.

I just can't tell her that yet.

I've got to be patient, even though patience really isn't

my strongest virtue.

She's got to want this for herself.

So I'll wait, as patiently as I can, and if she decides to take another position, I'm going to pursue the fuck out of her.

If she thinks I'm going away, even if she decides to work elsewhere, she really doesn't know me at all.

BRACKEN RIDGE
REBELS
ARIZONA
M · C
REBELS

CHAPTER 12

REBEKAH

I leave the motel in a daze. I can't believe what just happened. It feels kinda surreal. The fact that I never thought I'd see him again, and then he shows up as my potential new boss? This could only happen to me.

The trouble with one-night stands is they can come back to bite you. And the trouble with Knox is he's just the type of man I want to take a bite.

He was even better than I remembered him. He may be larger-than-life, but he also reminds me of a gentle giant. His soft smile, his kind eyes, his gentlemanly gestures. The way he has the ability to light a fire inside of me, just by being himself.

The way he hugged me… dammit, I can still smell his cologne. Like a schoolgirl, I feel like I never want to wash my shirt again.

And now this beautiful creature is offering me a job?

Being awkward in front of him, that was a first for me because I don't often get tongue tied. But it won't change the fact that I need cash, and he's throwing in medical benefits?

Can he really afford that?

I mean, is he just saying that because he wants me to help him and judging by the huge amount of work there is to be done, he needs someone today, not tomorrow.

I've never heard of anyone, except corporate jobs and big-name companies, offering healthcare benefits, and especially not independent small businesses.

He's obviously just being nice. It's what he does. And now I have to imagine him as my boss?

Being tempted by him every day?

Having to smell that musky, sexy as fuck scent and try not to look dreamily into his eyes?

I don't know if that's even possible.

I've got a little bit of money saved, but I didn't want to dip into my rainy day fund. I never want to rely on anyone, so that's why I don't touch that money, unless we're in dire straits.

Worst of all? I didn't even get to tell him about Brayden. He's a big part of my life, the focal point of my life; everything I do is for him and his future. Making him happy and providing a loving home is my priority.

In not telling him about my son, I also didn't explain why I would have to leave momentarily to collect Brayden from school, at least until he's settled in. Knox may not be happy with me leaving the office in the middle of the day, but it's non-negotiable. And most employers are flexible these days with working moms and dads.

I never ever thought that I would be a single mom, but at the end of the day I didn't plan Brayden's pregnancy.

When I found out, it was the happiest day of my life. It was also the saddest because I knew that things were not working with his father, and I was on the verge of leaving him even back then. So when I found out I was pregnant, I stayed to try to make things work, and it was the biggest mistake of my life. The only thing I can be grateful for is that my son was too young to remember any of the stuff that happened, and that's how I want it to stay. He never got to meet his father because I got away before he was born. Ran and never looked back.

A cold shiver runs down my back and I stop my wayward thoughts. I can't do that. I won't go back there.

I get home and prepare a salad and make lasagna from scratch because I know that will take me a while and it will also take my mind off things so my brain doesn't explode.

When I pick up Brayden from school and we get home, he's immediately suspicious. We only have home-made lasagna for very special occasions.

"Mom?"

"Yes, honey," I reply, checking the envelopes that came in the mail. Damn. First utility bill.

"What's going on?"

I glance up. "What do you mean?"

"We're having lasagna," he says, like it's obvious.

"I wanted to make something nice for you," I say, casually.

"Huh."

"You make it sound like I've got an ulterior motive."

"What does that mean again?"

I take a seat next to him at the kitchen table, where he's finishing his homework.

"It means that you offer to do something to gain favor with someone, to get something in return."

He turns back to his notebook. "Are we celebrating then?"

"Actually, we are," I say, clapping my hands together. "I got offered not one but two jobs today."

"Way to go, Mom!" He gives me a high-five. "Where abouts?"

"The Coffee Bean and the Bracken Ridge Motel."

"Which one is paying more money?" That's my boy.

"The motel."

"What vibe did you get?" I swear my kid is trapped in a forty-year-old body. He's all into the vibes and reads way too much stuff on quantum physics.

"Um, it felt... good, I guess." I am seriously going to hell for this. "The owner is a really nice man."

"So, did you take the job?" he presses.

I shrug. "I'm still deciding."

He frowns. "What's to decide?"

"Well, there's a lot to consider and both are willing to be flexible. I still have to pick you up from school."

Brayden rolls his eyes. "Mom, I'm ten years old and my school is literally a five-minute walk from home. You don't need to pick me up." I love hearing him say the word home. Even if I have dragged him around half the countryside for most of his life.

He'll never know just how much I'm willing to do to make sure he's safe and happy. I know he worries about me. It's like he's taken on that role as his job, but all I really want him to do is be a kid and enjoy his childhood. Make it something to look back on with the kind of fondness that will carry him into manhood and beyond. Like any decent parent, I want what's best for my kid. I will do anything for him.

I just hope this is the last time we have to move.

"I know it's not far, but you're still finding your way around the town, and I would worry."

"So, I'll text you when I finish and then when I get home," he says, casually. "It's not a big deal. I'm not a baby anymore, Mom."

"I know you're not a baby," I say, brushing his hair off his face as he pulls back and avoids me. "But you're my baby, you always will be."

He snorts a laugh. "Even when I'm fifty?"

"Even then."

"Seventy-five?"

"And beyond."

He grins as he keeps looking from his textbook to his notepad. His neat writing definitely didn't come from me. I watch as he takes his time, making sure that his writing stays steady on the lines. He's meticulous. Even doing a simple task like homework is done with the upmost precision.

"Mom?"

"Huh?"

"You're staring."

Oops. I smile to myself. "I can't help it, you're as cute as a button."

"Can Rawlings and her friend Layne come over to play?"

My kid's always gotten along with girls a little better than boys. He's a sensitive soul and while he loves outdoor activities, he can sit inside for hours and read or help me in the kitchen when we bake. I know I got lucky with him.

"If their moms say it's okay, but not too late."

He fist pumps. "Yes!"

I laugh. "I'm glad you're making friends. Are there any other kids in your class you've made friends with?"

He shrugs. "Some of the kids already have their own group of friends."

I try not to let his words hurt my heart. He'll be friends with anyone; he doesn't have to hang with the cool or popular kids. If anything, he's a loner. Tagging along with likeminded children who stay out of the way of the kids who rule the school.

Sometimes I have to remind myself that he is stronger than he looks, but the mama bear inside me wants to protect her cub.

"Well, I'm sure they'll come around once you've been in school for a little while."

He doesn't seem too fazed by it. "It's fine, Mom. Don't worry."

"Do you like your teacher so far? She seemed really nice."

"Ms. Delaney is cool," he says. "She's much nicer than Mrs. Goober…" That's his old teacher, and she was a witch.

"Gruber," I correct. "Ms. Delaney gave you a lot of homework, and you still think she's cool?"

"She makes her classes fun. We have a pop quiz on Monday on Ancient Rome I need to study for."

"Ancient Rome?" I ask. "It's a good job you're dedicated. Is it fun having a brain that works like that?"

"It's really cool. Ms. D wants to make a time capsule. We'd put all our wishes inside, bury it, and years later, we dig it up and read what we wrote and what we left there."

"That does sound really fun," I concede, happy that he seems to be fitting in fine. "Better make sure you write each and every wish down and really feel it with all your heart, Bray."

He meets my eye. "You're not going to cry, are you?"

I snort a laugh and push up from the table. "No, but if you keep up the cheek, mister, you won't be getting any lasagna."

Late into the night, I toss and turn. Unable to get to sleep.

This isn't like me. I've been sleeping fine lately, even after the move.

I check the time: 2:24 a.m.

I roll over one more time, like that will help.

Then I remember Knox's texts from earlier:

Knox: It was so good seeing you today. I hope you weren't put off by the mess. Or by me.

I'd laughed because I could never get put off by him. As much as I know I shouldn't get involved if I know he's going to be my boss, I also have some pretty vivid fantasies I still want fulfilled.

I'd replied back. Who is this?

Knox: Uh, I hope you're kidding.

Me: *smiley emoji* yes, sorry. I wasn't put off by the mess or by you, but I have questions if that's all right?

Knox: Shoot.

I'd really wanted to ask what would happen with us. Would he still take me on that date he promised? Where would we go? Then I'd reminded myself that by being my boss, any kind of relationship was bound for failure. We'd just be basing it on sex and, if I'm being honest, I'm looking to settle down, not have one-night stands with strangers. As amazing as Knox is, I'm not looking for casual sex. I'd lost my head with him; he was easy to get lost in.

Me: I know I said it today, but I don't want things to be awkward. If I come and work for you, I'm not sure if we'd be able to… just work together.

Why could I almost picture him smiling that shit-eating grin he's so good at while watching me with those intense blue eyes.

Knox: I've been thinking about that too.

Uh huh… and?

Knox: I think we could be friends.

My heart plummets. Friends? Friends? What the hell is he talking about?

Knox Steelman isn't anybody's friend. Well, certainly not mine.

I don't know why the words hit me so hard. I guess I thought we had a connection.

Me: You do?
Knox: We could try.

Did I even want that?

For the sake of my kid, I need this goddamn job. When I weighed up the pros and cons earlier, the position at the motel clearly came up trumps. I may not be able to stop picturing him naked, but I have to fucking try, don't I?

Me: I guess we could.

I hope he picks up on the apprehension. I hope he knows that I don't really mean it.

That I'd much rather him take me out on that date, then we'd make out a little bit after, and I'd string him along on the next date until he was all over me, begging me to let him take my body.

But I can't do any of that.

I'm a responsible adult with bills to pay and a kid to raise.

We had one hot night, and phone sex. That's it.

I always make the mistake of reading too much into things, and this is no exception. If he really did want more, he wouldn't have offered me the job, he'd have pursued me instead. And he wouldn't have suggested we try being friends.

I feel gutted. I thought we had a connection. I thought he felt something too?

Now it all just feels like quicksand and I'm in the middle.

Does he just want me to be his receptionist and clean all this crap up? Get on top of things… and not me? I could slap myself silly for that thought. But it made sense that he needed someone, anyone, to help him.

Knox: Are you still there?

Me: Yes, but it's late, I'm going to go to bed.

That wasn't entirely the truth, but I really couldn't face any more disappointment.

I knew for a fact I needed to pull up my big girl panties

and stop being a crybaby. I was a grown-ass woman. A badass. I can handle this.

This was nothing compared to the obstacles I've had to face over the last decade.

This was just another bump in the road, one that was easily fixable.

Knox: You'll give me your answer tomorrow?
Me: Yes, definitely.

He started to type, but then the grey bubble went away. What was he going to say?
Then:

Knox: Goodnight, Red.

Holy fuck. I know what he's got on his mind when he calls me that.
This is so fucking unfair.
I press my legs together and take a couple of long breaths.
Keep your shit together. Do not crumble.

Me: Goodnight, Knox.

And we'd left it at that.

He wants to try being friends. I try to rack my brain around exactly how that would look.

Me being his employee and having civil conversations every morning about the weather or what I made for dinner, all while I make his coffee.

I think I might tell him to go shove it up his ass.

I can't figure out if he's actually serious, trying to be Mr. Nice Guy, or if he really just does want me to work for him and nothing else.

I eventually fall asleep, more tired and confused than I've ever been before.

BRACKEN RIDGE
REBELS
ARIZONA
M · C

CHAPTER 13

KNOX

Friends?

I have no idea why I even said that. Of course I don't mean it, but I think it's what she wants to hear.

She wants to take the job but doesn't want things to be awkward with us, and rightly so.

How could it not be, though? I wonder. Most people haven't seen their new employee naked or have the memory of them sitting on your face.

I internally slap myself.

That's all I've been doing for the last seven hours: thinking about her every goddamn moment and what she's going to say.

I've memorized every contour on her lovely face.

The way her brows rose ever so slightly when she saw me behind the desk.

The way her cheeks flushed pink after we hugged.

The way her smile brightens her entire face. I wish she'd smile more.

In fact, I could make a full-time job out of trying to get her to smile just to see the reward when she does.

She's just so lovely.

The more I think about us in bed together and what I'd like to do to please her the next time around, I'll need to take a cold shower. And the more I know that this is a bad idea.

I should call it off. If she decides to actually come and work for me, there's no way I'll get any work done, not if I'm left to my own devices. Maybe with all the work to be done outdoors, I can be outside for most of the time, and I'll be too preoccupied.

I know I sound like a fucking pussy, but she has me wound so tight. I've never felt this way before.

And that's not like me.

I keep my cards guarded and close to my chest. I'm never open with anyone, and I already told her about my mom. That's a pretty big deal.

I think seeing her every day and not being with her in the way I want to would be something more like torture, not at all pleasant.

And now she thinks I really do just want to be friends.

I don't. I want so much more.

It makes no sense why I'm feeling this way, why I want

to know everything about her, what makes her tick, her likes and dislikes, what she does in her spare time.

I want to know.

But that's not what a boss is supposed to do.

So she needs to work somewhere else, and if she did, would that mean she'd give me a chance?

I'm so fucking confused over being the good guy and the bad guy all at once.

I did the unthinkable and jerked myself off in the shower thinking about her. The fact that she seems mad at me didn't help. I don't like that idea. I like it when she's happy.

I bet she doesn't even want to be friends. I bet she thinks I'm a complete jerk.

That I only want her to work for me and pretend this thing—whatever it is—never happened between us, but that's not the case.

She seems like a woman who is quite capable of making her own decisions.

Now I don't even know if she'll want to speak to me.

The next day isn't any better. Especially when Hutch, Steel, and the V.P., Brock, show up at the motel, wanting to know my answer.

Brock shakes my hand firmly; his biceps are about as thick as my truck tire. What the hell are these boys eating?

"Knox," I say.

"Heard all about you." That doesn't sound good.

I run a hand through my hair. "Well, until a few weeks ago, I didn't know I even had any family, much less a brother and sister."

"You sure you're related?" Brock looks between us both.

"According to the paternity test," I say.

Hutch chuckles. At least we've advanced from everyone wanting to throttle me.

Deciding the staff room is too small for the four of us, I invite them into my apartment, knowing Evie will be all over anyone who comes inside. She's a real people pleaser and thinks everyone she runs into is here to be her friend.

Other than going to sit in one of the motel rooms, I've got no other options.

Luckily, I keep my place neat and tidy. Even with the few boxes still strewn around, it looks presentable.

As soon as we walk through the door, Evie is at my feet, wagging her tail and pushing her head into my leg and making a whimpering sound. I bend down to pat her as she continues her ritual, like she hasn't seen me in a while, when realistically, it was only ten minutes ago.

"Guys, this is my baby, Evie."

Hutch and Brock exchange looks. I don't know what that's all about, but Hutch smirks and Brock mumbles, "This should be good."

Steel bends down and Evie moves over to him, pushing

her head into his hand as her tail wags like she's going for a gold record. I watch the exchange curiously as I quickly realize Steel is a dog person.

I'm shocked when he scruffs her neck, muttering to her under his breath, and I even see a trace of a smile as she whimpers in absolute submission.

"Great guard dog," Hutch says as I stand.

"Yeah, she's good at licking people to death."

"How old is she?" Steel asks, surprising me once more.

"She's five. She was a stray who hung around my house back in the city. She was skinny, had a broken leg that never fully healed, and she was full of mange, never seen anything like it. Took a while for her to trust me, but we kinda got an understanding going on. The rest is history."

He grunts. I'm assuming that means he approves, but I can't be certain.

Then he says, "Got a Pitbull, Lola, who was in a dog fightin' ring."

I wince. "That's fucked up."

"Not as much as the assholes that ran the ring."

Ouch.

"Also got a mixed breed terrier, Rocky. Owners left him at their rental and never came back. People are so fucked up."

"Tell me about it. Evie almost didn't make it. She had corrective surgery, but the bone never healed properly."

"Damn shame, she seems happy enough."

"She should be, she eats better than I do."

Steel grunts a laugh.

Okay, dogs are another safe subject. I make a mental note of that.

Brock gives me an eyeroll.

"Down to business," Hutch says, clearing his throat.

I gesture to the table. "Can I get anyone a coffee, tea?"

They all decline.

Evie goes to lay on her bed where she can still see us, and I take a seat at the table, where I left the business plan I wrote up last night.

It took me a while, but I've managed to map out exactly what we need to do, approximate costs, and a tentative timeframe for when the renovations should be finished. I'll take a hit when the motel is closed for the renovations, but it will give me a chance to catch up on things. I've already started redoing the interior of the rooms, including replacing doors, closets, and cabinets, fixing light fixtures, retiling the bathroom, replacing broken items.

I've always worked hard, but I've not stopped since I got here. The added stress of losing the office manager is something I didn't need, but it was necessary. If I'd known about the motel in the beginning, I'd have done something about it sooner.

I pass Hutch the proposal. He takes out his reading glasses, slides them on, and starts to read. Brock sits to his left and Steel to his right. And I hover because I feel nervous about how this is gonna go. I guess it'll go one way or the other.

Steel glances up at me, but before he speaks, Brock says, "Can you take a seat? You're makin' me fuckin' nervous."

If I knew which way this was going to go, I wouldn't be so goddamn nervous. But if I don't get an investor soon, this business will go under, and I'll be forced to sell.

I know the potential it has, and I've never given up on anything I've done before. I've always given a hundred percent and faced any obstacles head on. But I've also never been in a situation where I'd be using someone else's money. That's a whole different ballgame.

The time passes as we sit in silence, albeit a little awkwardly, until Hutch passes the proposal to Brock.

"I'm impressed," he says, taking his reading glasses off. "You've done a lot of homework; the agenda has a lot of valid ideas and reachable goals. However, it is a lot of money. Money I don't just like throwin' around on a business that may go under and on a man I barely know."

"We'd have a contract," I say. "And the business won't go under, we both know that."

"What we won't know is if the locals will embrace it. They've had to put up with an eyesore for years," Brock says. "And people talk in this town. They know everything about your business before you even do."

"The motel won't cater to locals, but for tourists. I do agree, we need to get the locals back on board, though. We could have an open house and invite some of them, host a brunch or something inside the conference room. One of the strategies I had for marketing was to offer the visitor center rooms to sell at the Skywalk," I say. "Most accommodation in the area will have online bookings, but they can also book direct and get a discount."

Steel frowns. "They got a conference room?"

"Yeah," I say. "It's being used as a pool house at the moment." Then to Hutch, I continue. "It's money you'd get back. You and I both know how valuable this place is and what we could do with it. I'm not afraid of hard work, I've done it all my life. I've already made headway on replacing the furniture in the rooms and fixing everything, however, it's gonna need a few weeks of cleanup before we can let customers in the place again."

Brock hands the papers to Steel. I guess the real test will be to see what my brother thinks in all of this.

"What if I said there are things I'd like you to consider before we front the money," Hutch speaks finally, his eyes meeting mine.

"Things like?"

"Helpin' around the clubhouse."

I stare at him, unsure what he means for a moment.

"Helping?"

"After the renovations are complete."

I run a hand through my hair. "You mean prospecting?"

"You sound about as thrilled as Steel was when I suggested it," Hutch goes on. "It'd be good for you to get to know one another. Plus, the club is always looking for members, especially ones who plan on sticking around and who have skill."

I rub my chin. I've never thought about it before. Not that I'm opposed to the idea.

"Does that mean I'd be indebted to you?" I ask, feeling like I know where this could be headed. "I ran with a club years ago, when I was a teen, similar kind of thing, and it wasn't a whole boat load of fun. I'm thirty years old."

"It'd only be for twelve months," Brock interjects. "If the club were happy with you, and vice-versa. My brother, Axton, is younger than you and he's only just been patched in."

Joining the club hadn't even entered my head. The thought of being a shit-kicker for the club, however, doesn't hold a lot of appeal. I do like the brotherhood, though, if I'm being honest.

That's why I hung out with the Phoenix Fury many years ago, before they disbanded.

I like the family aspect of this club. From day one, when Steel came to interrogate me at the gate that night and Hutch and a few of the other brothers came as well, I knew

they had each other's backs. Hutch seems like a fair man.
I've only heard good things about him from around town,
so that can't be a bad thing. I just don't like the idea that I'd
owe him.

Yes, I'd owe him the money back, that's a given, but
giving my time to prospect? I'm trying to picture what that
would look like.

I don't want them thinking they own my soul. That ain't
happening.

The fact they've considered me joining their club does
make me feel like Hutch may see something in me, even if
Steel doesn't, and a part of me feels good about that.

I never had a father figure I could look up to, and that's
a hard limit for me. It's something I've struggled with for
a long time. I was a nice kid. My mom said I was a sweet
little boy, a tough nut. But my father didn't see it that way
and nothing I ever did pleased him.

I haven't thought about this in a while. I kinda buried all
those shitty childhood memories with him and never being
good enough.

Now I see Steel suffered the same fate, maybe we have
a lot more in common than I first thought.

"Which club did you run with?" Steel asks gruffly.

"Phoenix Fury, back when Tex was just appointed
Prez," I say.

"Fuck," they all mutter at the same time.

"I know they broke apart some years back and Smokey started a new club. Sons, right?" I go on.

"Yup, Smokey's a good guy," says Hutch. "One of the few people this club trusts. If he can vouch for you, we'll talk about makin' the prospectin' lesser time or waiving it altogether. Not sayin' you'd be patched in and just given the keys to the kingdom. If you want it, it still has to be earned. Nothin' comes free in this club; we all pay our dues."

"I'd need time," I say. "To think about it. I will be spending a lot of my time here until I can afford to hire more staff. I do have a new office manager starting, I hope, so that'll take care of the office."

"I'll send Kelsey over," Hutch tells me. "She's been workin' on reception at Lily's salon, so she can fill in on days off."

"Appreciate it." That's a weight off my mind. Then I add, "So, what did you think about everything else?"

"The profit projections look good. The business plan is solid. If we can maximize on the upcoming events taking place in town over the coming months, then we may just have a chance to break even sooner than planned," he replies. The hairs on my arms stand on end. He's giving me the money? Albeit, at a price, but still. A hundred thousand dollars?

Then I wonder… is it legal money? I don't want dirty money; it goes against everything I believe in. As much as I want this, I don't want drug money.

"The club is…" I pause. "Not a one percenter club, am I right?"

Steel and Brock snicker. Hutch looks me right in the eye; he's good at intimidation. "We're legit. One day, I'll tell you some stories that'll make your hair stand on end about my time before I started this club. We've all got families, kids, businesses, people we care about. We don't deal in drugs and guns. Not much fun thinkin' about spendin' your life in a concrete cell now, is it?"

"Definitely not," I say, relieved. "I respect that."

"I'll have my lawyer draw something up in the next couple of days," Hutch says as my heart thuds in my chest. We're really doing this? "In the meantime, drop by the clubhouse on Friday night. We're having a celebration for Grizz's 70th birthday."

I don't know who that is, but it could be a good idea to snoop around a little bit.

"All right."

"Lily's going to be dropping by," Steel says out of nowhere. "She wanted to come yesterday, but I told her no. There's no keeping her back forever, though. She can be a little bit to handle."

"Or a lot," Brock pipes up. "Like most of the women in this club."

It feels too good to be true, but I won't look a gift horse

in the mouth, and I'll look over the contract and make sure there's nothing untoward in it. Hutch may look trustworthy, but I don't need any complications where any of that is concerned. Best to be on guard and let the chips fall where they may.

I could see myself in the club, and my motorcycle certainly wouldn't complain.

I look back across the table, hardly able to believe it. "So, we have a deal?"

Hutch's lips twitch as he reaches across the table, and we shake. "We have a deal."

Lily stops by on her lunch break and doesn't let go of me. I usher her into the break room as she cries and tells me how much I'm like Steel, minus the long hair.

"I always wanted another brother," she tells me earnestly. "When I found out, I didn't know what to think. I never knew my real dad. Hutch is like everyone's surrogate father, so I've grown up with him looking over us all. I'm lucky in so many ways, but even luckier now I have you." She squeezes me again around the middle and I don't quite know what to do with her.

She's nothing like Steel. She's dainty with long, chestnut-colored hair, the same blue eyes, and she's short. I tower over her.

"I can say it came as a complete shock," I say, when she finally let's go. "I always wanted a little sister, so this is kinda cool."

"You have to come over for dinner, with me and Gunner, and Steel and maybe Mom. I don't know how you'd feel about that, but she wants to meet you."

I look at her quickly, alarm in my eyes. "She does?"

She nods. "My mom is the greatest person alive. She was upset when Steel told her about what that douchebag Hank did, not that she was surprised; she had suspected he'd been cheating on her for years, she just never dreamed he'd have a secret second family. You see these things on television, but you don't actually think something like that is going to happen in real life."

"It is pretty nuts," I agree. "The lies he told and how he hid everything, it's damaging to those he left behind. I want to move on from it. As I told Steel and Hutch, I came here to settle down, get to know you—if that's what you both want—and God willing, start a family of my own."

She looks at me warmly, her eyes glassing over. "Of course it's what we want. Even Steel. He'll come around. He seems like a hard person on the outside, and he can be pretty mean, but his heart is in the right place, Knox. He means well. He's just not very good at affection or emotion."

"I kinda gathered that."

We both chuckle.

Thank fuck, I don't see much of my dad in her at all. She must take after her mother.

"I'd love to come to dinner," I go on. "I know it's gonna take some adjusting, but Rome wasn't built in a day, right?"

She claps her hands together. "I love dinner parties. I'll text you the details, but I'd like to do it soon. I have so many questions. I can't believe I have another brother!"

I smile, she's a ray of sunshine. Lily, my little sister.

It all feels like it's falling into place. I couldn't have imagined it going any better.

I would go out and celebrate tonight, but I have a self-defense class that I'd agreed to help out with at the YMCA. I saw a flier a couple of weeks ago and thought it'd be good giving back to the community. This one was close to my heart.

They do self-defense for women and also for kids.

"Totally!"

"I will be coming to the party for Grizz on Friday," I say. "Maybe we can have a drink then?"

She hugs me again and kisses me on the cheek. "I'll be there. Sorry I have to rush off, but the salon is short staffed at the moment so I can't stay for long."

"It's fine," I say, as I walk her to the door.

"Friday?" She turns and gives me a bright smile, her eyes still watery.

"Friday," I confirm.

She gives me a thumbs up, and then heads out.

I meant what I said. I feel like everything is just as it should be.

I check my watch and realize that Bekah hasn't called or dropped in yet to tell me her decision.

Maybe she really is pissed at me.

I wish she fucking wasn't. I don't want to make things difficult for her.

I won't cave.

By the time I lock up the office and head out shortly after, she still hasn't rung.

And I think this time, my day really was about due to take a nosedive.

BRACKEN RIDGE
REBELS
ARIZONA
M · C
M · C

CHAPTER 14

REBEKAH

I text Knox, feeling terrible that I didn't see him today, but I had to go up to the school. Brayden got into a fight, and I had to go and sort it out. I let him know that I had an emergency, but I'm okay and I'll talk to him soon.

Sitting in the principal's office on his third day of school doesn't exactly fill me with confidence, but when I saw the other kid, who was twice his size and sporting a bloody nose, my eyes went wide.

"Brayden? What the heck?"

He folded himself into my arms, something he rarely does, and told me that the kid was picking on him and Rawlings.

I didn't know what to do, how to react. Brayden's never been in this kind of trouble before; it's out of character for him.

Before we could even say anything, Rawlings came barreling into the office to see if Brayden was okay and told me firmly that the kid in question, who was being whisked away to the infirmary, was the class bully and he had it coming.

Brayden was also sporting a black eye.

Tears welled in my eyes, but Brayden held his own. "He deserved it, Mom," he'd said as I reasoned with myself that this was not his usual behavior and it seemed like self-defense.

Nobody wants to believe their kid is capable of being violent, but the kid in question was a bad egg. You could see it in his face when he passed us by.

"But now Brayden's the talk of the entire school," Rawling's went on excitedly. "Nobody's dared to take on Big Tim. He's mean and horrible, and even some of the teachers are scared of him."

"That's still no excuse," I said to Brayden, wondering if I even meant that. "You should always stand up for yourself, but you're supposed to go get a teacher if someone is picking on you, not take matters into your own hands.

"There wasn't time, he was already swinging," Brayden told me. "He's mean to everyone. Kids hide out in the library, so they don't get cornered by him in the playground."

I need to talk to the principal and Big Tim's parents. If they don't take it seriously, I'll open a can of whoop-ass.

I'd crouched down, assessing his black eye. "We need to get that seen to."

"Can't I just go home?"

I shook my head. "Brayden, you need to tell me what happened."

He was about to when the door burst open and a very large, scary looking man with the words 'Bracken Ridge Rebels' on the patch of his vest came marching in.

My eyes nearly bulged out of their sockets.

Rawlings turned and ran to him. "Daddy! Dad!" He picked her up and she wrapped herself around him, not breaking a stride as he reached me. His face furious.

Holy shitballs.

I swear everyone in that waiting room shriveled up and diverted their eyes when he walked in. I held my head high. One of the things that I've learned to do over the years is to try not to show any fear. I like to think I've gotten quite good at it.

He narrowed his brow, giving me a chin lift. "Your kid start this?"

I put my arms around my son as he stood in front of me protectively. "Certainly not, some kid called Big Tim picked on Brayden and punched him."

He brow furrows. "That little fu-"

"Dad!"

He cleared his throat. "Fudgehead. I've already had words with his mom, and I went easy, being he's got no father figure in his life, but this time…"

"I don't want any more violence," I told him as his eyes

flicked back to mine.

"I'm not going to fu…fudging hit a woman for Christ's sake. What kinda guy do you think I am?"

I glanced down at his patch. "I don't know, but it says you're Brock, V.P., whatever that means. I'm Bekah, Brayden's mom." I stuck my hand out to shake his.

Where I come from, it's polite to shake hands, even if they're big, scary looking bikers.

He frowned, wiped his hand down his vest to clean it, then clenched his very large hand around mine. His hands were rough and calloused, like he'd worked hard his whole life.

"Brock, obviously, I'm her dad, amongst other things. And V.P. means Vice President. My club is the Bracken Ridge Rebels. You've probably heard of them."

"Dad has a really fast motorcycle," Rawlings piped up, still in his arms. She clearly adores him. "Mom won't let me ride on it, but Dad said he'll get me my own bike when I turn eighteen. I've told him only if it's pink. Right, Dad?" She giggled like she knows this will annoy him.

"Apparently," he grumbled. He seems to do that a lot. "The women in my life seem to know exactly how to wrap their old man around their little fingers."

I rolled my lips inward. So he's a big teddy bear, really. See, nothing to be afraid of.

"I met your wife the other day," I said, referring to

Angel. "She seemed lovely. We exchanged numbers so the kids can have a play date."

He regarded me for a few moments, then said, "That woman will talk your ears off if you let her. Whatever you do, don't go to one of the girls' poker nights. Not unless you like sporadic, tequila-induced vomiting."

"Dad? What's—"

"Button it," he told her, letting her back down on the ground.

I smiled because I didn't know what else to say.

Then the principal came, and we all had to go into mediation.

To say that I needed a lie down when I got home was an understatement.

Brayden didn't get expelled because they believed him when they said it was self-defense, and if I'm not mistaken, Brock gave him a look of approval that I'm certain the teachers and the principal himself didn't miss. Big Tim didn't have a broken nose, thankfully, but he was given a suspension and they were working through mediation with the mother.

I took Brayden home because he'd had enough excitement for one day and I still couldn't believe my kid had been punched in the face. He'd given back as good as he got, which was something, but it still shocked me to my core.

"I'm fine, Mom," he said when I kept fussing. In fact,

he seemed quite pleased with himself.

"I still don't like the idea of you using your fists to settle an argument," I say. "Even though I know things can escalate pretty quickly."

"This kid's been awful to everyone for a while, and he didn't like that the other kids were talking to me and not paying attention to him."

Clearly, it's a case of sour grapes.

"I'm so sorry this happened to you," I say, feeling emotional. The nurse checked him out and gave us some paracetamol and said to go to emergency if he felt faint or lightheaded when we got home. "This isn't a good start to the school year."

He shrugged, like it was nothing at all. "I think now that he's been confronted, and taken down a notch, he might be a bit nicer to everyone from now on."

I shake my head, smiling. This is my kid; he thinks like a forty-year-old who's done the rounds.

"I understand if you have reservations about going back," I begin.

"I don't, Mom. He might be big, but like Brock said, the bigger they are, the harder they fall."

I can't believe he just said that.

I face palm myself. "I don't think we need to be taking advice from Brock. I'm sure he's used to settling things with his fists, but my ten-year-old isn't."

"It's fine, Mom, you worry too much."

"That's my job," I remind him. "You're the most important thing to me in the world."

"Shit happens, I'm fine."

"Don't swear," I chastise. "I don't want to hear bad words coming out of your mouth, young man."

"I'm sorry, but I'm just saying that it's true. Stuff happens. Big Tim may not even be allowed back in school at this rate."

Most kids would be scared of their bully returning, but not Brayden. I want him to know that he doesn't have to put on a brave face. I'll pull him out of school if I have to.

"I'll have to cancel tonight's class," I say, reminding Brayden that I had volunteered to lead a self-defense class at the gym.

I thought it'd be perfect since I've gotten my black belt in taekwondo. It took a good number of years, but I feel like I could definitely offer something to the class. There is nothing more empowering than a woman being able to defend herself. It's something that's close to my heart. While my abuse by my ex may not have always been purely physical, the emotional upheaval he put me through will always be etched into my soul.

He'll always own a part of me in a way and I hate he has that power over me. Even now, ten years later.

"No, Mom. I'm fine. If anything, I should probably

come with you and pick up a few more tips."

I shake my head. "Very funny."

"I'll come then, and watch you."

"Brayden, you need to rest."

"Ma! I want to!"

My phone rings, seeing who it is I pick up, "Hey, Angel."

"Hi, Bekah, is everything okay? I heard from Brock about what happened."

"Everything's fine," I say. "Brayden's just resting, but he's doing okay. I think I'm more in shock than he is." I move off the couch and walk to the kitchen to fix Brayden a snack.

"That kid is trouble," she tells me. "But from what Brock said, I don't think he's gonna be a problem for much longer. He just needed a kid to put him in his place. What annoys me is the teachers turn a blind eye."

"I know," I say. "Brayden's never done anything like that before. It's completely out of character for him."

"He's a strong kid, just like his mama."

"I don't know about that." I laugh. "I think he might be putting on a brave face."

"I'm not putting on a brave face!" Brayden calls out. I turn around and give him a look, and he pipes down.

Angel laughs. "Like I said, just like his mama. I can tell."

"It's always scary for the kids, I hope Rawlings was

okay," I say, taking out the bread to make Brayden a peanut butter sandwich.

"She's fine, she couldn't stop talking about it all afternoon. Which is why I'm calling. Are you still teaching class tonight? I understand if you're not."

"I should really stay here and be with Brayden."

"I'm coming, Mom!" he yells out again.

"As you can probably tell, there's no keeping him down," I muse.

"Well, it's at six-thirty at the gym. I've rounded up a couple of girls who could do with a few lessons on chokeholds and strangulation techniques."

I slap my forehead. I think Angel might have mistaken what tonight's class is actually for.

"Or rather, how to get out of a situation like that."

"Right. Well, if I don't see you there, we'll catch up for coffee this week, if you're free."

I have to get back to poor Knox. Anguish washes through me as I think about him waiting for what I'm going to say and how much shit he has to do without the office manager there.

He didn't reply to my text earlier.

"I'll shoot you a text. I'm not sure what day I'll be starting work."

"Sounds good, see ya."

"Bye, Angel."

I finish making Brayden's sandwich and walk it over to him.

"I want to go see you in action," he tells me. "You've been so excited."

I have, but I don't want to leave him alone after he's had a head injury, and he should really stay home.

"I think it's for the best, baby. There'll always be next week."

"What if I feel better later?"

"We'll see."

He smiles, taking a big bite out of his sandwich.

As long as my kid's okay, I can tackle anything life throws at me.

I decide to let Brayden come with me; the class is an hour. He's been doing fine on the couch and hasn't had any signs of concussion or anything bad, but I'm still worried about him. The fresh air may do him good.

We put on our jackets, and I drive us to the gym.

I am apprehensive but also excited to be getting out and about and doing something for a worthy cause. Giving back is something I always said I would do, and this is exactly what I had in mind. I'm passionate about helping other women, especially in domestic violence situations.

I grab Brayden a can of soda from the vending machine, and he goes to watch the muscleheads through the clear window in the weight rooms.

When we arrive, I see Angel and a bunch of her friends. I'm introduced to Lily, Sienna, Kennedy, and Cassidy. I also learn that they're all with members of the Bracken Ridge Rebels.

These men must be like the Magic Men of the biker world to snag these hot chicks. Maybe I need to get myself over to the clubhouse… then I think of Knox and his recent involvement with the motorcycle club. As I said, I don't know much about the club, and I don't hold any judgment. Once we got past Brock's fierce appearance and obstinate personality, I learned that he's actually a pretty nice guy. Gruff, but any guy who loves his family and shows attention and affection to his kid tells you everything.

"Welcome to the best place in the world to live," the dark-haired one named Lily said. "I'm Steel's sister. He's the big mean-looking one with a temper and a permanently furrowed brow."

"You mean meaner looking than Brock?" I laugh.

"Yep, my old man is Gunner. He's gorgeous. Here, let me show you a picture."

I smile as she pulls out her wallet from her purse and flips it open.

Wow. They do make them hot around here. He's blonde,

tanned with some facial hair, and a smile that could melt your panties right off. He reminds me of Charlie Hunnam.

"Wow, Lily, he's gorgeous."

"Oh, he knows it," she says, tucking her wallet away. "He models and has his own pierced jewelry line."

"You're forgetting Gunner after Dark," Sienna pipes up, then behind her hand, she whispers to me, "A naughty website where you can see him completely naked for money."

My eyes go wide.

"Not completely naked!" Lily defends. "You don't see his… you know what… I told him that is where I draw the line. If he wants to go on Only Fans, he can find another broad. That hot dog is mine."

The girls snicker, and I do too. They seem like a cool bunch. Maybe a little wilder than what I'm used to, but I dig that. I've always been a little off the radar myself, ever since I ran away from home. Having Brayden slowed all of that down and I'm thankful for it. I came out the other end, and I thank my lucky stars every single day.

We enter through the hall, and once I see Sally, the coordinator, she waves me over.

Sally also runs the Faux-Paws dog rescue, which I recently learned was established by Steel, the club's enforcer.

I leave the girls, check on Brayden who's still within eyeshot, and head on over.

"Hi, Sally," I say with a smile. I wore my workout gear; leggings, a long-sleeve fitted top, and my sweater. It's warm in here so I start to peel the layers off.

"Hi, Bekah, so glad you could make it!"

"Of course," I reply as I follow her over to where the others have started setting up the mats.

Then we move to the store cupboard to grab some pads. "I've been looking forward to it."

"You should meet our wonderful coordinator. You two might get along quite well, with you being a black belt and him being a kickboxer..." Uh oh.

We don't even get to the doorway, and I hear him talking.

How can I be this unlucky? Like, seriously, am I being punished or something?

"Knox," Sally says, waving her arm over to me. "Have you met Bekah? She's here to help with the class."

He turns, and our eyes meet. As usual, a bolt of electricity hits me square in the face.

Every time I see him, it's like this. He's so fucking gorgeous. It's like he just gets hotter every time I see him.

His lips twitch, and he does that one eyebrow thing. "Yes, we've met. How are you, Bekah?"

I tuck a lock of hair behind my ear self-consciously. "I... uh... good, thanks. How have you been?"

"Good. I didn't know you were coming tonight."

This is awkward.

"Angel rang and reminded me. I had a lot going on today. I thought this might take my mind off things."

Sally smiles, then goes and busies herself elsewhere.

He steps closer. "Is everything all right? When you texted, I was worried. I'm sorry I didn't text back. I got stuck outside for most of the day after my morning meeting, and my phone went dead."

"Everything's fine," I say as he watches me intently. This man… "I promise."

"Listen, about what I said about being friends…"

"It's okay, I understand. I know it makes things complicated. You need somebody who can do the job and those people are hard to find."

He smells like a fucking dream.

"But I was foolish to say it. I thought that perhaps I could do it, and be your boss, but I'm not so sure I could." He looks down my body. "Especially when you're dressed like that."

My heart fills up just that little bit more.

"That's where I come unstuck," I whisper, checking to make sure nobody is listening. "I really want the job, and I also really wan—uh, I." I rake a hand through my hair. "What I mean is, if I weren't working for you, would we go out on a date?"

His eyes burn into me, telling me that he would most

definitely not take me on a date, but instead, he'd keep me in his bed all night long. I know the things he can do with that mouth, those hands, that big cock of his. My cheeks flush.

"We'd do whatever you wanted to do," he says, his voice low. "If that's spending the afternoon in b—"

"Mama, where are you? Mom?" I hear Brayden, and my body freezes. Shit.

Knox looks over the top of my head as I hear Brayden getting closer and I turn to look.

Then, without looking back at Knox, I say, "I'm in here, Brayden."

When I turn back to Knox, he has a puzzled look on his face. "You have a kid?"

Here we go.

"Yes, I, I was going to tell you about him…" I trail off, knowing that I'm the worst parent in the world.

Brayden is already coming up behind me as Knox watches him, and I can't tell if he's really pissed off or if he's just in complete shock.

And frankly, I don't know which is worse.

BRACKEN RIDGE
REBELS
ARIZONA
M · C
BRACKEN RIDGE
REBELS

CHAPTER 15

KNOX

I stare at the kid. With the exception of having light brown hair and freckles, he looks just like her. He also has the same hazel-colored eyes and mischievous smile.

He looks at me, and I look back at Bekah.

"Uh… Knox… this is Brayden… my son."

I hold my hand out. "Hi, Brayden, nice to meet you." I notice he's sporting a bruised eye.

"That's a cool name, Knox," he says, giving me a firm shake. "Are you part of the biker gang in town too?"

I chuckle.

"Brayden!" I say. "It's not a gang, remember, it's a club."

"Okay, club." He rolls his eyes, and I can't help smiling.

"No, I'm not, but my brother is and my sister grew up with the club," I say. It feels weird saying that I have a brother. "I just moved to town."

"So did we!" he says, giving his mom a huge,

appreciative smile. He adores her, that's plain to see. "We've got a pretty small house at the moment, but it's cool. My bed folds out and it's like having a sleepover because I get to roll it up in the morning and you'd never know it was a bed, and we have a yard and Mom says we can get a basketball hoop so I can practice."

"Sounds like you're settling in just fine." I look at Bekah. She's looking a little nervous and avoiding my gaze. "I've got an old basketball hoop that's at the motel, nobody uses it. If your mom says it's okay, maybe I could come and fix it up for you?"

His eyes dance with delight. "That would be so cool! Mom, can we put up the basketball hoop?"

"We'll see," Bekah says. "I'd have to check with the landlord first, sweetie." She finally looks at me. "Thank you for offering, Knox, that's really… nice."

I watch her curiously as Brayden bounces on his feet, all excited about the basketball hoop.

It's no stress to me. I've got so much shit lying around in storage at the motel, I'd be happy to offload most of it.

"Anytime," I say, giving her a small smile.

To Brayden, she says, "I think you should go take a seat in the studio and get comfy for the next hour, okay?"

He takes another sip of his soda and beams at his mom. "Okay, but can I tell Knox how I got my black eye?"

Bekah gives him a look.

"What happened, bud?" I press. "Looks like you've got a real shiner coming up."

I feel Bekah's eyes on me, but I don't look at her.

"I made the class bully's nose bleed when he started a fight, and then he got expelled."

I give him a high-five.

Bekah's eyes go wide. "That's not exactly something to celebrate," she says, looking at me sternly. "Violence is not always the answer."

Brayden gives me an eyeroll behind her back, and I chuckle.

"That's true. I just liked hearing the part where the bully was bleeding." I give Brayden a wink, which I know won't help my cause.

He saunters off, and she says, "I better go help set up the mats…"

Grabbing her wrist, I pull her back toward me.

"You've got a kid?" I sputter again, when he's out of earshot.

"I know, I was going to… Look I was, Knox, I just… every time I tried to say something, we got interrupted."

I frown. "You think I wouldn't be okay with it?"

"That's not it," she whisper-shouts. "But let's face it, most men aren't, and they see it as baggage. I didn't tell you that night because I didn't know if I'd ever see you again. It didn't make sense to say anything. We had a great night, and then went our separate ways."

Ouch. I don't add that the whole time we went our separate ways, I was fucking miserable.

"I get that, but it's kind of a big thing to not tell someone when you see them again unexpectedly. How hard would it be to say, 'hey, Knox, how you doing? Oh, and also, I have a kid, he's really great…'"

"Why does it matter? I mean, you're making it a big deal."

"It doesn't, I promise you, I love kids. I just find it odd you didn't mention it earlier."

I don't want to make her feel bad, so I add, "He seems like a great kid."

"He is a great kid. We're a package deal, which is why I keep people at arm's length. Listen, I'm sorry, I thought we were one night and one night only…" she whispers, getting haughty all over again. "I had no idea that we'd be living in the same town, and I'd be working for you, and we'd be at the same self-defense class together. Coincidence or not, you have to admit, it's all a little freaky."

Curious, I give her a look. "There's no coincidence about it. We were meant to meet like this. Out of all the places and all the towns anywhere in this country, we end up in the same one? That has to mean something."

"I'm not ashamed of my kid," she says. I see that look in her eyes and I know she's telling the truth. She's self-protecting. And I don't have to be a genius to know that some guys have had an issue with it before. "I just wanted to figure out us before I even went down that road. I didn't want to blurt out my life story to the first guy that came along who I like…"

I stare at her, stunned. Is that how she sees me? I mean, I'm glad she likes me, obviously, but I sound like a real jerk in her eyes.

"I have no objection to you being a single mom," I say, a little angrily. "So, when you say that most men aren't okay with it, I'd appreciate it if you didn't put me into the same category as every other schmuck you've ever known."

"I didn't mean to. I will always protect Brayden, and that's what I thought I was doing."

"By keeping me out? One day, you'll learn, Bekah, that not all guys are total assholes. Some of us are just looking to find the right person and settle the fuck down with and be happy. Hard to imagine, right?"

Her mouth hangs open. "Guys like you don't exist," she carries on. "You're not supposed to exist!"

I frown, not knowing what the fuck she's ranting about, and then Sally decides to come back and sidles right up next to Bekah.

"Ready to get set up?" she beams.

I smile at her, as if there's nothing to see here. "Ready when you are."

I don't get to say anything else because Sally leads Bekah off back into the gym, and I'm left scratching my head, wondering how I'm the bad guy here.

I truly wasn't trying to make her feel bad, and now I don't get the chance to make it right.

I run a hand through my hair as I follow them out, carrying a bunch of mats with me to lay down on the floor, muttering under my breath.

I try, and fail, at keeping my eyes off Bekah. It's a little hard with her dressed in that outfit. The tight material enhances all of her curves for my viewing pleasure. Her cheeks are flushed now from our little spat and she looks a little bewildered. I feel it deep in my gut that she's very protective, but something more, like she's almost told me too much by me knowing she has a son.

Not for the first time, I feel that she's terribly afraid of something.

I'm distracted by being introduced to more women from the motorcycle club. They swarm around me as I start setting up. Sienna, Steel's girlfriend, lingers when the others go off to take their places and get ready for the class to start.

"So, how are things going?" she asks, a small smile on her lips.

"Uh, pretty good, thanks. Have you been to one of these classes before?"

She shakes her head. "No, but Steel makes sure I carry

pepper spray wherever I go."

"Well, that's a good start, but it's always beneficial to know what to do if someone approaches you by surprise."

I know there's something else going on from how she's listening, but her mind is clearly elsewhere.

"That's definitely a good skill to have."

I smile. "Something else on your mind?"

She clears her throat. "I'm just gonna go ahead and say it… Steel can come across as being a little gruff," she says, as I give her a side-eye. "And he is a little intimidating at times."

"You think?"

She laughs. "But he has a good heart, deep down, he just doesn't always show it. He's indifferent to most people. He likes his immediate circle and doesn't let people in easily, unless you're the four-legged variety."

"I kinda got the idea he was a dog lover when he played with my dog and asked me more questions about her than he did about me." I laugh.

Sienna rolls her lips. "That sounds about right."

"You don't have to worry about my feelings," I tell her. "I'm a big boy, I can handle it."

She nods. "Of course you are. I just don't want you to run away too soon. Steel's always had his club brothers, and Gunner—Lily's ol' man—they've been tight since Gunner was small, but I know he's curious about you. He just takes a little while to warm up to the idea."

I nod. She's giving me the heads up, I get it. "I've no plans to go anywhere, it'll take time. What Hank did wasn't cool, but here we all are. We can't change what he did, we can only move forward."

"I agree. It'll be great if you can hang around the club a little."

I know she likely doesn't know anything about them asking me to patch in, so I keep my mouth shut. I know how motorcycle clubs work to some degree.

"I'm coming to the barbecue Friday, so it'll be good to finally meet everyone."

She smiles. "I'm so glad that you came to town, Knox." She gives me a squeeze on the arm. "It's going to be great for everyone."

She takes off to find the others and a warm feeling washes over me. Deep in my gut, a family is what I want, what I've always wanted, and something I know that has been missing in my life.

Maybe I did come here to attempt the impossible, but at least I'm trying. At least this way, I will know. I can see me having a relationship with Lily, for sure. She's easygoing and very sweet. Steel, however, the jury's still out on that. Time will tell.

My eyes flick to Bekah. She gives Brayden a smile as he waves and continues to play on his Nintendo switch.

I'm still reeling from her comment earlier.

Guys like me aren't supposed to exist? What the fuck is that supposed to mean?

She's making it sound like I'm some fucking saint or something, and I'm not. I'm far from perfect.

I just wanted to be honest. If I had an issue with her having a kid, I would be truthful.

What's worse, Sally suggests that since Bekah is a black belt, it'll be perfect if we demonstrate the moves. She seems to think that's a good idea and neither of us can argue in front of the others.

Yeah, really fucking perfect. She looks like she wants to stab a pencil in my eye.

We start by demonstrating the chokehold. Being this close to her without the thought of choking her for real while I rode her from behind is enough to make me want to explode.

Now I have to put my hands on her in front of the entire class and pretend that it doesn't affect me.

If I make it out of this class without bursting into flames, I deserve a goddamn medal.

I demonstrate the different moves, explaining the importance of using your legs or feet to kick them first to try to hurt them enough to loosen their grip. I also show them the technique of trying to move your head to one side, creating a little space between your neck and their hold, then bringing your arm over theirs to try and pull their arm away.

"Obviously, we don't want you to hurt each other, "I say. "So go easy and see if one of the techniques might work for you."

Everyone pairs up, and I turn to Bekah, my arm still loosely hung around her neck.

"Should we see what you've really got? Since you're a black belt and all?" I mutter in her ear.

"You really don't want to mess with me tonight," she replies coolly.

My dick stirs.

"You owe me an apology," I say. "Which I'm willing to collect."

She snorts. "For not telling you I had a kid?"

"No, for insinuating I'm an asshole."

"I did not mean to insinuate that," she pleads, her tone hushed. "I don't think that."

My grip softens. I don't want her to move away from me. I'm enjoying her being this close, but I know that's for other reasons that I can't show in front of the class.

She turns in my arms. "My turn?"

I spread my arms wide. "Go for it."

She reaches for my neck to choke me from the front. "One rule of thumb for a successful choke is to hold and press the neck for at least fifteen to twenty good seconds."

"You're not supposed to be enjoying this," I tell her. "But if by cutting off my circulation means that you get all this pent-up rage out of your system, then go for it."

Even though we're supposed to be walking around, making sure the class does the techniques safely—like Sally is so diligently doing—instead, we're too caught up in each other to remember to do what we came here for.

I bring my arms up, knocking her out of the hold as I take a few steps back. "Gotta put a little more fire into it, Red," I say, a smirk on my lips. "Which I know you have."

We take our places on the mat again, and I pull her easily into my arms, her back against my chest as I wrap my entire arm around her neck. "What are you going to do now?" I mutter in her ear. The subtle scent of her faded perfume permeates my nostrils.

There is no sweeter scent than this woman, even when she's infuriating.

"Show you what I'm made of?" she fires back, and before I can retaliate with a smartass reply, she drops, pushing back against my shoulder, then kicking my knee. And when I buckle, she flips around and trips me. I fall on my back against the mat with a thud, and she falls too, landing on top of me, straddled across my knee.

I stare up at her as she stares down at me, then applause erupts around the room.

"Very nice!" I hear one of the women from the club yell. "That's one way to keep a man down."

Her cheeks are flushed, and I resist the urge, with every

fiber in my being, to place my hands on her ass and squeeze. I'm so hard right now, it's ridiculous.

She gives me a sarcastic smile, hops off me, and then proceeds to take a little bow in front of the class.

Someone else calls out "girl power," or some shit as I pick myself up off the floor.

"I think you're taking this a little more seriously than most," I say, dusting myself off as the class gets back to it. "Ten points for creativity, though."

"I should get eleven points for knocking you on your ass. You are a lot bigger than me." I can't be sure, but her eyes momentarily graze down my body and land on my dick.

"Maybe I let you trip me because I knew you'd fall too."

"We both know that's not true." She folds her arms over her chest like that'll save her.

"Are you going to come work for me?" I blurt out. The angst is killing me.

"I was, until…"

"Until?"

"I want the job, I just don't want things to be weird between us…after…everything."

"It won't be weird."

She nods, though I don't know if I believe her and frankly, I don't know if I even mean it.

I run a hand through my hair with frustration but I try not to show it. "Let's move on from that, start from scratch.

Hi, I'm Knox, and I really like you and I'd like you to come work for me."

Her eyes go wide as she looks around, making sure nobody heard. She clears her throat.

"Fine. Pleased to meet you, Knox. I'm Bekah, and I have a ten-year-old kid. And I need a job."

My lips twitch. "There you go, wasn't so hard, was it?"

She rolls her eyes. "Do you want me to drop you again?"

I think our spat is over, but I can't be sure. What I can be sure of is Colt standing in the middle of the gym, staring at us.

What the fuck is his problem?

I move, standing in front of Bekah as I give him a chin lift. "Got a problem, Colt?"

"Bekah?"

Oh.

She shoves around me and gasps, both hands going over her mouth.

"Daniel?"

Who the fuck is Daniel?

He starts to walk toward her. Wait. Daniel… she's mentioned him before, her cousin…

Relief floods through me that he's not some ex-boyfriend or lover who I've got to fight.

"Is it really you?"

Tears leak from her eyes. "Oh my… it's me," she cries. "I'm so… I'm so happy to see you, what are you doing here? Your name is Colt now?"

He pulls her into a massive bear hug as she sobs into his shoulder, her words undecipherable.

"I'm here, Bekah. I've waited so fuckin' long for this moment," he murmurs.

"I never thought this day would come. I looked for you."

"I looked for you, too."

They pull apart, and Bekah wipes the tears from her eyes.

I've never seen her look so vulnerable. I only know her as a feisty, strong woman who knows what she wants and goes for it. This side shows me so much more.

Not that I didn't already know. I realize there's more to this woman than meets the eye.

BRACKEN RIDGE
REBELS
ARIZONA
M · C

CHAPTER 16

REBEKAH

I can't believe my eyes as Daniel—Colt—cups my face. He has a dark but amused expression on his face. "The second I saw you knock Knox down on his ass and heard that smart mouth, I knew it was you."

He's a lot bigger than I remember. He's always had a strong build, but his shoulders are wide set and he's got more muscle. His raven-colored hair falls gently over his face as those green eyes I remember so well take me in. I've missed him so much.

I smile up at him, amongst my falling tears. "I guess some things never change, huh, cuz?"

"This is Daniel?" Knox interrupts, standing beside me like a bodyguard. "The guy you told me about, right?"

I didn't miss the way he pulled me behind him when my cousin came stalking toward me, protecting me. It made goosebumps appear all over my body and my annoyance with him, and mainly myself, disappeared. His possessiveness is executed in a different way to what I've experienced before. I can't explain it, or the fact I like it, and that confounds me all over again.

"I had no idea this little town was going to be the best thing that ever happened to me." I hold my hands up to my face and sob. Nobody knows me like Daniel does. Nobody comes close, and he's here, right in front of me, alive and well.

He puts an arm around me, and we move off to the side as the others watch on curiously, but Sally continues on with the class, getting everyone's attention back to the front. When Knox sees that I'm all right, he goes off to help Sally as Brayden runs up to me.

"Mom? Who is that?" he asks, looking up to the giant who has me pulled against him as Daniel tells me over and over that he can't believe it.

"This is Daniel," I say. "Remember, I've told you all about him and his brother Elijah, who went to be with the angels." I swallow hard as Elijah's face comes into view. I can't go there right now. After all these years, it still hurts.

"This is Daniel?" Brayden looks him up and down and his eyes go wide. "What are you lifting?"

We both burst out laughing as my cousin looks toward me, shaking his head. "Chip off the old block?"

"You got it. Takes after his mama."

He bends down to Brayden. "You can call me Colt. Your

mom and me go way back. We used to work in the fields together, and she'd run out there in her pretty dress and get it all dirty and ruined, and she'd get a telling off, but she'd just go ahead and do the very same thing the next day."

I laugh at the memory. "Papa wasn't happy."

"Nope, he wasn't, but it never stopped you."

All the memories of our upbringing surface quickly, and I'm glad I've had years of practice at banishing the unpleasant ones. Those can stay locked away where they belong. I only choose to remember the good days in the field, with my two cousins who I loved dearly. Seeing Daniel—Colt—is just the icing on the cake for me. Life couldn't get any better right now.

Brayden looks up at me. "That's really cool, Mom. I knew we liked this place for a reason." He moves over to me and gives me a hug. I run a hand through his hair and wipe my face again.

"Here, honey," I hear Angel say behind me, handing me some tissues. "Typical Colt, making all the girls cry."

"Hey, this is for good, not evil," he says, giving her a devilish grin as I thank her, feeling stupid for crying in front of everyone, but this is monumental.

Cassidy comes over and Colt puts an arm around her. "This is my ol' lady, Cassidy."

"We've already met, and please call me Cass," she says, giving me a wink. "But I didn't know you were his cousin then, obviously. This is crazy. Colt talks about you all the time and what you guys got up to as kids back home. We've tried so hard to track you down, Bekah, that I feel as if I know you."

I start to well up again, and Cassidy smiles sympathetically. "That's so sweet of you to say. I've also looked for you, but I don't have any social media, so that makes things a little hard."

With my ex being the way he is, I never take any chances with having too much information out there. It's just too risky. I used Mallory's Facebook account a few times, but nothing ever panned out. I thought it was a lost cause. There was no way he was going back home; his parents had no idea where he was living now.

"You guys will have to come over for dinner. How about we grab a pizza after this, if you're up for it?" she asks, looking up to Colt who's nodding.

"Can we have pepperoni?" Brayden asks, much to the amusement of us all.

"Of course, if your mom says it's okay," she replies.

"We'd love that, thank you," I say. "We've so much to catch up on, I don't even know where to start."

"Me either." Colt chuckles. "Ten years is a long time, Bek, but I think we'll manage somehow. You always did talk way too much."

I punch him on the arm playfully, feeling like we're

already back into the old swing of things.

When I glance over at Knox, he's watching me. He gives me a soft smile, which I reciprocate.

I gave him a bit of a hard time, and in some ways, he's right; I did treat him like all men are the same. I know they're not. But I've lived under scrutiny and judgment my whole life. If he knew, he'd understand. He'd probably pity me, and I don't want that either.

I don't know what to do with him. That's the bottom line.

But I'm sure as shit gonna make it my mission to find out.

The evening is a blast. I caught up with Colt, as he likes to be called now, for a couple of hours, both of us still hardly daring to believe that we're here, in this place, and it feels absolutely amazing.

"I knew I'd find you one day, Bek," he said when we were relaxing with pizza back at his place.

His dog Bella came up to me and sniffed my feet, then proceeded to slump down on them. Apparently, it's a thing she does. I reached down and pet her head.

"Me too, I always looked for you everywhere, hoping one day our paths would just cross." All night I've been crying and hardly daring to believe it in case I'm dreaming the whole thing. But he's here, and I couldn't be happier.

"I didn't know you changed your name, that didn't exactly help the search."

He'd shrugged. "I hate social media, never go on there, but like Cass said, we tried. I used hers to look for you. I even went to a P.I. one time."

I'd frowned, not yet quite willing to tell him about my past. It was too soon, and I didn't want to bombard him with my problems on the first night of our reunion.

"We were meant to find one another, it's as simple as that," I'd said, feeling it deep within me.

"We were," he agreed. "Do you miss it?"

I made a face. "Sometimes, if I'm honest, but I mean the times I had with you and Eli."

He nods. The pain in his eyes will always be there, as it will be for me too. We loved him. We always will. Nothing can ever change that.

"He's watching over us."

I know this is so hard for my cousin. "He is. I really believe it." I held his hand while we sat and talked until it was time for Brayden to go to bed.

Later when we're home, and I'm exhausted, I pull my phone out and rest it on the side table. Climbing into bed, I see a message pop up on the screen.

My heart jolts when I see it's Knox.

Knox: My ass is still kicked, just in case you wondered.

I can't help the grin on my face. He's too adorable to stay mad at.

Me: I'm sorry, sometimes I forget my own strength.
Knox: Very funny. I don't want to mess with you in a dark alley. Maybe you could be my security instead of my receptionist?

My heart hammers in my chest. I'm going to be working for him. Lord help me.

Me: A promotion already? Anyone would think you're playing favorites.
Knox: You're the only applicant that didn't have a record.
Me: I feel so special.
Knox: Good workers are hard to find.

I remember him with his mouth on me, his hands, everything, and I stop myself from writing anything dirty.

Me: I should ask for more money then. I smile, waiting for his response.

Knox: I would've paid it.

There's that jolt again, the electricity that is so apparent between us, even when he's not even in the room.

Me: What time did you want me tomorrow?
Knox: All day, every day.

I smile, knowing this is not good if we're supposed to be platonic work colleagues.
I have no idea how I'm going to negate this.

Me: Knox, we're trying the friends thing, remember? Now you're my boss, though, do I have to call you Sir?

The grey bubble appears, then disappears, then starts again. This goes on for several moments, prompting me to type back.

Me: Cat got your tongue?
Knox: You call me Sir and I'll put you over my knee.

Holy shitballs.
I press my legs together.

No, no this can't be happening. Not like this. I've spent the last few days actually convincing myself that we can do this, and yet every time I see him, I'm convinced that that's the wrong decision. And then I change my mind. And then I go over all the things I already know, weighing out the pros and cons. We both know that realistically the attraction is too much, but we're both trying to fight it.

When I knocked him down on the mat tonight, there was an unmistakable hunger in his eyes as he looked up at me. He did not mind one bit, and frankly, neither did I, even if at the time I was still mad. The sexual tension is palpable, like nothing I've ever experienced, and that scares me a little.

The flame between us only burns hotter, even when we disagree.

I still feel bad about not telling him about my kid, but it couldn't be helped. I will protect my son with every inch of my life. Let's face it, my taste in men in the past leaves a lot to be desired.

From what he has shown me so far, I know he's a good guy. I think I can trust him, but there will always be that part of me that stays reserved. Ready and waiting. Fight or flight. I suppose once someone has been in an abusive relationship, a piece of your heart will always be missing. And a part of me is scared that if Knox saw to the heart of me and realized just how damaged I am, he wouldn't want me anymore. And sadly, I would accept it. My feistiness and courage have only just woken from a deep slumber, and it's taken a long, long time to get it back. I don't want to lose it again. I can't.

Not for my sanity's sake. Not for my son's, but most importantly for me.

I will never be in that position again, with nowhere else to go, sleeping on my friend's couch, always looking behind me, never quite sure if he was going to show up.

Sometimes I can't even believe I got away from him. It frightens me what he's capable of and how obsessed with me he was.

I have to understand that this is a different time, a different place, a different man. One I could quite easily overlook because of my own self-preservation. I don't want to get hurt again; I'm terrified of it. And if my walls come down too much, I know I will fall for Knox.

Maybe I already did the night we first met.

Now everything has become more complicated, yet I can't stop myself from wanting what I want.

And I meant what I said: that men like him don't exist. In my world, that is one hundred percent true. Even if part of me craves a family and a man to protect us and watch over us. Is it so wrong to want those things? Is it so wrong to picture in my mind's eye? Because I know we've lived without a man for so long and I've survived, but I can't honestly say I've been happy. I can't honestly say it's been all smooth sailing, though I'm proud of where I've come from. I wouldn't change anything because I wouldn't have Brayden.

Knox: Did I scare you off?

I gather myself, realizing I've been daydreaming again.

Me: No, Sir.
Knox: You really don't take hints too well, do you?
Me: No, I'm very bad at listening.
Knox: Should I be rethinking your employment?
Me: I'd hold off. Find someone better, then fire me.
Knox: You're not making this easy on yourself.
Me: Well, you brought up spanking.

I smile to myself. I know I'm pushing the limits.
I know what I saw tonight. He was protective; in a way that made my heart melt, not in a way that meant I was trapped. I didn't know until tonight that there was a difference.
I guess I'm still learning things about myself that surprised me.

Knox: You're a bad influence.

Me:Getting back on track, what time do I start tomorrow?

Knox

What time is school drop off?

God, could my heart melt any more?

Me: 8:45
Knox: Does 9 o'clock sound good?
Me: Yes…
Knox: Don't say it.
Me: I won't, but I'll be thinking it.

I snuggle down into the pillows, knowing tomorrow will be a challenge, but I'm up for it.

Knox: Me too. Goodnight, Red.
Me: Goodnight, Knox.

I resist the urge to write Sir. I want him to hear it from my mouth instead.

I fall asleep quickly, remembering everything about tonight. Feeling so light that I could just melt away.

Things are finally turning around for us; things are really starting to look up.

I hope this is a sign of better things to come and that the

past is truly behind us. It feels like a new chapter and I'm gonna take all the opportunities that come with open arms. I owe it to myself. That strong, confident, and outgoing woman who knows what path she's on and where she's headed.

If I can just keep my hands off Knox, then I may have a fighting chance at keeping my job.

Though something tells me I'm going to be calling on The Coffee Bean to beg them for a job so I can do very bad things to Knox without him being my boss.

I fall asleep with that very notion on my mind, not knowing which way it'll swing in the morning.

I get to work on time, as punctuality is my specialty. I also pick up coffee from the takeout van parked at the top of the street, remembering that he took cream and sugar in his coffee that day in the lunchroom. I order a cappuccino and hope for the best.

"Good morning," I say, when I walk through the front door. Knox is behind the desk, and when I get closer, I see he's on the phone. He frowns when he sees me, but motions for me to come over. He answers a few questions, unable to really give any detailed information, and I set the coffees down as I watch him.

When he finally hangs up, I can't help but giggle a little bit, even though none of this is funny. I actually feel really sorry for him. He's pale and looks incredibly frustrated.

"I don't know who thought it was a good idea to let you loose on the phone or the computer, but I'll just say I'm glad I got here when I did."

He puts his head in his hands. "You've no idea, this is so stressful."

"I know how I can make it instantly better; you're closed for business, right? You're only taking inquiries?"

He nods, looking defeated.

I know the general public, so he probably just had his head chewed off again.

"Where's your phone system? Does it have an answering machine?"

"It's right over there, and I've got no idea, but I want to throw the fucking thing out the window."

I tut, moving over to the phone cradle as I take a second to figure it out. It's a fairly new system, so it shouldn't be that complicated.

"First order of business," I say matter-of-factly. "We need to switch the phone on to answer only with a detailed message about being closed for renovations. I can do that for you now, if you'd like?"

His eyes go wide. Poor Knox. He looks like a deer caught in headlights.

"Yeah, that sounds fucking amazing."

I roll my lips. "Uh, less of the F-bombs. Not a good habit to get into if customers are around."

He chuckles. "Yes, ma'am."

"When are you planning on opening again?"

"Late February."

Christmas is literally two weeks away, so that gives us eight weeks to get everything done. I know I can sort the mess in the office today, then work on filing and tidying up tomorrow. I can check emails the day after and spend time going through bookings and whatever else he has for me.

"Perfect. I'll redirect them to the website, assuming that it's up and running and doesn't let people book at the moment?"

"Lucky for me, the software company did all of that before Vi left. Customers can book from March onwards, with the new Skywalk opening, which will be a big draw card. I can only hope the renovations will be complete."

"Excellent." I take a moment to figure out where the answer button is, click around, and then begin. "Thank you for calling the Bracken Ridge Motel. Please note that the motel is currently closed for extensive renovations and remodeling. We will reopen with brand new rooms and facilities on the 1st of March. At this time, we are only taking bookings and inquiries from our website. We are booking up quickly for the grand opening of the Skywalk this coming spring, and all the details and room rates are on our website. Your call is very important to us, so if you have any questions, please feel free to email us directly and we will attend to your query promptly."

I hit end and then listen to the recording back to make sure I don't sound like a freak.

Satisfied, I turn to Knox. He's already out of his chair. "You did all of that and you haven't even put your purse down?"

His eyes scan down my body and I feel that thrill go through me.

Business, I tell myself. This is business.

"You're playing with the big guns now, boss," I say with a small smile. "Where would you like me next?"

Things are about to get interesting.

BRACKEN RIDGE
REBELS
ARIZONA
M · C

CHAPTER 17

KNOX

Where would you like me next?

I try not to come in my pants at the very thought of where I'd like her next. If I go down that road, we won't get anything done today except fuck on the desk. And I'm not so sure Bekah is really up for that anymore since we're trying the friends thing and attempting to be civil. I am, after all, her boss.

I've never had so much restraint in all my life.

If she does call me Sir, though, I will have no choice but to do what I promised and spank her ass.

I swallow hard as her hazel eyes assess me, amusement laced in her expression.

"I'm not gonna answer that."

"Good because I can clearly see we won't get anything done with a desk looking like that. If you're happy for me to tidy this up, stack up all the paperwork so we can go through it together, and I can throw out whatever is junk, make a tray for bills and things to be paid and another for things I need to respond to. Then I'll give everything a good clean."

"Uh, that sounds good."

She hands me a coffee, and I sip it gratefully. "Is it too much to ask you to pick up coffee and pastries or lunch for the boys while they're working?"

She snorts. "How many of them are there?"

"About twenty-five or so."

"I think we could buy morning coffee once a week like a treat. They can supply their own lunch, and I can find an urn and make coffee here. It'll be too much to do that every day."

"Wow, you're bossy."

"No, I ran a tire shop really well. I know how much stuff costs and you have no income with the doors closed so we have to manage every penny."

I like the way she says "we."

"A woman after my own heart."

"I will pick coffee up for us, though, if you're paying."

I grin. "Would you like a proper tour?"

"I've already seen the staff room, and that needs a good clean."

"I don't expect you to come and clean, Bekah."

"Well, you have cleaners, right? You could pay them cash to come in and overhaul the staff room and bathroom, which I'm assuming is in no fit state to be used?"

"You could say that."

"I'll call whoever you like to arrange it, then we can keep busy getting on top of things here."

I wish she'd stop saying on top of things. The only thing I want on top of me is her.

Moving those hips, those tits, that fucking dirty mouth…

"Knox?"

I blink. Oops.

"Yeah?"

"Something's scratching at the door."

"Oh." I jump up. "It's my dog, Evie, she can hear my voice through the door. She was buried in a giant pillow when you were at my apartment that night, she doesn't let anyone get in the way of her power naps."

She smiles. "That is kinda sweet."

"Well, my apartment is attached to the office, so after a while, she gets antsy when I don't show my face."

I open the door and Evie pokes her head through, heading straight over to Bekah.

"Oh, she's so gorgeous!" Bekah says in delight as Evie rubs her head on her leg, and she finally drops her purse and bends down to pat her.

"She knows it. She'll have you eating out of her paw before long, don't be fooled."

She scratches her gently behind her ears, telling her what a beautiful girl she is.

I smile, knowing how good Evie is at making people do whatever she wants, just by being her.

"She's adorable. I can see how she'd fool me, three seconds in and I'm done."

I chuckle. "Evie wins again."

I spread my arm out. "This is my apartment, excuse the mess."

She peeps inside and gives me a smile. I'm not going to show her around in here; I just wanted Evie to give her seal of approval, and it looks like she has.

"Very convenient that it's not a long commute to work."

"You can say that again."

I've only just noticed she's wearing a skirt. Well, that isn't true. I noticed her legs before when I was on the phone, but I was too busy trying not to give myself an aneurism in the process.

"I'll get the kitchen and bathroom cleaned today," I go on. "If you like, I can show you what I've been doing in one of the rooms with the remodel. Deanna is coming over this week to look at decor. It'd be good to have a second opinion."

"I'd love that," she says. "Lead the way."

We leave Evie to go and explore, and when I show Bekah the closets I've been constructing, along with sanding back some of the furniture, I think she's quite impressed.

"Obviously, we need new beds and mattresses, and the sink and toilets will all be replaced, the whole nine yards.

But with new carpets and lighting and fresh paint, it'll look like new."

"It's going to be so great, Knox. I'm really happy for you."

I turn to her. "Thanks, I've been so excited about this project ever since I got here. To see it all coming together is a dream come true."

"Just to think some developer would have bought it and bulldozed the place," she agrees. "It would've been a crying shame. Once everything is up to date, we will have to schedule a photographer to come and reshoot the room photos to update the website and third-party booking channels."

"Hey, that's a great idea." She thinks of everything. I love how fucking smart she is.

Even dealing with the phone was such a simple solution. I just didn't know what the fuck I was doing. I'm more of a hands-on kinda guy with tools, rather than computers and goddamn phones.

"Happy to help. I've got so many ideas running around in my head. The storage room we saw the other day, all that stuff could be moved into the shed, and you could make that into a function room, catering to businesses, banks, corporations, and workshops," she goes on. "They could book out all the rooms and get a package with the Stone Crow for meals, since it's right down the street."

"How come I haven't thought of that?"

"Because you've been busy holding up your motel with

your own bare hands?"

Warmth washes over me. This is who she is, always trying to make other people feel better. That urge to reach out to her, to take her in my arms, almost overwhelms me.

I can't do that, though. She's my employee…

"It has been a little stressful," I concede.

"If you like, I can call the cleaners and anything else you need doing, you just have to ask. I'm here to help." I know she genuinely means it.

"Thanks, Bekah, I really appreciate it."

We walk back through the grounds as I point out the different things that will be going on, like a new sign, garden beds that will be replanted, and paving to be replaced.

I know we're going to blow through a hundred grand like there's no tomorrow, so hopefully it'll be enough to get everything done.

"It's going to look amazing," she says. "You're putting some heart and soul back into the place. With all the people helping and the club pitching in, it's going to be great."

"Thanks for your enthusiasm. I feel like it is really happening now, after not knowing for so long if I was going to close the place down and sell it. I'm glad I didn't."

"I'm glad you didn't either."

I hold the door open as she moves back inside.

"I really wanted to get things moving before Christmas, as there will be at least a week where work will cease for the holidays," I say. "And I don't expect people to work during that time."

"I'm happy to," she replies with a shrug. "I've never really celebrated Christmas very much, not since I left home, and even then, it was much simpler than the customs that are traditional everywhere else. Brayden loves it, so I do a little something for him with the tree and a few presents to make it nice for him, but… Christmas is around the time I left home… for good, so it brings back memories."

She looks down at her feet, and I know that this is extremely painful for her.

"I'm sorry." I don't know what else to say.

"It's okay, I've no reason to be sad. I've made a good life for myself, and now I've got this amazing new job, I'm meeting new people, and I've got Colt back in my life. Things are good."

I want to ask her how she feels about me, but I don't want to be pushy.

My phone rings, pulling me from that thought. It's one of the contractors so I have to take it.

Bekah moves off over to the desk and begins to tidy up.

And that's how it goes all week.

We fall into easy banter, and she laughs a lot.

The reception area already looks good just from the junk being removed. There were old chairs that were no longer usable, an old computer, and bags full of old documents with nowhere to land. It seems Vi was a hoarder of epic proportions.

The carpets will be replaced along with the linoleum in reception and the breakroom.

I feel so good about where things are headed. Everything has become so much clearer.

Except for what to do about Bekah.

We've been getting along so well. I've kept my distance, though I don't really want to.

Being around her like this, getting to know her a little more day by day, it's been fantastic.

She's been showing me how to use the computer, sitting close to her while she demonstrates. Having to witness her in a skirt every single day, even though it's wintertime and her legs should be covered, is absolute torture.

I don't know how much more of this I can take. My hands are itching to touch her, feel her, make her squirm.

I was wrong to think that we could do this. I can't, yet she's such a valuable asset that I don't know how to turn things around.

And what's more, she still fucking flirts with me, especially over text.

She has yet to call me Sir to my face, but I know she's storing that up and the bubble is gonna burst when she does.

On Friday, after a busy week of construction, I lie down on my bed as a text comes through late.

When I see it's Bekah, my heart does a little flip.

Bekah: Are you up?

Me: Always.

Bekah: I just wanted to say think you, Knoxy

Huh? Knoxy?

Bekah: I mean, thank you, it's been a gret wick

Bekah: *great week

Me: Are you drunk?

Bekah: A little bit

Me: Where are you?

Bekah: I'm at home with Jack

My heart pounds in my chest.

Me: Who is Jack?

Bekah: Jack Daniels, silly

Me: Where's Brayden?

Bekah: Asleep. I'm not drunk, you ass!

Me: Sounds like you might be.

Bekah: Well, I'm not. I was just trying to be mice

Bekah: *nice

It's cute how she sends corrections. I chuckle imagining her tipsy, that would be a sight to see.

Me: Jack, huh? Hardcore

Bekah: I'm my own crown of thorns. I mean ouch, right, that would hurt?

I think I like drunk Bekah. A lot.

Me: I guess it would

Bekah: So, what are you doing?

Me: Attempting to sleep

Bekah: *laughing crying face*

Me: Why are you sending me a laughing emoji?

Bekah: Because I like the idea that I woke you up

My dick starts to stir. I like everything about her, that's nothing new.

Me: that's not nice

Bekah: I'm a bad girl, remember

I swallow hard. Oh boy.

Me: I remember, you corrupted me

Bekah: Are you kidding me right now????????

Me: That's a lot of question marks, assuming you're upset with that statement

Bekah: You spanked my ass and ate my butt hole

I burst out laughing. Oh no, she's gonna regret this tomorrow. She is hilarious.

I should shut this down, but I'm having way too much fun.

Me: You shouldn't taste so good
Rebekah: Knoxy…

I imagine her touching herself.

Me: Knoxy?
Rebekah: I think it has potential for a nickname
Me: I think it has potential to get you another spanking

Shit. Now I'm down the rabbit hole, and I can't even blame alcohol.

Rebekah: I didn't even call you Sir

I close my eyes.
Being her boss is one thing, but being her Dom…

Me: You know what that word does to me, and you know what I said I'd do to you if you said it
Rebekah: You're my boss now, you can't do anything.

I smirk.

Me: Oh really?
Rebekah: Yep.
Me: Wanna bet?

The gray bubble appears, then disappears again.
A few moments later, she replies.

Rebekah: I'm naked

My eyes go wide. That escalated quickly.

Rebekah: Tell me what you want to do to me

Shut this down now! She's intoxicated.

Me: I don't think that's a good idea, when you're…
like this
Rebekah: We should change your name to
grumpypants who doesn't know how to have fun.
You're my boss now so that means it's a no fun
zone, right?
Me: No, I just don't want to take advantage of you
Rebekah: I miss your cock, Sir

No, she did not.

I move my hand down to my cock. It's hard and I make matters worse by fondling myself.

Me:I need to hear your voice

A few moments later, she calls.

"Fuck, you're beautiful," I tell her.

I shouldn't, I really need to tell her good night.

"I liked it when you went down on me without having to ask," she whispers. "This is so unfair."

I chuckle. "Like I said, you should never have to ask."

Remembering that just makes my hand work faster as I pull on my cock harder.

Fuck yeah, that feels good.

Then she shocks me all over again when she says, "What if I don't want to be friends?"

Why is she torturing me this way?

"Red, you're driving me crazy."

"Tell me," she insists. "I want to know what you'd do to me, your bad little girl who doesn't listen."

I groan. "I'd worship that body of yours, making sure every single inch of you is covered in kisses. I'd devour those soft nipples that turn hard under my touch, coating each one with my tongue, sucking them into my mouth while I finger that sweet, tight little pussy. You'd like that, wouldn't you, baby?

"Oh, yes."

"Are you touching yourself?"

"Yes. Are you?"

"What do you think?"

"I think that you can't keep your hand off it. I wouldn't if I were with you."

I want to go to her so badly, but I know that she may be making a mistake when she's inebriated. I don't want to be the guy who takes advantage of a woman, no matter how fine she says she is. No. When I take Rebekah again, she'll be one hundred percent sober.

My hand starts to work faster.

"Are your fingers inside?"

She groans. "Yes."

"Fuck yourself and imagine me, Red. Imagine it's my tongue doing what I did to you that night all over again, in and out, in and out, my thumb pressing your clit until you explode on my tongue."

"Oh, Knox, oh, oh…"

"Pull your nipples," I growl. "I'm so hard for you, Red, so fucking hard. Come for me, tell me how good it feels."

"Knox!" she cries. "Oh yes, yes, ohhhhhh."

I close my eyes, pulling myself faster and squeezing tight until I start to come. I squirt cum all over myself as I groan her name over and over, pissed that it's my hand and not her pussy.

"You'll be the fucking death of me," I mutter.

"I like hearing your voice when I come," she says.

I refrain from groaning. Any more talk like that and I'll go over there right now and whisper dirty things in her ear just so she'll do it all over again.

I don't want this to end.

I have to take a stand. First thing Monday.

"I like hearing it too."

"I better go," she whispers after a few moments of silence.

"Goodnight, Rebekah."

"Goodnight, Knoxy."

I smile. Fucking Knoxy.

She may have started this, but I'm finishing it.

I can't be around her and not touch her. To ever think I could is a fucking joke.

I just hope she feels the same way about me when she's sober.

BRACKEN RIDGE
REBELS
ARIZONA
M · C

CHAPTER 10

KNOX

After what we did on Friday night, let's just say it's been one hell of a frustrating weekend.

Working all week together, our hands accidentally touching when we both reached for something. The close proximity, it's almost too much.

Not to mention the whole self-defense thing where she straddled me in public. Then I've had to put up with her in her little pencil skirts and see-through white blouses, which I'm certain she wears just to tease my cock.

It's enough to throw me over the edge.

And the edge is where I stay, until she arrives at work with our coffee ten minutes early.

My voice hoarse, I say, "Good morning, Bekah."

She places her travel mug down on the desk next to her computer, but doesn't look at me.

"Good morning, Knox."

My eyes travel down the length of her body, checking out all the contours of her ass that I'd love to have my way with. She's even wearing heels. I imagine her kneeling before me just wearing those. With her back to me, I adjust my dick through my jeans.

This is not a good start to the day.

"I don't know how you expect me to get any work done, coming in here looking like that," I say. The words are out before I can stop them.

"Listen, about Friday night."

"Oh, you actually remember?"

Her cheeks flush slightly. "Of course I remember."

"You think that's appropriate when I'm supposed to be your boss and not be staring at your ass all day after the shit we pulled over the weekend?"

She shrugs. "You wanted to try being friends, remember?"

I steel my jaw, gritting out, "Yeah? Well, that ain't working out so good."

"Clearly not." She darts her eyes down to the bulge in my jeans. I feel like a fucking rampant teenager when she's around, unable to control my bodily functions.

I saunter toward her, my arms folded over my chest so I won't reach for her. "Is that right?"

She turns, steeling her back straight as she faces off with me. "Uh huh."

"If anything, I should be mad at you. You're the one who drunk dialed me."

"I wasn't drunk, I knew what I was doi—" She stops herself.

Hmm. Interesting.

"So, what you're really saying is you enjoy cock teasing me just because you can?"

I step closer, invading her space. She doesn't get it. Just as she didn't get it when seeing her as a mom only made me want to put a fucking baby in her belly, and I can honestly say I've never had such a strong feeling before. I don't know what to do with any of it.

"No, I didn't do it on purpose."

"Why, do you drunk dial all the guys you want to play with?"

Her eyes go wide, but I don't care anymore.

"You're still mad at me about the kid thing," she bleats. "Just admit it."

"You're really clutching at straws now, Bekah. I love kids. I don't know Brayden, obviously, but he seems like a good kid. Stop deflecting."

I'm so fucking hard, and I'm so fucking close to taking her over this desk if she doesn't keep that smart mouth shut.

"I'm not?"

"Oh, really? Are you sure you're not trying to push me away because you're scared of being hurt?"

Her mouth falls open. "No, that isn't… that isn't it."

"You want the truth?"

"That'd be nice," she mumbles. "Though I'm not sure I want to hear it."

"Seeing you as a mom with Brayden that night was the most amazing thing I've seen in a long time. I want that someday, Bekah, with the right woman… I've always wanted a family, to be a husband, and a father. And fuck me if I didn't see you, for one second, pregnant and barefoot with my kid inside you, and it's ridiculous when we've been together once and now we work together, and it's all I can think about. I'm a fucking mess thinking about you all the time, and I don't know what to fucking do about it."

Her mouth opens and closes again. "Knox?" She swallows hard.

"Don't say my name like that."

"Like what?"

"You know what, you know what you do to me."

"Sir?"

"Bekah," I warn.

"You saw me… like that?" she whispers. "Barefoot and pregnant, with your kid?"

Shit. Now she's gonna be the one running like a country mile. She's gonna think I'm completely nuts.

I run a hand through my hair, closing my eyes momentarily. "I shouldn't have…"

"Say it again."

My eyes pop open. Huh?

I quirk an eyebrow. "What?"

"Say it again, Knox."

I try to keep my hands off her, I really fucking try, but I relent, brushing her hair back off her face as my fingers lightly brush her skin. "I saw you barefoot and pregnant with my kid inside you."

She bites down on her lip. Oh, fuck.

My resolve shatters.

My mouth finds hers as her hands reach and pull me by the lapels of my shirt, our lips crashing together. She groans when our tongues meet and one hand cups her face, the other reaching down to squeeze her breast. It's like sweet heaven.

"I have to have you," I mutter, in between kisses.

"Take me then."

Fuck.

I pull myself away, charge to the door in all of five steps and lock it, ripping my shirt off as I round the desk again. She stands there, staring at me.

"Bend over, back to me, ass out…"

She bites down on her lip as I come closer. I pull her lip free and bite down gently on it.

"You know what that does to me, too, Red."

I spank her ass as she begins to turn, and she yelps.

Without waiting, I yank her skirt up, pulling her stockings down and her panties all the way to her ankles. She leans over the desk, her ass sticking out as I put both my hands on her. "Spread your legs wider."

She does so, gasping when I move one hand between her legs.

"Have you been a bad girl, Red?" I mutter in her ear, unbuckling my belt as I unzip my jeans and yank them and my boxer briefs to my knees. I'm hard as a rock.

I give myself a couple of pulls as I check out her ass, fondling her with my free hand.

I spank one cheek. "Answer me!"

"Yes!" she cries. "I've been so bad, Knox. You need to punish me."

I smile. I could line up right now and push into that soft, sweet center and worry about my own release. It's what she deserves after the last few days of teasing me, something she's becoming an expert at.

I reach around and start to unbutton her blouse. "All you do is tease me," I tell her. "In your little outfits, tight skirts, and sheer blouses, where I can see your nipples, tossing that beautiful hair over your shoulder, giving me looks when you think I don't notice. Is any of that being a good girl?"

"N…No," she stammers. Once her blouse is halfway unbuttoned, I open it enough so her tits can be free. When I yank down her bra and cup her breasts, her head leans back onto my shoulder and she moans. I start to pluck her nipples, my cock sliding into the crest of her ass as she writhes and moans in my arms. This is exactly how I like her. At my mercy.

"Why am I gonna make you beg me to come?" I demand.

"Because… because I was rude and jumped to conclusions about you."

I smile, nipping her neck, my fingers playing her like a guitar. "Why else?"

"Because I wore a tiny gym outfit and flaunted it in your face."

"Mmmhmm." I'm glad she remembered that.

"And… and I wore this skirt on purpose to tease you because I knew it was too tight."

"What about that see-through blouse? You want everyone to see your tits?"

She gasps. "No," she stammers again. "Just you."

I run my nose up her neck. "You're my dirty little slut, aren't you, Bekah?"

She groans when I pull her nipples harder, and she sticks her ass out farther.

"You've wanted me to do this to you ever since you came in here for your interview, didn't you?"

"Yes," she whispers. "I did. I wanted you to take me on the desk."

It's like music to my fucking ears.

"That's not a good girl, Red, that's a very bad girl, and you don't seem to be learning very well."

I reach down and fondle her ass. I'm gonna make her so goddamn wet, she's gonna be bouncing on my cock for days.

"Spank me," she cries. "I want it."

I kiss her neck. She's so hot for me, and I fucking love it.

I do as she asks. Reaching back as I hold one breast in my hand, I spank her left ass cheek, and she yelps. Then I spank the right, loving how her white ass turns pink almost immediately.

"You can't stop thinking about it, can you? About what I can do to you."

"Knox!" she moans when I spank her ass again, harder this time.

"You want to come so badly right now, don't you, Red?"

"Y-yes. I need it."

I reach between her legs and feel how soaked she is. Swearing under my breath, I drop to my knees and spread her farther apart.

I run my nose through her wet folds, taking her in as my tongue darts out to skim over her clit, and she groans loudly. She's so damn close that the moment I touch her, I know she'll explode.

"This pussy is mine," I tell her. "You got that, Red? Mine!"

"Ahhh!" she groans when I plunge my tongue into her hole, fucking her with it as she starts to ride my face. I keep her open to me with both hands as my fingers begin to rub her clit as she moves her hips, gaining friction. "I'm gonna come, Knox!" I stop, and she makes a sputtering noise. "Knox?"

"You think bad girls get to come?" I say, running my tongue over her back entrance as she gasps, bending over farther. She tries to reach one hand around to rub herself, but I smack it away.

"Let me come! Please, Knox!"

"You want this cock, baby?"

"Yes!"

"Then don't be a bad girl, take your punishment."

I smack her ass again, then kiss each side gently as she moans.

I start to move my hand over my cock. I've never been this hard. I'm ready to explode, but I want this for her. Making her wait will only build up her orgasm and it'll feel that much better.

I start again, fucking her with my tongue as she gains friction, and then I stop.

"Knox!"

I bite her ass cheek, still stroking myself as I move my

tongue to her back entrance, licking all the way up to her clit.

"You're so wet, baby," I say, plunging two fingers into her pussy as she rocks back against me.

"I want this pussy so hot for me."

"It is hot and wet for you. Please, Knox!"

I've teased her enough; I know when she's at her limit. I remove my fingers and suck on her pussy lips as she starts to gasp and groan. I suck her into my mouth, then move up to her clit and lick in soft, slow circles, enjoying her taste on my tongue. She moves to look over one shoulder, watching me as our eyes meet.

I start to fuck her again with my tongue and she turns back to the desk, gripping it with both hands as she sticks her ass out. And then I let her come.

She goes silent for a few moments, then lets out a sensual, loud, pleading mewl that will stay with me forever. Her taste changes as she orgasms, my fingers tapping her clit lightly as she releases, calling "Knox, Knox, Knox" over and over.

Satisfied, I stop, rub my fingers through her pussy, and stand.

"Taste yourself," I say, pressing my fingers to her lips. She takes my fingers in her mouth and sucks them, her tongue swirling, before she bites the pads gently. I need her mouth on me.

"Suck my cock," I tell her. "Get on your knees."

I spin her around to face me, and I rip her blouse in half and unfasten her bra, tossing it across the room. She reaches for my cock as I bend to take one hard nipple into my mouth.

Her other hand reaches for my hair as she grips it hard, and I just about spurt all over her.

"Knox, you're so good," she pants. "So, so good at this."

"You like me making you wait, baby?"

"That was intense."

I smile, kissing her as our tongues meet, and she slowly works her way down my body till she's kneeling between my legs. My cock's hard and heavy as she takes it into her mouth, and I start to breathe even heavier watching those lips take my length as she starts to suck.

I wasn't planning on this. I wanted to take her hard and fast. Fuck her into next week for making me wait this long, but now I want to take my sweet time, because after this, we're going up to my apartment so I can fuck her in my bed.

"That's it, Red." I grip her hair. "Take all of me, baby."

She groans as I move my hips, in and out, in and out. I hiss, closing my eyes. I know she's gonna make me come like this, and I wanted to empty myself inside her, but this just feels so good.

Her tongue flutters over my sensitive tip, making me

see stars, and when she squeezes my balls with just enough grip, I start to unravel.

"Gonna come, Bekah," I groan. "Gonna come in your mouth…"

She sucks harder, gripping me at the base and tugging on my balls at the same time. I spurt my cum down her throat. Reaching down, I hold myself over her hand and pull out so I come on her lips, chin, and face. I can't even describe how hot she looks.

"Oh God," she cries when I'm finally empty. She's dripping in my cum. I reach for my shirt and wipe her face quickly and gently, bringing her to her feet as our lips meet.

I taste myself, but I don't care. I need so much more.

"You tempt me so bad, baby," I tell her. "I'm still rock hard. I want your pussy to squeeze the fuck out of my cock."

"Hurry, Knox," she says, "I need your cock inside me, now!"

I turn her around, bend her over, and shove my cock deep inside her. I still, and we both groan at the same time, letting her adjust to my size. She wiggles her ass as I pull out and push back in again.

"You're so wet, baby," I whisper in her ear.

"I love tasting your cum," she tells me as I move my cock in and out of her. "I can't get enough of it."

"That cum was supposed to be inside you."

"I'm sure there's plenty more where that came from."

I chuckle, moving my hands to her hips. I smack one ass cheek as I move in and out of her faster, holding her so she's bent farther over the desk on her elbows, her ass in the air.

Chasing another release, I want her to explode all over my cock.

Knowing she wants it inside her spurs me on even more. She gasps as I pound her, the stapler and some other shit falling on the floor as the whole desk moves as we do.

In and out, I pound her little pussy, loving how she takes me, how she wants it.

I like having nothing between us, it feels so much better.

My balls slap her pussy as she starts to convulse beneath me. I'm hitting her sensitive clit, and when she gasps and then goes quiet, I know she's about to come. She's loud, pounding her ass back into me as I shoot my load inside her, calling out her name as I release on a violent shudder.

I stand behind her for a moment, my hands gripping her hips, and we're both naked and panting. Though she still has her shoes on, her tights around her ankles, and her skirt rucked up around her waist.

"You'll be the fucking death of me," I tell her.

"This all started because you had pretty eyes," she says back, out of breath. "So technically, it's your fault."

I kiss her hair. "I need to clean you up so we can do all of that again."

BRACKEN RIDGE
REBELS
ARIZONA
M · C

CHAPTER 19

REBEKAH

I suppose I brought it on myself. If I'm honest, I did want Knox to notice me. He's an ass for thinking I wore a short skirt just for him, but I'd be lying if I said that I didn't wave it under his nose a few too many times.

The chemistry between us is just too consuming to ignore and the sexual tension is off the charts.

When I let him take me over my desk, make no mistake, I wanted it. Even though I knew it would change everything between us, and there was a chance I'd have to leave my job, it takes job training to a whole new level.

Knox carries me into his apartment and up to his bedroom. Evie glances up at us from her large bed, dropping her head back down and rolling over. Clearly, sleep is more important at this time of the morning.

"What about work?" I pant, as Knox continues kissing me.

"Fuck work."

"But we've got so much to—"

He spanks my ass lightly. "No work talk while I'm making out with you."

"I'm technically on the job."

"Good thing I turned the closed sign around then."

I smile at him, and his eyes crinkle as he grins back at me. "Don't take all the credit, I left that amazing and detailed answer message."

"It's like you've been running the place for years," he tells me, warmth in his tone.

"We shouldn't be doing this, Knox," I whisper, as if someone will hear us. "You know how hard it'll be for us to stop."

"I don't want to stop. Don't tell me you're turning back already?"

I shake my head. "No, but working together will be a conflict eventually."

"So? We'll settle any arguments in bed."

"That's not exactly how relationships work. We're supposed to be getting to know one another."

"Fine, I'll tell you what to do, and you'll go behind my back and do what you want anyway. See, I already know all I need to know."

I smile at his accurateness. "I'd ask you first."

"Of course you would," he says with a sarcastic tone.

"I'm pretty good at organizing."

"No, you're excellent at organizing."

I can't help but feel that flutter in my stomach when our eyes meet. "Wait till you see how I filed everything in alphabetical order instead of shoving it all in the filing cabinet."

"A woman after my own heart."

When Knox kisses me, it's with his whole being. It's really the sweetest thing ever.

Until he throws me on the bed.

Climbing over me, he pulls my panties and my stockings all the way off, followed by my skirt.

"Are we really going to have sex all morning?" I giggle when he starts kissing me starting at my ankles, working his way upwards.

"No, we're fucking, there's a difference."

"Do you think we should address the elephant in the room?" I ask, squeezing my eyes shut as his mouth works its way north.

Seeing Knox over the top of me, completely naked, fondling himself as he kisses every inch of my body makes my skin tingle with want.

This man is like nobody else.

"What's that, baby? We've already established you can't work for me while I'm between your legs."

"Such a romantic."

He settles between my legs as I reach for him, cupping

his face as our lips meet.

"You were saying?"

"That whole thing, about you… putting a baby in me." I bite my lip as he grins.

"You think I was just saying that in the heat of the moment?"

"Weren't you?"

"Honestly? No."

I blink, thinking I'm mishearing. "You want to knock me up?"

"Eventually."

My eyes go wide as I sit up. "Knox?"

"I said eventually. And I know I should keep that shit to myself, but you should have seen how beautiful you looked bent over that desk with your skirt around your waist."

I know he's trying to be playful, make a joke out of it, but when he said that—and I made him repeat it—it got me off so badly. Even if it is a crazy notion. Not only do I barely know him, but we're running and jumping straight into the deep end.

"It's just… we don't know each other, not really."

"What's your point?" He starts to kiss my neck, spreading my bent knees wider.

"My point is, we've not even gone out on a date, and you want me to be the mother of your unborn child?"

"Children," he corrects. "But we can start off at one."

I slap him on the arm as he grins again. "Can you be serious?"

"I am being serious," he replies. "If you think that's too much, too soon, I respect that. So do I, if I'm being honest, but I can't help how I feel."

God. Hearing him say that, it makes something come alive in my core. I can't believe how much of a turn on that is.

"I've read about men like you." I point my finger at him.

"Men like me?" He bites my pulse point.

"Men who have breeding kinks."

He bursts out laughing. "Breeding kinks?"

"Don't laugh, it's a thing."

"Where did you read that?"

"In a dirty romance book."

"A very reliable source then." He chuckles again.

"Hey, don't knock dirty romance books. They're every man's best friend if he wants to know how to really please a woman."

He runs his tongue up my neck. "I think I've already mastered that goal."

"You're very sure of yourself."

"I know what my cock does to you."

I swallow hard. I can't argue there.

He starts to slowly make his way down my body, nipping, teasing, sucking. Taking one nipple into his mouth, he sucks gently, his hand lifting and squeezing my other breast. Still sitting with my knees spread wide, I rest back on my hands, giving him full access to my tits as he sucks one and then the other, making hot as fuck noises as he pays each one attention.

One hand snakes down my body to cup my pussy. He mutters something against my lips for a fraction of a second before moving farther down, nipping at my navel, swirling his tongue over my skin, taunting every muscle in my body until it's under his command.

He just came inside me, and he doesn't give a shit about putting his mouth between my legs.

I cry out as he starts to lick my folds, eating me out as I stare down at him, my knees closing as I resist the urge to come too quickly. He uses his hands to press my knees back out and holds them there, going in for the kill.

He sucks each of my lips until I'm quivering, laving every inch of me. Spreading my pussy with one hand, he starts licking my clit rapidly over and over until I'm squirming and wriggling beneath him. When I start to come, he sucks me into his mouth and inserts a finger inside me. My ass lifts off the bed as I rub myself on his face, and I swear I almost see God.

"Knox! Oh, Knox, oh, oh…" my orgasm goes on and on, and I grip the sheets with both hands as I throw my head back.

When I'm done, he looks up at me, and I need him

inside me now. Pulling him by his head, our mouths crash together once more as I taste both of us on his tongue.

He plunges into my mouth as he lays me back, and my hands sweep over his broad chest and biceps.

"Fuck me," I wail.

He grins. "Fuck me instead." He flips me over and pulls me onto his lap, my hair swinging loosely over one shoulder. "You want me to fill you with my cum again, baby?"

"Yes!" I groan, grasping him at the base, using his tip to pleasure myself as I rub his hard length through my folds. I'm so damn wet.

He sits back on the pillows and watches me fondle him and myself at the same time.

"Touch your tits," he tells me. "Wanna fuck them so bad."

I move one hand to my breast and touch myself, rubbing my erect nipple until he sits up and takes it into his mouth and sucks hard. I love it when he plays with my tits.

I rub up and down, enjoying how stiff his cock is, until I can't take it anymore, lifting up and sinking down on him.

He lets go of my nipple and hisses, both hands moving to my hips.

"You're so big," I groan as he starts to guide me back and forth, his eyes devouring me as he watches my expression. I've never been with a man so intense, not like this. He loves to watch me coming undone.

"You're so beautiful, Red. You like all my hot cum inside you, don't you?"

I close my eyes as we get into a maddening rhythm. "Yes, oh yes, I need it, Knox. Fill me."

I cannot believe how much I'm turned on by his dirty words, and I didn't know until this moment that the breeding kink thing is so hot when it's with him.

He starts to move me faster, lifting my hips this time up and down. "Ride my cock, squeeze that tight pussy, baby, milk my cum, all of it."

This fucking man!

I grind down on him, riding him hard as my tits bounce up and down. He sits up again, coming face to face with me, his hands still digging into my hips.

"Tell me, Red, tell me how much you want me to put a baby inside you."

I make a mewling noise that isn't of this world as I'm so close to erupting. "I want it, I want it so bad… oh, oh, yes, right there, right there…"

He starts to groan, his piercing blue eyes on mine the whole time as we fuck like maniacs.

Oh God, this is so good. I'm right on the edge.

"Barefoot and pregnant won't stop me, baby," he growls. "I'll still do everything I'm doing to you now. Ride it harder. Fuck me like you want my cum."

"Oh, oh!" I grind down, my clit hitting his pubic bone as I orgasm loudly, calling his name for the whole of Bracken Ridge to hear.

He comes too, grunting his release as he pumps me long and hard, his cum spilling out of me as he slowly stills when he's finally empty.

I fall against his chest, completely exhausted. He lies back down and brings me with him.

"That's so fucking hot, Knox," I pant.

"You like breeding kinks, praise, and degradation in bed, now that's fucking hot."

I snuggle into his shoulder, totally relaxed. "You're a bad influence."

"No, you are, coming in here in those tight little skirts, which by the way, are only now for my viewing pleasure."

I laugh. "Now you think you get to tell me what to wear?"

"Yeah, I didn't think so." He holds my chin so I look at him. "But know this, if any other man touches you, talks to you, or even looks your way, Bekah…"

I smile. "You're such a brute when you're all possessive."

"It's my job to keep you safe."

"I may remind you that we're not official, so technically, it isn't your job…"

"It's my job if you're gonna agree to be my woman."

I look up at him. "I want more than just sex, Knox. This

is wonderful, amazing, sexy, and all of those things, but I don't just want to have sex and nothing else. I want to get to know you. I don't even know basic things, like your favorite TV show or your favorite color."

"Modern Family and blue," he replies.

I do a double take. "Modern Family?"

"What did you think I was going to say?" His eyes dance with amusement.

"I don't know, maybe like the Sopranos or Yellowstone or something."

He snorts a laugh. "What's your favorite show? Please do not say Married at First Sight.

"Fine. Love Island."

"Tell me it's not true."

I laugh. "The Vampire Diaries."

He groans. "Seriously?"

"Have you seen the eye candy on that show?"

"So are you team Damon or team Stefan?"

"So you've watched it then?" I muse.

He rolls his eyes. "I haven't watched it, but I'm also not living under a rock."

"Team Damon, all the way."

He shakes his head. "You really are the bad girl."

"Says you, who just pulled my underwear down and my skirt up to fuck me in his office."

"It's your office now, so that means you have to wipe it."

I giggle, then I sober as we both fall into a comfortable silence. "I meant what I said, Knox. I've had my share of wild times in the past, but I mean it when I say I want more than that. I want to find someone to spend my life with. I know that's heavy when we haven't even gone on a first date, but I want to be upfront about that."

"Not as heavy as me admitting I want to knock you up."

I cup his face. "That was pretty hot."

Was it just a kink thing?

He answers my question by saying, "I meant what I said too. I've always wanted a family, a wife and kids. I almost gave up looking. Nobody ever came close until I met you, Bekah. And I plan on taking you out on that first date. Wherever you want to go, let's do it. I'll make it special, for both of us, because I haven't been on a first date in a long time."

I stir in his arms. "You're my first real date in ten years," I confess.

"For real?"

"For real."

"I'm sorry that some douchebag treated you bad, baby," he says, my heart melting. "You deserve everything your heart desires. Ever since I met you, I've had this protective thing for you that even I don't understand."

His words warm me right down to my toes.

I know I've never felt this way about anyone before.

I know falling for him is a bad idea this early on when we know nothing about one another aside from our attraction.

Still.

My heart melts.

I'm falling for him, in a big way.

My heart wants what it wants and everything about him screams come to me.

"To start the story, I should tell you… I grew up Amish," I say, hiding my face.

"What, really?"

I nod. "I ran away from home… that's a whole other story, to be honest."

He watches me carefully. "I would never have picked it."

"Kinda shocking, right?"

He smiles. "A little."

"My ex," I begin, then take a second to swallow hard, knowing that this is a hard limit for me. "He wasn't a good man. I met him when I was still with the Amish. He was with the English, which is what we call everyone else who isn't Amish, and we ran away together." Concern laces his face as I continue. "Things were good for a while, until I realized that the religion he did practice was… more like a cult… one that I almost didn't escape from. I went from one prison to another in some ways. Then he started to get physical…"

Knox sits up and pulls me closer to him. "He hit you?"

I nod.

"It was for my own good, he said, to get the bad demons out of me, which is ironic since he's the one who convinced me to leave home to be with him. I was so besotted with him, I couldn't see straight. I thought that's how relationships were. I'd seen how my father treated my mother… I didn't know any different."

"Bekah, I'm sorry. Where is he now?"

I shake my head. "Back in Idaho."

"And Brayden is his?"

I nod. "He never knew him. I didn't want Brayden growing up with those people. Their beliefs were just damned crazy. I knew that he would eventually hurt Brayden because he never wanted children and would often ramble about him being the devil's child."

He stares at me, and I shake my head. "I'm sorry if this is too much."

He cradles me to his chest. "It's never too much, baby. You can tell me anything."

"So, I ran. I never saw him again, though I know he was looking for me. Nobody leaves the circle. Not without good reason, and he believed that knowing all their intimate secrets and weird rituals would therefore put them in danger. He even talked about…"

He rubs my back, holding me tight. "Mass… suicide. They believe that Jesus is the second coming and he will be back to save us all, that sacrifices have to be made, in the name of our savior. I read up on it one day when I went to town. We weren't allowed internet or a telephone, so I had no way of talking to anybody outside the circle. He isolated me. Took me away from my family, who ironically were far safer to live with than him, and then brainwashed me. And for a while, it worked."

I know this is a lot for him, and I won't blame him for running.

"That's intense," he says. "Fuck me, mass suicide? How long were you with him for?"

"A little over a year." Tears well in my eyes. "I kept running because I truly believe that he would have tried to kill us eventually. You don't understand how fucking crazy he is, what he'll do to be 'saved.'"

"That's fucking nuts. I won't let anything happen to you, Bekah. You're safe with me. You'll always be safe with me."

I close my eyes, taking in his scent, his warmth.

"He had a possessiveness over me that also wasn't normal. It was obsessive. Sick. He wanted to go with me everywhere. Chose my clothes. He did my hair. He controlled every aspect of my life. And I let him, because I thought he loved me. I'd only ever seen my father beat my mother, so I had a warped sense of what love truly was."

He strokes my hair, letting me ramble. "But you got out,

you got away, Bekah. That's all that matters. And you did it all by yourself, with a child."

I nod. "I know. I should give myself more credit. But I've lived in fear for ten years. He came looking for me at my work one time. Somehow, he tracked me down. I came this close to running right into him, and it wasn't the first time."

"So you believe he's still looking for you?"

"I believe he won't quit. He's crazy. Since coming here, it's the only place I've ever felt safe," I say. "You don't know what that's like after ten years of hell."

"You're a survivor," Knox tells me. "You've come this far all by yourself, and you should be proud of that. You got away. And now you also have me, and the club. They're slowly becoming my family, too. Since coming here, I've learned about what family is really all about. It's taken me this long, thirty years, to understand it. To feel safe, as you say. To feel like you're finally home. My situation is nothing like yours, but I've never felt that I belonged anywhere."

"Same here. I think it's why I gravitated to you. I know you'd never let anything happen to me, and that's a lot to put on a person, especially one you don't know."

"That's a man's job, despite what all the feminists might say. What worries me more is I was rough with you, Bekah, the spanking…"

I turn and cup his face. "I like that," I whisper. "That

kind of punishment, it turns me on, but it's not done to hurt me, it's for pleasure. Something else I've never known because… when you're inside me, everything feels different. It's like we're connected. Like everything just fits. Like we've known each other forever.

"Maybe we have. I feel it. I fell in love with you the first night I saw you," Knox blurts out, surprising me. "I don't care how much of a sap I sound like. I knew then and there I wanted to be with you and get to know you. There was something about you that gripped at my heart. Then when we got together that night, I felt that spark inside me that I've not felt in a very long time. I couldn't stop thinking about you. I wanted to come to you, but I knew that I was risking everything, and I'd been hurt in the past…" He swallows hard. "I should've taken the chance."

I close my eyes. Wondering if this is all a dream and I may wake up from it soon.

"It's all right," I say. "And I feel the same way. When I'm with you… I can't describe it. It doesn't make me want to run, and that's something I have to get used to. Feeling safe."

"I will always keep you safe, Bekah. Always."

I know he means it.

To even be able to say that is such a sweet release, one I didn't think I was holding on to so tightly.

Am I finally home?

Is that ridiculous?

With a man I barely know, but feel so close to already?

So many emotions swell through me, but I push them aside.

I want to enjoy this moment before all my insecurities decide to invade my thoughts.

I want to bask in it, for just a while longer.

BRACKEN RIDGE
REBELS
ARIZONA
M · C

CHAPTER 20

KNOX

There're revelations, then there's… that.

Amish? And then she joined a cult, without knowing her ex was an obsessed stalker.

No wonder this woman is made of pure steel; she's had to be to stay alive.

Some confessions are hard to hear, but that takes the cake.

She ran from this man to protect herself and her unborn baby?

When I think about someone hurting her, anger shoots through my body, making me want to kill someone.

The fact she's scared of this man doesn't sit well with me.

He's the reason she's always been on the run, looking over her shoulder, moving from place to place. I shake my head at what she's been through.

"I've never told anyone, aside from my best friend Mallory," she tells me softly. "It's not exactly the kind of thing you go shouting about. People are already judgmental enough."

"It's pretty intense, babe. I can't say I've ever heard anything quite like that before."

"I was so young and naive. I'd never had a real boyfriend before," she goes on. "My world started and ended with him. And because he was religious, like I was, I didn't see any wrong in it. I didn't see his fanatical side until it was much too late."

"I thought my ex was bad."

"Not a crazy cult leader with obsessive tendencies?"

"Sadly no, she cheated on me, though."

"What? Wow, that woman must've been crazy."

I shrug. "I always had a tendency to pick the wrong women. Women who were emotionally detached or unavailable, I don't know why. Maybe a part of me wanted to fix them. Be the hero in their eyes. After a while, I just stopped trying. I used women for sex, as they did me, and I had no feelings at all." I rub a hand through my hair. "Then it all caught up with me. I guess when you hit thirty and you're still single, have lost your parents, and are starting from scratch in a completely different job, in a new town, shit kinda gets real quick."

"I think it's very brave, Knox," she whispers.

I kiss the top of her head. "I don't know about brave, baby, but I do know that nothing changes unless you make a change yourself. I wallowed around for a long time, thinking the world owed me. Wondering why I wasn't good enough, why I attracted the wrong women every damn time. But I never really looked inside myself, you know? It's a scary place. But as soon as I did, I got the truth. The real truth. I knew everything I wanted was there if I really wanted it. I just had to go get it. And that's what I'm doing, or trying to do."

"You must miss your mom."

I'm stunned she mentioned it. Everyone else skirts around it, pretending it didn't happen.

"Every day. But she'd be the first one to tell me to pick myself up off the ground, stop wallowing, and change it. She would've liked you, Bekah, a lot."

"She raised an amazing man," Bekah says, her eyes warm. "A good man with a big heart."

I smile. "That's always been my downfall."

"Having a big heart?"

"Yep. For those who don't deserve it. I'm a sucker. I gave second chances when I shouldn't have. My ex, she hurt me over and over, and I kept taking her back, knowing we'd never work. Not realizing I was worth so much more than that," I say. I never wanted to unload this on her, but we've all got baggage in some form or another. "Then one day, I just said no more."

"I'm so glad you did."

"That's the funny thing, when you stop taking less than you deserve, the whole world opens up."

She strokes my face. "That's so true. I knew when I left… him, that I'd been living under a black cloud for way too long. I was scared for my life, and I knew it was no way to bring a child into the world. So I ran."

I hold her tighter. "Bekah, you never have to run again, not if you don't want to. I know we don't know each other that well yet, but I know what I feel and it isn't just sex. It's so much more than that."

"I feel it too," she breathes, and I feel relief wash over me. "I really do."

Could I really be this lucky?

"I'm tired of chicks saying I'm a nice guy, but then think they can treat me like shit. I've never hurt a woman intentionally in my life. All the casual women I've been with, we both knew it was just sex." I know I don't have to explain myself, but I want to. "I've always wanted to settle down, but with the right person. Which is why I've been single for a long time. I just couldn't put any more effort in when it wasn't reciprocated. It was too taxing on my time and energy, and I was sick of cheaters and women who dicked me around."

"I have no idea where the hell you came from, Knox, but I'm glad no other woman snapped you up before I came along."

"You've no idea how that feels to hear that."

She snuggles into my shoulder. "What's your real name, Knox?"

I grunt a laugh. "You don't think my mama called me Knox?"

She shakes her head. "Nope."

"It's actually John."

"Get out?"

"Yup."

"You look more like a Knox than a John."

I squeeze her around the middle, and she squeals. "I look more like a man who wants more of your body, Red."

She slaps my hand away. "We should get some work done, before I finish my shift."

I grin into her skin. "I should give you a bonus, you suck cock real well, baby…"

She slaps my arm. "Sexual harassment in the workplace is a federal offense."

"So is looking that hot in a pencil skirt."

I want to lie like this forever and just be with her, in this soft bubble of bliss. But unfortunately, we do have to get back to work, and in a short time, Bekah has to go and collect Brayden from school.

I wish it didn't have to end, but at least I know where we both stand.

"You know you can always tell me anything," I reassure

her when we get dressed. "Don't feel that you can't. As long as it's not a guy hitting on you, then we're good."

She pads around the side of the bed, picking up her discarded clothes. "That's awfully decent of you."

"I know, quite gentlemanly of me, isn't it?"

"You're something else, Knox." She smiles softly, but I can see the hurt and pain in her eyes, and I want to take it all away.

I frown. "Is that good or bad?"

"Good," she insists. "But with that monster cock of yours, I can guarantee I won't be walking right tomorrow."

"You're still walking." I shrug. "Can't be that bad."

She pulls on her bra and clips it at the back, and then keeps hunting for her blouse. I don't go to help her, it's way more fun watching her fumble around half naked, not knowing her blouse is back in the office.

"If I call in sick tomorrow, at least I have an excuse."

"I won't be accepting excuses, Bekah." I grin. "Especially if you keep wearing those pencil skirts and see-through blouses. By the way, it's in the office."

Her skin flushes ever so slightly. It's cute how she blushes. "Would you mind?"

I smile. "Sure." Ducking out of the room and down the stairs to retrieve it for her.

I find it right where it landed and take the stairs two at a time. I watch as she dresses and ties her long, red locks into a ponytail, I come up behind her and pull her against me, her back to my front.

"Knox," she breathes as I kiss her neck gently.

"I can't stop touching you," I say against her skin. "What are you doing to me?"

"We need to get back downstairs. For real."

"Yes, ma'am."

I fasten my jeans and run a hand through my messy hair and tug on her hand as we reluctantly go back to work.

Just as I enter through the adjoining door from the house, Steel's coming through the front door of reception. I forgot I've given Hutch a key so they can come and dump supplies in reception until we need them.

Bekah and I freeze, like deer caught in headlights. It also doesn't hurt that I'm still tucking my shirt in.

I glance at Bekah, and I doubt Steel would know she had her hair in a bun this morning and now it's sweeping halfway down her back.

He frowns, glancing from Bekah to me, then I see the slight twitch to his mouth and his eyes begin to crinkle at the sides. I don't know if I'll ever see Steel smile, but this was pretty damn close.

"Everything okay?" I ask as Bekah quickly makes an exit into the lunchroom.

He comes toward the counter. "Fine," he grunts, then adds, "How long you been fuckin'?"

My eyes go wide as I look tentatively toward the lunchroom to see the door's closed. Thank fuck.

"Uh, it's not like that."

He grunts again, scratching his chin, and this time his lips curl up into a smile. Then he slaps me hard on the arm and says, "Proud of you. She's a fox. We can't hold the fact she's related to Colt against her."

"That's true, but yeah, let's just keep this between us," I mutter. I need to get him out of here before Bekah comes back. "What's up?"

"Boys are about to bring in the cement bags around the back. Once they've done that, the shed's gonna be full. Probably be a good idea to put some of the equipment in here for safe keepin'. Brock's managed to score furniture from a warehouse that's closing down, and he'll be sending you pictures to make sure it's what you want."

"Can you forward them to me?" a dark-haired woman asks, walking in the door and giving us both a smile.

"You must be Knox?" she goes on. "I'm Deanna, Hutch's daughter."

I hold my hand out. "Nice to meet you, Deanna. I hear you're going to be redecorating. I've seen some of your design ideas, they're great."

She gives me an even brighter smile. "How long have you—"

"Don't even think about it, D," Steel says sternly.

I frown.

"Shut up, Steel," she replies, giving him an eye roll. "I was going to say how long have you been in town?"

"Same difference," he grunts.

I clear my throat. "About a month, actually."

"That's funny, I haven't seen you around."

"I don't get out much," I reply.

"The rooms are that way." Steel points back the way she came in. "On the back of the property."

"Stop being a stick in the mud, Jay-Jay," she taunts. Clearly, these two have known each other a while.

I give him a side-eye. Jay-Jay? I muffle a laugh. Is that short for Jayson?

She's brave, I'll give her that.

Just as I'm about to excuse myself to make sure Bekah is okay, she comes through the lunchroom door and gives Deanna a small smile.

"You must be Rebekah?" Deanna practically throws herself into Bekah's arms.

Everyone sure is friendly around here.

"I am," she says, looking a little tentative."

"Colt has told us all so much about you. I'm Deanna, by the way."

"Nice to meet you," Bekah says.

I can't miss the slight blush coloring her cheeks after our mid-morning fuckfest. I try not to settle my eyes on her for too long, it's better that way.

"Why doesn't Bekah show me the rooms," Deanna goes on. "We can catch up and have a little girl time. You're coming to the barbecue on Saturday, right?" She links her arm through Bekah's, and Deanna leads her to the door.

When they're out of sight, Steel says, "Fuckin' women."

I chuckle. "Whirlwind Deanna?"

"You got it. Take one hell of a man to tame the beast. I was gonna say she'll corrupt your girl by the time they get back, but it looks like you've already taken care of that."

"I met her before I moved here," I say, not that I need to tell him shit, but for Bekah's sake, it's best I explain. I don't want him or anyone thinking she's easy, or available. "We met by chance and didn't know we'd both moved to the same town."

"That's a stroke of luck, if you like her, that is."

"I like her, a lot."

"Better not bring her to the club then," he muses.

I know why.

The Phoenix Fury was the same, and probably a lot worse. I saw women being treated like shit at the club. Smokey was one of the good guys, even if he would rip your tongue out for stepping out of line. He didn't tolerate the women being hurt or abused, it's where him and Tex butted heads. Tex didn't give a shit how he treated women. The shittier the better was his attitude.

"Not claiming her, if that's what you're saying."

He turns to me. "Why not?"

"For one, I'm not a member, and if I was, you'd make me a prospect. As a prospect, I'm not entitled to shit much less an ol' lady. Bekah ain't fair game." My blood begins to boil.

Steel gives me a brief look of satisfaction. "You're gonna fit in well around here, little brother," he says. It's the first time he's acknowledged he even has a brother, so that in and of itself is some kind of miracle. "And Colt won't let anyone get to her. Most of the brothers have ol' ladies anyway, and the ones that don't, well, you seem like you can put up a fight if you needed to."

I have no idea why this amuses him, but at least we're getting somewhere.

"If anyone even fucking looks at her, I'll make sure they're using a straw to drink out of for the next few months."

He gives me a squeeze on the shoulder. "The men of this club are protective, and I want you to get fuckin' serious, Knox. You can't really be in business with the Rebels and not be one of us. If not for yourself, do it for the club."

I flick my eyes to him. I don't even know what to say. "I thought you hated the idea?"

He shrugs. "You've proved you're not a pussy boy by

stickin' around when shit hit the fan. You could've walked away from this joint and sold it and ran. You didn't. You didn't take the easy road out, man's gotta respect that. You're in up to your eyeballs and now we're joinin' you in the chaos. You just gotta decide what it is you want. If it ain't with the club, then you better tell me now."

"Straight between the eyes," I mutter, not that I expect anything less.

"I want you in the club," he says. "We need members that are upstanding and wanna contribute. And with Bekah by your side, you could make a real go of it."

"You don't even know her," I reply. "Neither do I, to be fair."

"You think I knew shit when Sienna came to town? I didn't even wanna know her. She owned the clubhouse for a short time and refused to take our offer." He chuckles to himself at the memory. "Didn't think I wanted her either, but then I didn't like any of the other brothers lookin' or tryin' to get into her panties. Didn't know what the fuck that was all about. So I made the moves. Tested the waters. Turns out, she thought I was all right. Some shit went down, we got through it. Women are complicated, bro, that's all I know."

"Never met anyone like her before," I say, daring to believe I could even have a conversation like this with him. He's barely said two words to me. But between dogs and his ol' lady, I see a familiar pattern with him opening up. She must be a good woman, to wiggle her way into Steel's heart.

"Felt the same way. She got a kid, right?"

I nod. "Brayden, he's ten."

"You like kids?"

"Yeah, always wanted a big family."

"Not me," he goes on. "Happy with my ol' lady and my dogs. If Evie's lookin' for a friend, we've got rescues at Faux Paws that need good homes."

"Might take you up on that, though I'd need a dog with a bit of energy. Might coax Evie to get off her bean bag and actually want to go for a walk."

"Boxers are beautiful dogs," he goes on. "Come by the center if you're serious. Just shoot me a text."

"I don't know how you do it," I say. When he frowns, I elaborate. "Be around dogs that have been mistreated or abandoned like that."

He looks away. "Sometimes it's hard. With Lola, the way she was treated still haunts me. Even gettin' payback on the assholes that did that to her didn't make it better. It gave me a few moments of satisfaction, sure, but Lola had a life sentence. She didn't deserve it. They almost put her to sleep, but I knew she had a fightin' chance."

He's a good man. I feel it. I know it.

"What gets me is how forgiving they are, you know? Someone ran Evie over and left her for dead with broken bones that never healed properly. Who fucking does that?

And she still trusted me to take her in."

He shakes his head. "Humans are scumbags, that's all I know." He gives me a look. "I want an answer by Saturday, about joinin' the club, got me?"

I had no idea up until this point that Steel felt so strongly about it. I don't know why he's had this almost sudden change of heart. Maybe Sienna said something, then again, I didn't think ol' ladies had that much say-so within the club ranks. Judging by this club and how protective they are of their women, I tend to think pillow talk is alive and well.

I nod. "Got it."

"You gonna keep pen pushin' in here, or come out and do some real work with the rest of us?"

I hide my smile. "Lead the way."

He grunts again and stalks off toward the door.

I may never figure my brother out, but at least we have some common ground.

That's a miracle in itself.

BRACKEN RIDGE
REBELS
ARIZONA
M · C

CHAPTER 21

REBEKAH

The rest of the week flies by, and I'm amazed by Friday afternoon how much I actually got through. Knox has been so busy with the renovations that I've barely seen him.

Our sexcapade, as I like to call it, hasn't been repeated since because we've both been too busy.

It's a little hard to get together with him after work, since I have a child and not ready to introduce Knox into our lives until I figure this out.

I know that we had some major confessions, but I also know that it takes time to get to know someone. The last thing I want is Brayden getting close to Knox, and then we don't stay together or make it work. I have to be sure. I've put Brayden through so much. We've moved a lot, and he's never really gotten to know any kids in school for long periods of time. I don't want to ruin his chance of happiness if things go pear-shaped with Knox.

I suppose I'm also guarding my heart. I know I've fallen for him, and though I'm not purposely trying to distance myself, I need to clear my head about what I want and how much I'm willing to give up for it.

For me, love has always come with conditions. I'm not used to a man wanting nothing from me, just to be with me. I don't know why all of a sudden, I feel like I don't have to run anymore. This place. This town. The people in it. I feel like I'm finally home, like for once, something good is going right for me.

Then, Friday night, everything changes.

I get a call from Mallory. "Turn on the television," she tells me urgently.

I'm making dinner, a glass of wine on the counter as Brayden does his homework at the table.

"Why, what's going on?" I panic.

"Just do it. It's him, Peter."

My eyes go wide and my heart hammers in my chest as I move toward the living room and do as she says. I flick the channels until I get to the news.

My eyes go even rounder when I see the headline: Religious cult brought to its knees as leader is charged with multiple felonies.

"Oh God." I slap a hand over my mouth. "Mallory?"

I can hear what they're saying, that he's been arrested… one of the counts is attempted murder and holding a minor against their will as well as multiple other offences they reel off while my head spins.

"He's going away, babe," she says, her voice teetering on the side of tears. "You're finally free of him. They found enough illegal activity going on there to shut the motherfuckers down once and for all. He's not gonna pray his way out of this anytime soon."

I sit on the edge of the couch as Brayden calls out. "Mom? Are you okay?"

I swallow hard for a second. "I'm fine, honey, just helping Mallory with something."

I don't ever want my son knowing any of this, it's hard enough with what we've already been through together without him knowing his father is now a cult leader who is now going to be in jail. No good can come from that, not until he's older. Then I'll tell him the truth.

"I don't believe it," I whisper into the phone. "Is it finally over?"

"I think it is, Bekah, and I couldn't be happier for you. That bastard is finally getting what he deserves."

I've not watched the news in forever because it's too depressing, but I watch as the footage shows Peter being arrested at the compound and put into the back of a police car.

Everything finally caught up with him.

"So they'll shut the compound down?"

"They don't have to. It burned to the ground already."

I move my hand to my chest and hold it there like I'm trying to keep my heart in place. "They burned the evidence." I shake my head.

"Of course they did."

"What the fuck were these people into?" she whisper-shouts.

"Like it's so damn creepy."

"Tell me about it. Why do you think I left?" I whisper back. "I truly think the cult completely brainwashed people. They chose us at our lowest point and most vulnerable, like I was, and then exploited every one of us until they got what they wanted. Until you were so overpowered and isolated from anyone who cared about you, it was too late."

"They're completely nuts, baby girl. They're even saying that these monsters had connections to child trafficking!"

I pinch the bridge of my nose and close my eyes. "I should have reported them years ago," I whisper. "I didn't know anything about that. But I could have done more to make sure nobody else had to suffer like I did. There were others like me who were brainwashed and never got out."

"It's all right, Bekah. You did what you had to do for the sake of your child. Look at you now. You ran while seven months pregnant and got away. You did it all by yourself.

You should be proud of what you've done and how far you've come."

"I am," I say, feeling anything but. "I just hate to think that other innocent people, and children were hurt and in danger because of him. I can never make that right."

"He will have his comeuppance," she says matter-of-factly. "I may not be religious but that doesn't mean that I don't believe in karma, baby."

I let out a small laugh, running my hand over my face as tears fall. "I can't believe he's finally being brought to justice." Guilt washes over me. I could have done something, I should have…

"He is and so are the other leaders who they managed to also arrest before they fled. They will all have their day in court."

I calm up. "Court? Oh God, Mallory, what if… what if they want me to testify?"

"Calm down, nobody knows your name, you didn't list that bastard on Brayden's birth certificate. Nobody knows, and it'll stay that way. I'll take it to the grave."

I let out a sob. "Mallory, I can never repay you…" What my friend has done for me, I can't describe in words. She makes everything better.

"You don't ever have to, we're not just friends, Bekah, we're family. I told you I'm a piece of work when it comes to protecting the people I care about, and I mean it. You're free. You don't have to run anymore. Now I want to hear all about Knox."

I let out a long sigh, shuddering at the thought that I can finally be free of this dark cloud that's been hanging over me. That no matter what happens, it looks certain that Peter will spend a lot of time in jail.

"You know all there is to know," I say after a few moments of gathering myself. I literally told Mallory everything, including him bending me over the desk when we should have been working. "I told you everything."

"Hmm, well, I can't wait for the next episode. I live for your wild adventures with Mr. Hottie Pants. It's so diabolical that he's your boss now. I fucking love it!"

"I've gotta go," I say. "I need some time to let this all sink in."

"That's understandable, take all the time you need. I want to bring the girls up for a weekend soon, then we can catch up properly."

"I'd like that so much. Thank you, Mallory, for everything."

"We'll celebrate with a bottle of wine when I get there."

"I love everything you just said."

We click off, and I sit there for a few moments, a shudder running through my body as I take it all in.

I'm finally free?

I weep tears of joy, knowing I can't alert Brayden. One

day he will know the truth, but now isn't that day.

* * *

Knox pulls me to him and holds me close.

It's late, and when I told him the news over the phone, he insisted on coming over.

Brayden was in bed, and we will have to be quiet to not wake him up.

We just sit there, on the edge of my bed while he lets me sob quietly.

"You don't know what this means, what hold he had over me, Knox," I sputter.

He soothes my hair and kisses my forehead. "I know, baby, but if it means you no longer have to worry anymore or look over your shoulder, then this is a good thing. Let it out. I can't even imagine what you've been through."

I hold on to his shirt, and I do let it all out, until all my tears are gone.

"I don't even know where to begin," I go on. "I left so much behind when I left the church, and I didn't realize until I heard Mallory say he's in custody just how much of a hold he still had over me."

This isn't me. I'm a strong person. I don't take no shit, but when it comes to this particular subject, I turn to jelly. I'm not afraid of him, not anymore, but I was always afraid of what he could do to Brayden if he ever found us. I know his sinister plans would not have ended well for either one of us. One more look at the news before bed and I saw the charges were upgraded to manslaughter. I couldn't watch any more. I went to the bathroom and threw up.

"I'm here, baby. He can't hurt you anymore, you or Brayden."

"I feel so guilty, all of those innocent people he fooled," I cry. "They all thought he was a direct link to God, that he did everything for the church and the members, but all he did was lie, cheat and hurt people."

He kisses me again, running his strong, warm hands over my skin. "You have nothing to feel guilty about. You did what you had to do, it was survival, Bekah. You had to look out for your baby and that's what you did. You're a strong, amazing, beautiful woman. And you're safe." He tilts my chin so I'm forced to look at him. "You're safe, Bekah."

I close my eyes and shake my head. "Hold me, Knox, please," I beg.

He peels back the duvet and I crawl under it. Kicking his boots off, he climbs in, still wearing his jeans and t-shirt.

The fact he's not using this situation as a booty call just warms my heart all the more.

This man is too good to be true. I can't be this damn lucky.

He pulls me toward him, my back to his front, and he wraps his arms around me.

"Sleep, baby." He kisses the top of my head.

"What about Brayden, in the morning?"

"I'll be gone by the time he wakes up. I promise."

"I don't deserve this."

He tsks. "Don't ever say that, Bekah. You deserve every good goddamn thing coming your way, baby girl. You deserve so much better than me, that's the truth. But you never have to hide from me, never, do you understand?"

I nod, even if I don't feel like I can give myself completely over to him.

I'm in love with him. There's no two ways about it.

This is the man I was meant to meet and spend my life with.

I feel it in my bones, from my head down to my toes. He's the man I'm supposed to be with.

I've never been in love before, not like this. I've also never had a man treat me this way. Like I'm precious. Like I mean something to him. It makes my heart dance.

"Thank you for coming over," I whisper.

"I want you to come on the run with me tomorrow," he murmurs. "I want everyone knowing that you're mine, Bekah."

My eyes spring open. "The run?"

"On my motorcycle, with the boys and the other ol' ladies."

My heart kicks up a notch. "I… I can't, Knox."

"Why not? Are you afraid of riding?"

I shake my head.

"What then?" he goes on. "Brayden has that play date with Rawlings and her friends, right?"

"I can't just go and leave him."

"He's ten and Angel will be there. Please think about it. I have to let Steel know if I'm joining the Rebels. He wants an answer."

I swallow hard. "You're going to join them?"

"Would it be such a bad thing?"

"No," I say. "They seem great, if it's what you want, but don't do it to please them. They need to accept you as you are and respect your decision if you decide not to."

He squeezes me again. "Those are wise words, Red." The way he says it, makes my heart swell.

He murmurs something else, but I drift into a deep, peaceful slumber and forget about everything.

I wake with a jolt. It's still dark. It takes me a moment to realize where I am and who is wrapped around me. My heart races in my chest as I realize I was having a bad dream.

Knox's arms are wrapped around me, his body warm as he holds me close to him.

The heat radiating off him is like no other. He stayed

with me all night, just to hold me.

Not expecting or wanting anything, just for me to have a good night's sleep.

My heart warms and I snuggle back against him, my ass pressing into him, and I realize he's removed his jeans. I turn, without waking him, to find he still has his t-shirt on and his boxer briefs.

I stare at his face, his strong jaw, his perfect lips, the way his hair falls softly on his forehead as he sleeps soundly. I could get lost in all things Knox. As if sensing my invasion of his space, he stirs, his forehead creasing and his lips twitching as he mutters something in his sleep.

I trail a hand down his chest and then run it under his t-shirt, feeling his abs.

He may have had the best intentions by sleeping in his clothes and holding me all night, but that's only got me more aroused than ever.

I feel his six pack, his chest, and pecs and how hard they feel under my fingertips. He murmurs again, and I watch with fascination as he sleeps soundly while I touch him.

I move my hand farther down, trailing through the slight smattering of hair below his navel.

I glance down as I cup his cock, pleased that it's hard under my touch, and I fondle him through his boxers. Cupping him, he murmurs, and as I glance up, those fierce, intense, sexy as fuck eyes stare back at me.

Uh oh.

"Red?" he murmurs as I continue my exploration of his dick.

I slide my hand under the elastic and grip him harder. He hisses a I enjoy the feel of him growing in my hand with every stroke, knowing I can give him so much more.

One hand caresses my shoulder gently and the other he moves to my breast and squeezes.

The slightest touch on my body sends a shiver running through me. I want his hands on me.

Scrap that, I need his hands on me.

I reach down and pull my nightshirt up, my breasts bouncing free. He stares at them and groans as he feels one hard nipple and my eyes close.

I begin to pull on his cock, squeezing it in my palm as he dips his head and his mouth wraps around my nipple.

Cursing, my free hand runs through his hair as I jack him off.

I lift off the mattress for a second, pulling my top off as I throw it, and he moves his head to my other hard peak, moaning softly as he sucks and licks and my clit begins to throb.

"I love this cock," I whisper as he moves his hand under the waist band of my pajamas. I open my legs to give him better access and he groans harder when he feels how wet I am. "That's what you do to me, baby," I whisper. "Even in my sleep."

He moves his mouth to my other nipple, pulling softly with his teeth as I groan, needing friction so badly. He circles my clit, running his fingers through my wet folds as I move my hips, trying desperately to gain my release. When he inserts a finger, then two, I clamp down on him as I start to unravel, my orgasms hitting me hard and fast as I ride his fingers.

When I'm done, his lips move to mine and his tongue invades my mouth as we grasp one another, my hand squeezing his cock frantically and him spreading my slickness everywhere.

"I want to suck your cock," I tell him, rolling him onto his back as he grips my ass, tugging my pajamas off. I kick them off as I roll on top of him and then kneel between his legs as he bends them, touching himself as I move my mouth to his tip and start to lick and suck just the end.

"Fuck," he hisses. "Red…"

With him, I feel wild abandon, like I can do no wrong. I swirl my tongue, lapping up his precum, taking him farther into my mouth as he grips my head and starts to fuck my face.

Yes! My core is on fire as I bob my head up and down, hollowing out my cheeks as I suck like a woman possessed. He groans, and all of a sudden, I'm being yanked off him as he pulls me into his lap. Sitting up, he presses his forehead to mine.

"That's a very naughty thing to do, Red, waking me up to suck my cock like a dirty little bitch."

I wrap my arms around his neck as I start to kiss him, circling my legs around his waist as his large, swollen cock hangs heavily between us. My pussy is dripping for him. I need him inside me so bad.

"I'm so hot for you," I whisper. "I need your fat cock inside me, baby."

He groans, reaching between us to pull himself a couple of times. "Sit on it, Red, take all of it, ride me, baby."

He doesn't have to ask me twice. I use his shoulders for balance as he holds himself at the base and I slide down on him, taking his engorged shaft until it fills me all the way inside.

"Oh…" I cry softly. "Knox, oh yes."

"You like that, baby?"

I nod.

"You want my fat cock inside you, fucking that tight little hole, don't you?"

I quiver at his dirty talk as it sends a ripple through me. I start to pull up off him slowly, then sink down again as he hisses.

"My pussy is so wet for you," I whisper.

He moves his mouth to my tits as I arch my back, wanting as much in his mouth as he can take. He sucks my nipple harder, cupping the other one as he moves between the two, kissing and sucking hard on one nipple, then doing the same to the other as I start to ride him back and forth, my clit brushing his pubic bone as I watch him suck my tits like a starving man.

"Got my cock so hard," he mutters, in between sucks. "Gonna fill your pussy with my cum, Red. You're gonna take every fucking drop."

I muffle my cries in his hair as I come, jerking and moving my hips faster as my release takes hold and he clamps down on my nipple even harder.

Then, he grabs my hips and starts to move me up and down, faster, harder, thrusting up into me as my tits bounce in his face.

We're frantic as he digs his hands into my hips, slamming into me over and over as I rock against him, enjoying how full he makes me. The look on his face as he stares at me, pumping his cock in and out as beads of sweat roll down his forehead... Fuck, he's hot.

"Baby," I mutter. "Oh yes, oh God, Knox, right there, baby, right there…"

I let go, squirting all over him as he loses it, my name on a low growl as he spurts his hot cum inside me, jerking and pumping until he stills and every last drop is indeed inside me, and I flop down against him.

He pulls me down with him as he crashes into the

pillows, both breathing heavy, both not getting enough of each other as we lie there, catching our breath. And I fall asleep almost immediately, with him still inside me.

BRACKEN RIDGE
REBELS
ARIZONA
M · C

CHAPTER 22

KNOX

I stare at my woman while she crosses the lot, headed directly for me.

"When the fuck did this happen?" Hutch frowns, his head tipping my way.

"A while back," I reply, unable to take my eyes off her. "We met before we ran into one another here. Call it fate. I never thought I believed in any of that shit until I met her."

He chuckles. "Another one bites the dust."

He turns to Gears, his ol' lady Amelia on the back of his Harley. "Ain't that right, son?"

Gears snickers, patting Amelia's thigh. "Got it in one."

I was introduced earlier to the other members of the club. One thing about the Rebels that sticks out the most as I get to know them is exactly how close they are.

The Phoenix Fury was never like this. All I saw with that club, minus a couple of the good ones like Smokey and

Hoax, was destruction at its finest.

Nitro sits to my left. He was a part of Phoenix Fury long after my time as a prospect, so I didn't get to know him then, or Rubble. Somehow, it just reiterates that I was always meant to be part of a motorcycle club. I never kept in contact with any of them so I didn't know until recently in a passing comment from Hutch that they've formed a new club; the Sons of Phoenix Fury.

As I sit on my Harley and Bekah moves closer to me, everything just feels like it's sliding into place. Her agreeing to come on this run with me says something and it also sends a message to the other brothers. I may not be a patched member yet, but my girl is completely off-limits. As Steel said, most of the members already have ol' ladies, but that doesn't mean I trust any of them. Not yet anyway.

If I do become a patched member and I have to claim Bekah, then I'll have to see how she feels about that. After the ordeal that she's been through in the past with a crazed and possessive man in her life, I always want her to feel safe.

I may feel possessive over her to a degree, but I always want her to speak her mind. Be her own person, and do what she wants to do. I would never get in the way of that. I would never get in the way of her and Brayden because I see what they have and it's a very special bond between a mother and child.

Yet, I can't help that feeling inside of me, the feeling that something is missing. I may have scared Bekah a little bit with my talk of having kids and settling down, but I'm not here to play games, and if it's not something that she sees in her future, then it's best to know now. I would love to have those things with her, even if I've known her for what feels like five minutes, but sometimes you just know. Sometimes someone just walks into your life, and everything falls into place, and I haven't felt that before she came along. I've never felt that pull ever before.

As she reaches me, she has a tentative smile on her face which I reciprocate. She looks beautiful, as usual; her hair loose and hanging down her back, her skin a little flushed, and bright hazel eyes that sing to the very soul of me. She's dressed in jeans, thigh-high boots, a hoodie, with a leather jacket over the top.

My ultimate biker girl.

A smile slowly spreads across my face as I say, "Hey, baby, looking good."

She looks down at her boots and then her eyes meet mine again. "Finally got a chance to bust out the boots. This seemed like a perfect opportunity to dirty them up."

I pull her closer, kissing her rough, knowing the boys are watching, and grit out, "That's not all I'm gonna dirty up."

I feel a hand on my shoulder as I turn. "You must be Knox? I've heard all about you. I'm Kirsty, Hutch's wife."

An attractive, blonde-haired woman probably about mid-fifties greets me with a big smile and flicks her eyes to Bekah, amusement sparking there.

I give her a crooked smile as she assesses me. "Nice to meet you, Kirsty."

She claps her hands together. "You must be Bekah?"

Bekah nods as they shake hands, stretching over my body as I hold Bekah around the middle.

"Very nice to meet you," she replies.

Kirsty has an all-knowing smile when she asks, "How long have you guys been together? I thought you just got here."

"Uh, we knew each other back in Phoenix," I say, giving her a chin lift. "Bekah also works for me at the motel."

"So I've heard. Been hearing great things about what's going on over there. Deanna is very excited to start after Christmas."

"Will you stop jabbering, woman, and get on the back of this fuckin' sled." Hutch sighs, patting the space behind him.

She rolls her eyes. "Just hold up, baby. I'm getting to know the newbies."

"They're gonna be oldies by the time you're finished grilling them, for pity's sake."

She assesses me for a second. "You do look the same," she says softly. "Minus the hair."

"Please don't tell him that, Mama Bear," Gunner says, coming up behind her and slinging an arm around her neck. "Hutch, if you don't get this foxy woman on the back of your sled, she's goin' on mine."

Kirsty laughs as Gunner kisses her on the cheek. "Where's Lily, sweetie?"

"She had to work today. Ridin' solo unless I get any takers?" He waggles his eyebrows at Kirsty.

She shakes her head playfully as he helps her onto the back of Hutch's bike.

"Every fuckin' little asshole always tryin' to steal my woman," Hutch complains. "Give me some sugar, you damn fine sexy woman."

She leans over his shoulder, and they share an intimate kiss. I look away, and Bekah hides her smile as her eyes move to mine.

Colt and Cassidy roll up next to us. Colt smiles at Bekah. "You okay?"

She nods. "I'm good."

"See you at the Canyon." They take off ahead of us.

"You ready?" I ask, giving her a chin lift.

"Ready as I'll ever be."

I pass her the helmet and watch with delight as she places it on her head.

I start the engine and my baby roars to life. I love everything about this motorcycle. The soft curves of its sleek body, to the loud rumble of the engine between my legs. Riding has always been a passion of mine and having Bekah on the back makes me wanna go harder and faster.

She holds on to me as she climbs aboard and then wraps her arms around me without having to be told.

My dick stirs to life and I've no idea how I'm gonna make it on this run without wanting to pull over and have my way with her. There's nothing hotter than Bekah wrapped around me on my bike.

She texted me this morning, saying that Angel was happy to watch Brayden while she came on the run, and Angel would bring the kids to the barbecue.

I squeeze one of her hands as she presses her chest against my back, and we follow Hutch and the others out of the lot and onto the highway.

I've always loved Arizona. The rugged mountain ranges, the dips and valleys of the desert, the colors that flicker across the sky at sunset. It's magical. There is nothing about this beautiful place that I don't love.

The wind whips by our faces as we travel south on the 101. It looks like we're heading up to Shotgun Canyon, and even though the weather isn't great, this will probably be the last run before Christmas. It's freezing out, but I don't seem to notice, not with Bekah pressed against my body. The heat rolling between us feels like an inferno, a fire that could never be put out. And I know that I'm exactly where

I need to be. There's a certain sense of freedom out here. With nothing but you and the road ahead, the cool breeze hitting you in the face, reminding you that you're alive. Your heart pounding in your chest because this could very well be the best day you've ever lived. It is whenever she's by my side, she makes everything better.

I try to remember a time when I felt this happy, and nothing comes to mind. The last year especially has been one of the hardest; losing my mom, leaving the city and all I'd ever known, starting a new business that I knew nothing about, and finding out I had a brother and sister in a strange town that I've grown to love. I should be grateful that at least something good came out of Hank's lies and betrayal.

Steel asked me this morning if it was okay if his mom came to the barbecue to meet me. I've been very apprehensive about it. I know it wasn't my fault that Hank did what he did, but he's still my father, and I don't want her to hold any resentment toward me. I really don't know what to expect, but judging from what Steel said, she holds no malice toward me and genuinely wants to put a face to a name.

It was always going to be awkward, me being the child that nobody knew about. What really gets to me is the fact that he went between two women and that Lily is younger than me. He was still with both women continually and that just makes me sick to my stomach. What my mom put up with over the years, it just isn't fair. He didn't deserve her. Now she will never get to see me settle down, get married and have kids of my own. I think that's what tears me up the most, that life is so unfair and so short; we need to make the most of it. Nothing has been more apparent since I lost her. I'm well aware of time being something we just don't have enough of, and I came here to start a new life with no excuses. I want to be with Bekah. I know that I can make her happy and give her all the things that she wants, I will spend my life being the best man I can be for her. Some men may balk at the fact that she has a ten-year-old child, but I couldn't be happier. Seeing the joy in her eyes when she is around her son shows me just what kind of woman she is and how strong she's had to be. I admire her strength, her resilience. I would love nothing more than to be part of her and Brayden's life, if she'll let me.

I would love the chance to be a father to him if that's what she wanted, but I understand we have to take baby steps because she's probably not quite ready for that.

I'm ready to jump, but I know that Bekah is much more reserved. I'm willing to be patient, even if patience isn't my strongest virtue. I just hope she gives me a fighting chance.

When I see something I want, I'm like a bull at the gate. I can't wait to get out. I can't wait to make it mine.

And I want her.

I want her and everything in between.

She presses her hand to mine as we ride, and I feel her chin rest on my shoulder.

We fit.

We just fucking fit.

And I couldn't be happier that she came with me today. It tells me she's serious about us, about sending a message, and that's all I need to know. She may not be cut out for MC life; it's too early to call it. But I need to know how she would feel if I did join the Rebels.

It's kinda backwards, but I want her to be okay with it, and if she's not, then I'll reconsider.

The men of this club are all in. They're here because they want to be and choose to be. They love their club and their women, but I've always given a hundred percent to everything except myself, always putting others first. This is about Bekah and me, and I don't wanna blow it.

As much as I want to join the Rebels and stand alongside my brother and be a part of a brotherhood, they'd shrivel up if they thought that I'm having second thoughts or was putting a woman first, before the club. But I don't care about that.

They're the ones who asked me to join, not the other way round.

This is gonna be done my way, or I'll walk away.

Whenever she's ready to take the next step, I'm here.

As we pull up at the lookout, I kill the engine and Bekah

slides up and over the bike. I grin as she takes her helmet off. Handing it to me, I push her hair back and cup her face. "You look fuckin' windswept and edible," I tell her, unable to take my eyes or hand off her.

She presses up against my leg and my bike as I stay seated. I need her between my legs, my cock pressed up against her, enjoying her warmth as we take our time to just breathe and enjoy the view.

I pull her to me and press my lips against hers. My kiss is urgent and demanding and she opens her mouth as our tongues collide.

"How was that, baby?" I whisper, our foreheads touching.

"Amazing," she breathes. "I love it, Knox."

"Not as much as I love seeing you in my helmet with your ass on the back of my bike."

She bites down on her lip, and I almost convulse. I'm rock hard.

"That rumble," she whispers. "It hits every spot."

My smile turns into a slow grin as I kiss her again, grabbing a handful of her ass.

"I can't wait to hit every fuckin' spot of that tight little pussy," I murmur, fondling her ass as she rests her hands on my shoulders. "Just like I did last night, except this time, I'll lick all my cum out of you and make you do it all over again."

Her eyes go wide as her cheeks flush, and I grin.

"Knox!" she chastises.

I kiss her nose. "What?"

"That's so damn sexy."

I kiss her chastely, then she steps back as I climb off the bike. Taking her hand, we walk over to the barrier of the lookout and take in the spectacular view.

It's beautiful up here, time stops. The desert meets the sky. Yeah, there's wildlife all around and lush greenery, which shouldn't be here.

"Wow, it's beautiful," Bekah whispers.

"Not as beautiful as you," I murmur, my hands on her hips as she leans back against me.

I don't remember a time where I felt so at ease with everything around me. It's a new experience and I like it.

I also like how she makes me feel, and I hope I'm making her feel something in return, though by the look on her face, I'd say she's happy. She can't stop grinning.

The idea that I had something to do with a smile on her face makes me feel like king of the world. It makes me feel like I can do anything. With her by my side, I feel like I could rule the world.

"It's so peaceful," she says.

"Nothing for miles, except the echo of the mountain ranges and the canyon below. It's like the desert is kissing the sky," I reply. "Like nothing can get to us up here."

"Nothing can," she says, her voice full of confidence.

I could spend hours in her arms and just be there with her, breathing and saying nothing at all.

The ride wasn't just intimate. It felt like we were really transitioning, enjoying the silence on the long, dusty road. When I thought there was nothing greater than being on my Harley with her, that was an understatement. Everyone else mills around, checking out the view, taking photos, and watching the canyon flow below us.

"You got that right," I reply, giving her a kiss on the back of the head.

She is correct, nothing is ever going to get to her again, not where I'm concerned.

"Did you ever think that this would be us?" she asks out of nowhere. "After our first night together?"

"Hoped is a better word," I reply. "I should've hunted you down sooner."

"Well, everything worked out, just as it should," she reminds me. "Like everything was planned out for us. We just had to get over the first few hurdles."

"One of those hurdles is Brayden," I say in her ear.

She turns in my arms. "What do you mean?"

"Don't laugh at me, okay?"

She squints at me, just a little bit, then says, "I promise I won't laugh."

"You're already laughing," I say, bumping my hips with hers.

"Tell me." She pretends to button her lips.

"I feel like I should ask him permission to date his mom."

She stares at me for a moment, then blinks a few times.

"Are you serious?"

"Isn't it the right thing to do?"

She cups my face at one side, pulling my head toward her as our lips meet, and she mutters against them, "You are the sweetest man to ever walk the planet."

I grin into her kiss, enjoying the feel of her lips on mine.

"And what do you think he would say?" I laugh. "He may not approve."

"He may not."

"Kids do love me, though," I go on. "I have that knack of being able to be cool but not be annoying."

"So you're saying you're a natural?"

"Something like that."

"We could always see what he says." She can't hide her smile.

I kiss her again. "We could. I just hope he likes me."

"Who wouldn't like you?"

"Plenty of people, but more importantly, if he doesn't, then we've got a problem."

She places her hands over mine as I fold my arms around her. "Knox, it's going to be okay. Brayden's cool, he'll be fine with it. If you want to ask him, then that would be really sweet, but the main thing is, I don't want his life turned upside down if he bonds with you and things with us don't work out."

"I get that, but I don't plan on being an asshole."

"Well, that is a good start," she muses. "We just have to take it one day at a time."

"You mean slow down a bit?"

"We could go on that first date?"

"We could all go to the movies. Brayden likes the movies, right?"

She squeezes my hands. "There you go again, being all sweet. Brayden is invited to our first date?"

I like how her warm hands feel in mind. "If that's all right with you? Maybe if I'm a good boy, I can sneak his mama a kiss before curfew?"

She laughs. "If you play your cards right."

"Or I could sneak into your room later and eat your pussy until you're screaming for more."

"Now you've got a lot to live up to."

The moment is perfect, just like her. In my arms.

We spend a little time there, then when everyone starts complaining they're hungry, we jump back on the bikes and take off for the clubhouse.

Nothing could top this day.

And nothing could alert us to the fact our whole lives were about to turn upside down.

BRACKEN RIDGE
REBELS
ARIZONA
M · C

CHAPTER 23

REBEKAH

Colt swings an arm around me. "You seem to be fitting into club life," he muses.

We walk around the top of the cliff, away from the others.

"It's not so bad."

He smirks. "Would a certain someone have anything to do with that?" He nods behind me where Knox is talking to Cassidy and she's pointing at something.

I grin. "Maybe."

He shakes his head. "You always had that streak of bad ass in you, Bekah, even back when we were kids."

"Don't remind me."

"I will keep reminding you because it's funny remembering you being ticked off because you had to go back home, covered in dirt without your shoes."

I shake my head.

It isn't such an awful memory, it was worth the telling off. I'd do anything to be with my brothers and my two favorite cousins, even if it meant I got a hiding when I finally made it home.

"The good old days," I say. "Being with you and Eli in the field."

"Tell me about it. I wonder what he'd think about me being in a motorcycle club."

I give him a smile. "He'd be happy that you're happy, I know that much."

"I hope you're right," he sighs.

"I am right. I know it."

He squeezes me a little tighter. "Means the world to me that we found each other."

I lean my head against his shoulder. "Me too, I still can't believe it."

The ride home completes one of the best days I've had in a while. Not only did we get to explore Shotgun Canyon and look out at the magnificent scenery, but I felt such a deep connection to Knox that I've never felt before.

I've never really felt like I belonged anywhere and trusting people has been a major hurdle in my life. But with Knox, I don't feel afraid. I know that we've got a long way to go and a lot to learn about each other, but that will come.

I press my body into his back as we ride, resting my cheek against his warmth, feeling content and happy. The exhilaration of being on the back of his motorcycle is an experience I won't forget. The freedom. The air in my lungs. The sheer bliss of it all.

Nothing could beat this.

There's a deep sense of relief that flows right through me riding like this. It's like all the problems and cares of the world just melt away. It's like nothing can touch you.

I've fought so hard and now to think that I've finally turned a corner and can move on with my life without fear, it brings me joy like I never imagined.

We slowly approach the clubhouse and pull into the lot at the back. I truly never wanted it to end.

The fact I know he was making some sort of claim when I first arrived didn't go unnoticed. I know that's how they work; I've seen TV shows and know how loyal the women of the club are to their men, and vice-versa. The truth is, I didn't mind.

I want everyone to know that I'm his and he's mine, because I sure as shit don't want any other woman coming along to try their luck.

Knox is mine. John.

I live up to my name where the red-headed temper is concerned.

When we come to a stop, I take a few moments to really let it all sink in. Slowly, I climb off the bike and pull my helmet out, shaking out my hair, a smile on my face. He smiles back at me as he reaches over and plants a quick kiss on my lips. I'm so wired from riding and being pressed against him, I want to whisper that we need to get going so we can continue this in private, but just as I'm about to open my mouth, Angel comes running around the corner.

As soon as I see the look on her face, I know something is terribly wrong. She runs right into Brock, and he holds her by the shoulders, but she's looking directly at me. Her face is red and angry, and she's crying.

Brayden.

Oh my God.

Tears stream down her face, and she starts ranting hysterically, saying that he's gone, over and over, as she tries to reach me.

I shake my head. "No," I say softly. "No!"

"Babe!" Brock says, trying to keep her contained. "What the fuck, is it the kids? Calm the fuck down... talk to me..."

She shakes her head. "B-Brayden, they... they... they took him."

I try to walk toward her, but my feet don't move, in fact, I start to fall just as Knox catches me, holding me up against his body as I try to remember how to breathe.

Somebody took my baby?

I try to form words, but I can't. It's then I realize I'm going into a full-fledged panic attack.

Cassidy is the closest and she reaches for me as Knox holds me against him. I start to shake, but I feel hot, then nausea hits my stomach, and I feel like I'm going to pass out.

Everyone starts to crowd around, and I hear police sirens.

"My baby?" I cry out. "Angel… Angel… tell me…"

"I left Kelsey at the house…" she goes on. I've no idea who that is. "In case he came back, but Rawlings… she was playing out front when I heard her scream. By the time I ran out, I saw the van speed away…a blue van…" She slaps a hand over her mouth like that will stop the churning in my body, the racing of my heart, and ultimately the end of me if I don't get him back.

"Jesus fuck," I hear Knox mutter.

I start to sob, but nothing comes out. My brain won't work, it's gone into shut down mode, along with the rest of me. Cassidy and Knox steer me to the closest picnic table to sit me down as they both tell me to calm down and to breathe.

This can't be happening.

"I used to have them," Cassidy explains, but she sounds far away. "For a long time, we just have to help her ride it out until she's over the worst of it… could be ten, twenty minutes, just keep talking to her."

After that, I only hear parts of the commotion in rapid succession.

"I had to call the cops… they can set up perimeters…"

"…some kind of panic attack…"

"They can't be far. I'll call Linc and get him to hack into the cameras on Brock's house."

"Fuck that, let's start ridin' now. There's only one way in and one way out of town."

"Why would they take Brayden?"

"If there's no ransom, that ain't good."

"…I don't know, we'll have to take her to the E.R…"

"…he's ten, dark brown hair, hazel eyes, Caucasian, about five foot…"

"…was wearing a blue hoodie with jeans and sneakers and an Arizona Cardinals baseball cap…"

"Just give her some room to breathe… we can get some answers when she's recovered."

I put my head in my hands and listen to Cassidy and Knox. Little by little, I start to breathe normally and the pounding in my ears seems to dissipate.

"Bekah?" I hear Knox say as he crouches in front of me. "Are you okay?"

I barely nod, swallowing hard as Knox brings a bottle of water to my lips, and I take a sip.

"Brayden?" I stutter his name, unable to bring myself to believe it.

"We're gonna get him back, baby. We're gonna make sure nothing happens to him, I promise you."

I shake my head. "You can't know that, Knox, none of you can! This has to be him. He must have found us."

"He's locked up, baby, remember?"

I shake my head more firmly. "You don't understand how they work. He will never stop, Knox, he will never stop looking for us."

"Are you sure it's…"

"I know it. I know it in my bones. It's him!"

I hear more talking, Knox giving someone the information that he knows about Peter, then he turns to look down at me. A cop car rolls up into the lot and stops beside Knox's motorcycle.

I can't even look.

Knox holds my shoulders. "Bekah, we're gonna need to know everything. Your ex's name, the address for the compound, where you think they could be…"

"I'll tell you what I know," I whisper. "But we need to go look for him. He could be… he could be anywhere!"

I reach for Knox, holding on to the lapels of his jacket. "It's gonna be okay." He looks up to Cassidy. "Stay with her. I need to talk to Jenkins." He nods over to the cop making his way over here.

I jump up, but Knox turns as I start to wobble on my feet. "I need to talk to him," I say.

He nods. "Just wait here, all right?"

The cop is immediately swamped by Angel, Brock,

Hutch, Steel, and basically the rest of the club, and everyone starts raising their voices.

I stare at the ground, my head in my hands. "I need to get out of here," I mutter to myself.

"Maybe he went back to Angel's…"

"The other club members are at Angel and Brock's. Kelsey is there now, she's the babysitter. Axton is a club member, along with Patch and Dalton, they're all good guys. They'll keep watch in case he does come back." She rubs my back, and I don't know how I'm going to survive the next few seconds, let alone minutes that pass by that my baby is missing.

Angel finally reaches me, Brock holding on to her as she bends down. Her face is red and she's shaking. "I'm so sorry, Bekah… I could see them from my doorway. We don't… we don't ever have things like this happen here…"

I nod. "It's not your fault," I find myself saying. "It looks like my past has finally caught up to me." I can't stop the tears falling. "I don't know what I'm going to do without him. He's got to… he's got to be okay…"

She folds me into her arms and squeezes me tight. "I'm sorry…"

"I just want him back, Angel," I whisper. "I just want him back."

When she pulls back, the cop called Jenkins approaches and starts to take Angel's statement. He wants a photo of

Brayden and all his particulars. I pull out a picture of us taken about six months ago and hand it to him. He looks sympathetic as I try not to meet his gaze.

He asks me all kinds of uncomfortable questions about Peter, and I have to answer them, with Angel and Cassidy listening.

"You should really stay home. If this is personal, then you need to be there in case they try to contact you."

I nod, though I have no intention of doing that. "You don't know these people," I tell him. "They're fanatics. They may still have Peter in custody, but that doesn't mean his minions won't do the dirty work for him."

He nods, writing in his notepad. "We're setting up a perimeter check and stop point fifty miles out of town, and I've dispatched all the patrol cars we have and called for backup from Mesa and Phoenix. The highway may be vast, but there isn't a whole lot of places they can hide." He glances at Angel. "I'll need to talk to Rawlings. Brock said she saw everything."

Angel nods. "She's inside with Ginger. She's pretty upset."

"We should take this down to the precinct," he says.

Hutch comes to stand next to Angel. "You can question her here or not at all," he says. "Kid's been through enough. The longer it takes to get what you need, the longer it'll be to locate Brayden. Let's get this over with and we can all start lookin'."

"All right, but a squad car will go over to your house, Angel. They'll need to collect any evidence, as well as surveillance if we have it."

"We have a camera right at the front porch," she whispers. "I swear, I did all that I could."

Hutch folds her in his arms as she cries into his chest, and I sit there numbly.

I need to move.

I barely register as Hutch takes charge, barking orders at his members as another two police cars show up.

I think about all the canyons and desert out in the wilderness where they could take my son, and I shudder. I have to get the fuck out of here.

There will be no ransom.

This will be Peter's parting gift before he goes to jail.

I have to get my son back.

I stand. "I have to go," I say shakily, waving a hand at him.

Cassidy and Angel share a look, and I move past them. "I'll be in touch if there's any news," Jenkins says as I give him one last look.

My head hurts.

"Bekah?" Knox says when I start toward the front of the clubhouse. He jogs to catch up with me as the others all start making plans. Harleys roar and Steel and Brock take off like bats out of hell. Maybe I should've got a ride with them.

"I need to go find him. I'm not sitting around waiting for him to magically come home, Knox. I won't do it. I need to be out there, trying to find him."

"We'll find him, baby, the cops are setting up…"

I shake my head. "I want him back." The words barely come out. "You don't understand…"

He pulls me to him and holds me tight, his body warm as he presses into me.

"I wasn't kidding when I said I'm gonna show you what you mean to me, Red, but you gotta let us take charge of this. The cops can only do so much. They can set up checkpoints and put alerts out about an abduction, but that takes time. Steel and Brock are already on their way out of town, and we're waiting on a call back from Steel's contact Linc. He'll access the security footage from the street and hopefully we'll get a plate number."

That at least makes me feel a little better, if not by much. "If you're asking me to go home and wait and do nothing, you're messing with the wrong woman," I say, my tone cold and cut off. "I've lived through this hell, and I'm not gonna take this lying down, Knox."

I hold on to my purse, knowing that the gun will change my life if I use it and what will happen if the cops find out. I learned to shoot a gun a while back, wanting to protect myself if something should ever happen.

I vowed if anyone would come for me or my kid, I'd

kill them.

I can't believe they've tracked us down, and if I know anything, Peter's disciples are just as fucking crazy as he is, if not worse. It churns my stomach to think that he's out there… right now… probably gagged or tied up in the back of a van somewhere.

Oh, this anger is quickly spreading into rage.

"I'm not asking you to, I'm trying to reassure you." His eyes dance with so much worry, I have to look away. "This club, they're connected, and they're all gonna help."

Closing my eyes, I nod and say, "We need to go."

He cups my face. "It'll be quicker on the bike, but the prospects will bring my truck south, so when we find Brayden, it'll be more comfortable for him to travel back in."

My heart almost leaps out of my chest.

When we find Brayden.

I press my forehead against his shoulder and sob. It all comes out.

Every ounce of pain and heartache that I have held inside comes rushing out.

This is all they get.

I'm done.

I'll have no more tears for any of it.

They're going to pay and pay dearly.

I know it won't get my son back, and I'm wasting time when I could be out there looking for him. But I can't help it. I need to get this out so I can think straight.

Ten years of living like a fugitive because the police never took me seriously and the fact the group hadn't committed any crimes, so they couldn't be charged, it has my temper flaring.

Nothing happens with cops until somebody gets hurt. Exhibit A.

And it's my fault. I put my guard down.

I let Brayden go to Angel and Brock's, but I barely know them. If I hadn't been gallivanting around on the back of Knox's bike… he'd probably still be here.

Make no mistake.

I will shoot them dead if I find them before the cops or the Rebels do. I know what I have to do.

When they came to my town, pulling my son off the street, abducting him… there's no coming back from that.

I need to find him.

I need to tell him he's safe, that he's loved, and that I'm going to fix this.

And fix it, I will.

All bets are off.

I don't tell Knox about the gun.

He'll only try to convince me to not use it.

I can't believe that after having the best day of my life, I'm now looking at the asphalt over Knox's shoulder as we drive to God knows where to look for my abducted child.

None of it feels real.

None of it should be real.

I didn't even register half of what just happened because I feel so numb inside.

Any slight bit of hope eludes me as we keep travelling on the highway, every car that passes on the other side a potential suspect, but where the fuck do we even begin?

I clutch onto Knox like my life depends on it.

We stop at a gas station. I hop off the bike and run inside, asking the attendant if he's seen a blue van with a little boy of ten years old, four-foot-eight with light brown hair and brown eyes. The description of the car is scanty, but it's all we have.

"He had on navy sweats, a gray t-shirt and a light gray hoodie," I say, not wasting any time.

The attendant shakes their head, giving me a sympathetic look. I scribble down my number and tell him if anyone comes in to call me, or 911, or both.

I turn and Knox is right behind me. "Steel just phoned."

My eyes light up as he moves me outside to talk in private.

"He said Linc got a partial number plate, and his guy is running it through their system. Ohio number plates, baby.

You were right."

"Of course I'm right!" I say, pulling at my hair. "This man was domestically violent toward me. He got off on making my life hell, making me think that I was worth nothing, that he had all the power and I needed him, and I believed it, for years. If he or any of them get their hands on Brayden… Knox, I will fucking kill every last one of them."

"Calm down, baby girl. I know that's easy to say, but we have to keep it together. He also said he followed the car to the outskirts of town. He didn't see them leaving on the 101, so they're still in Bracken Ridge."

"Fuck!" I yell. "I'm going to go out of my goddamn mind!"

He grips my shoulder, his eyebrows knitting together. "We need to keep moving. We'll turn back."

"What if he's wrong?"

"He's not wrong. And in any case, Steel and Brock are ahead and the cops are setting up roadblocks. Missing kids around here won't go down well. Hutch was organizing a search party as we left. The whole town will be on board."

I nod. "I knew there was a reason I loved this town."

He cups my face. "Come on, we'll search everywhere until we find him, I promise. I won't rest until he's back in your arms."

I pull him to me as he looks down at me with concern. "I love you, Knox," I say out of nowhere. "I just wanted you to know that. In case… in case anything happens."

He stares at me with a look on his face that's a mixture of shock and bewilderment. "Baby, I love you too, so fucking much." He brings his lips to mine and kisses me like I'm going to break. It's not the usual kind of kiss I get from him, but right now, it could go either one way or the other. "And for the record, nothing is going to happen. You and Brayden are the two most important things to me. I loved you that first night and every night after. Nobody makes me feel how you do, Bekah. When this is over, we'll go somewhere, just us and Brayden and Evie. I'll fix this."

My eyes well up again with his sincerity. All I can do is nod as he kisses me on the forehead and grasps my hand, pulling me with him.

My heart races at our confessions. I know it's not just adrenaline. I love this man with all my heart and soul. And he loves me, and my kid.

We're coming, Brayden. Just hold on a while longer, I tell myself over and over.

I love you. Mom's coming. And Knox too.

We'll make this right.

We have to. We just have to.

BRACKEN RIDGE
REBELS
ARIZONA
M · C
M · C

CHAPTER 24

KNOX

Nothing could've prepared me for today's events. Seeing the worry and fear on Bekah's face was one of the scariest things I've ever experienced.

To think that this kind of thing could happen, that whoever took Brayden and had been watching him and Bekah, just makes me want to commit bloody murder.

I feel terrible for Angel, she was so distraught. I feel for Rawlings too, having to witness what happened and then relay it all the police. I can't even imagine what's going on in her head right now.

I know Bekah blames herself, but whoever snatched him knew what they were doing.

This is a small town where everybody knows everybody, and I'm sure from time to time, bad things do happen, but this is a little too convenient.

They were after Bekah, to hurt her, that was their sole

purpose, and in retaliation, they could hurt Brayden. Well, I'm not gonna let that happen.

The problem is knowing where to look. The one thing about this community is that everybody rallies together. And I know that right at this very moment, as we head back toward Bracken Ridge, that everyone will be out looking.

The concern and shock I saw on the other faces around the club made me realize that this club is so much more than a brotherhood. They are a family, and I want to be part of that family. Bekah has no family to speak of either, other than her cousin, and the look on his face told me he was all in.

I let out a slow breath. Bekah telling me that she loved me… that was probably the best thing I've ever heard. Hearing her say that…I could never love anyone else. From the moment I saw her in the bar, it's always been her. And having her wrapped around me, even in her fragile state, makes me want to burn everything down to the ground just for her. I will not hold back if anyone gets in my way. I will get her kid back.

We will find Brayden, and that's all there is to it.

As she clings to me, I can feel her shaking, and it's not from the bike.

When she had a panic attack, fear ran through me that she was in this much pain. There was nothing I could do to take it away. So keeping my promise to get her son back is what I can do to show her how much I care. How much I want us to be a family.

I know how much her son means to her; he's her world. Brayden is her entire life and I'm not gonna let someone take that away from her.

I meant everything that I said.

I want to be a dad.

If Brayden does accept me, then I'll work on it. We can take things slow. Not having a father figure in his life may be an adjustment for him, and to Bekah, and I don't want to overstep, though I do want to get to know both of them better.

I'm willing to do whatever it takes.

The adrenaline coursing through me could fuel a rocket. But I have to be calm for her. I have to be strong for her.

Losing my shit is exactly what we don't need. I need to save all that pent-up energy for when we find those fuckers.

When we drive back to main street, I can already see a commotion going on. There is a roadblock already set up in the street, people are passing around fliers, and that makes me realize that this whole fucking town is gonna be looking for him. This is what we need.

This is what true community is all about, and it's why I moved to a small town in the first place.

I'm sure I hear Bekah whisper or murmur something. I just pat her hands with one of mine, and keep riding through town, even though I don't know where the fuck I'm going.

The trouble is, I don't know where the fuck to even start looking. If they've been tracking Bekah for a while, then they'll know where she lives. So maybe it was a good idea for her to stay at home, not that I'll be able to keep her there, but the chances are the kidnappers may realize they can't get out of this mess or leave town, therefore, they may let Brayden go.

Another part of me shuts off to any other possibility.

"Where are we going?" she asks as we make our way through town.

"To your place. I think we just need to regroup. I'll call Steel and see if we have an update from Linc."

It only takes a few minutes before we arrive. Bekah takes off her helmet and waits for me to dismount.

"I don't see what being here will achieve," she says, shaking her head. "We need to be driving around, looking for the car."

I hold up a finger as my phone rings, it's Steel again.

"Linc got a lead," he says. Thank fuck for that.

"Out with it."

"Linc got a signal off a mobile device that he thinks belongs to the car. It went east off Regent Street and out to the road that leads to the old quarry. This was right after he got snatched. Thinkin' they got trapped in, with nowhere else to run. Why the fuck they didn't go for the highway, I don't know, but they clearly didn't plan on Bracken Ridge having state of the art surveillance."

Dread fills me.

The old quarry?

"Fuck," I say.

My eyes dart to Bekah as she tries to grab the phone. "What's he saying?" she cries, frustrated. "Have they found Brayden?"

I shake my head and instead I put the speaker phone on so she can hear. "Baby, they've got a trace on the car, so we're gonna head there now." Then to Steel, I say, "You're on speaker, we can be at the quarry in five minutes."

"The quarry?" she gasps. "Why would they…" She doesn't finish the sentence as she moves her hand to her face and cups her mouth and nose, letting out a strangled noise.

"Hutch, Colt, and the rest of the club are already headed that way. Didn't wanna involve the pigs, but Jenkins was still there with Rawlings. No doubt he'll be tailing them," Steel goes on.

"Isn't that a good thing?" Bekah blurts out. "We want the cops there… don't we?"

Steel grunts. "Sweetheart, when you snatch a kid or have any kind of unwarranted dealings with family of the club, you commit the ultimate sin. First rule is, you don't mess with women and kids. People have bled for less. We don't fuck around like the cops do."

Her eyes go round. "But I'm not family." She hugs herself, and my heart breaks all over again.

"Well, my brother is, and that means you are too, by association. You're his woman. That's how this club works. We act first and ask questions later, and we're gonna do everythin' we can to get your kid back. Me and Brock are headed back, and we'll be right behind you."

I pull her to me, cupping her face with one hand.

"Thanks, Steel, we're on our way." We hang up, and I tilt Bekah's face to mine. "Let's go, baby, we can't waste any time."

She nods, her face paling, but she manages to keep it together.

We hop on the bike, and I break several driving laws just getting across town.

Nobody goes out to the quarry anymore, not from what I've heard. Mining stopped some years back, though I've heard kids go out there to party and make noise where nobody can hear them. But it's a deserted mine pit, nothing more.

When we make it to the road that leads to the old quarry, I can feel Bekah's grip getting tighter on my jacket.

My heart races as I hear motorcycles right behind me in the distance. There is no greater sound in the world than the fucking cavalry arriving.

Having Steel call me his brother and say Bekah was family was a revelation.

I know I've been trying hard to keep in with the club, now we're business partners, but to hear him acknowledge me as his brother, it was like nothing else.

If I ever needed any reassurance of his loyalties, then that was it. Fuck knows with the club here to help find Brayden, there is no stone that will go unturned.

I turn to Bekah as we get to a gate that's flapping loosely in the wind. "You okay?" I ask.

She nods. "I just want to get there."

I toy with waiting for the others and going in alone, but I've got Bekah to think about, not just myself. I'm not even fucking armed, aside from a knife I keep in my saddle bag.

I've never liked the idea of carrying a gun, but now I wish I'd taken up target practise because I'd feel a whole lot better with a piece in my hand right about now.

I surge on, taking it slower over the dirt. I see fresh tire marks, and I know we're getting really fucking close.

The quarry is large, expansive, and pretty beat up. There is a vast, wide plain one way, and a huge dip with different levels leading down into a pit the other way.

Where the fuck is the car?

I scan around the area, not seeing anything in my immediate line of sight.

But there are plenty of places to hide out here.

Maybe they didn't head up here after all, maybe they took another detour. It isn't as if there are any cameras up in these neck of the woods.

Panic rushes through me as we ride through the narrow drive, dodging rocks and debris.

What the fuck am I missing?

Then, I see something move in my peripheral.

As I turn my head, I hear the gun go off, and I swerve instinctively as Bekah screams.

"Fuck," I cry. "They just shot at us!"

Then another shot goes off, and another. The bullet ricochets off the large boulder I'm heading toward as I pull my Harley behind it, thanking my lucky stars we've got somewhere to shelter.

"Holy shit," I mutter as Bekah hops off and I stand my bike up and try to peek around to where the car is parked. "They're fucked no matter which way you look at it. The boys are right behind us." I turn, but Bekah isn't there. "Bekah?"

She starts to run toward the car as I chase after her.

"Please!" she cries. "I'll give you anything you want!"

"Bekah, no!"

The gun goes off, and I duck as I keep running, then I realize that the gun going off is in Bekah's hands. She owns a fucking gun? Where the fuck did she stash that?

The car starts up, and I can make out two people in

the front.

"Brayden!" Bekah yells as I reach her, throwing my arms around her as she cries out.

"Mom!"

He's still alive. He's still fucking alive.

"I'll fucking kill you!" she screams as the car skids and takes off the way we just came, leaving a gust of sand in their wake as we come to a stop.

"Bekah, what the hell?"

"Brayden!" she stammers. "He's alive."

"Give me that fucking gun!"

"I'm going to need it when I shoot those bastards for taking my son," she tells me.

She puts the safety on and takes my hand as we run back to the bike. I climb on, and she follows behind.

"The gun, Bekah," I say again.

She grumbles then, albeit reluctantly, she hands me the piece.

"Could have fucking been killed," I say, taking off just as fast as Bekah wraps her arms around me and tells me to hurry.

The drive up here was steep and there are a lot of corners and plenty of areas to slide off the road. There's a reason nobody is supposed to be up here.

Then it hits me. They're not after a ransom, they're not even looking to get away with abducting Brayden and getting out of town. They came here to use the quarry, and I swallow hard at that realization.

This can't be happening.

I pick up speed, trying to gain some distance while every cell in my body is alight with the fact that Brayden is still alive. I've never been really religious, but I pray to God that this fucking ends well. He's right there, almost within reach.

Bekah's arms squeeze even tighter as I ride as fast as I can, speeding through the barrier we crossed earlier, rock and dirt spraying everywhere as we get closer.

I feel Bekah press her chin into my shoulder. I know she's on edge, she just shot a fucking gun.

Then I hear the rumble of straight pipes getting closer.

There ain't no sweeter sound.

I accelerate when we take the next corner, and then it all happens so fast. We watch the car skid sideways taking the corner too fast as it spins out of control, careering toward the edge, hitting the guard rail, then plunging over the barrier.

Bekah screams as the noise rings right through the trees, and I watch in horror as the car slides down the embankment.

A few moments later, we pull up and Bekah jumps off the bike, tears streaming down her face as she screams, "Brayden!"

I'm two seconds behind her as the car literally hangs

over the ridge, the front end pointing down toward the ground, the cliff so high that the ground is a mere speck in the distance.

"Fuck!" I yell, my boots skidding in the dirt as I move to the side of the vehicle. There's no way down the ledge to get close to the door or window to haul him out.

"Mom!" Brayden bangs his hands on the back window as Bekah cries out. She tries to reach for him, and puts her hands on the trunk, attempting to climb onto the back, but I stop her. The car is unbalanced, her additional weight will tip the car over the edge, and it's literally see-sawing like it could give way at any moment.

"Bekah, it'll tip over," I say, holding her by the wrist. She's impulsive and adrenaline is pumping through her right now.

"Baby! Are you all right?" she breathes, her hands covering her mouth as all the blood drains from her face. "Brayden? Talk to me!"

"I'm okay, Mom. Hurry!"

"Wait," I say when instinct takes over. "Brayden, don't move, stay right where you are, buddy." The car sways every time he moves and one slight movement any which way could have dire consequences.

Bekah looks at me frantically. "Knox?"

There's a crack in the glass from where the car hit the guard rail and it gives me an idea.

"He's gonna have to kick the spidered glass to get out,

baby," I say.

Tears roll down her face as she nods, realizing it's the only option.

"Brayden," I say as he peers at me through the window. "Gonna have to get you to very carefully and slowly kick the glass window out, okay?"

He nods. "Okay."

"Just go carefully," I warn again. "Slowly."

I glance to the driver's window and one of the men starts to rouse. The other one could be dead, but I can't quite tell at this point.

Bekah squeezes her eyes shut as I get as close as I can to the trunk.

Then Brayden's foot kicks the glass once, twice, and each time he does it, the car sways.

"Good boy," I tell him. "That's really great work, bud. I'm gonna try to peel back some of the shattered glass okay?"

"Okay, Knox."

He's so fucking brave. Pride swells in my chest as he watches me, his eyes big and round, his face dirty, with blood trickling down.

"He's hurt!" Bekah cries. "Baby, Mommy's right here, it's gonna be okay, baby."

All I can think about is getting him out before the car plummets down the side of the ridge and smashes into a million pieces. As I peel back the glass, some of it's shattered, some of it still attached and forming jagged edges. I don't want him to cut himself to smithereens, but he needs to reach for me.

"Take my hand, Brayden. Reach to me." I lean over the back of the trunk as Bekah pleads with him. Just as he does, one of the men moves in the front. I hear him swear, then he starts to try to get into the back, rocking the car, and it sways and groans in protest. My eyes go wide as the trunk starts to tip.

"Brayden!" Bekah screams.

"Jump to me, bud! Fucking jump. Now!" I yell.

He climbs up to the edge of the back window and jumps, landing in my arms just as the car careers down the cliff and smashes into the rocks as it bounces off the side, plummeting to the ground. An explosion sounds when it finally hits the ground.

I guess they got what was coming to them.

Silence follows for a moment as I hold Brayden and Bekah wraps her arms around him, crying.

The sound of straight pipes behind us doesn't even register.

He's alive.

He's safe.

That's all that matters.

The rest can wait.

BRACKEN RIDGE
REBELS
ARIZONA
M · C

CHAPTER 25

REBEKAH

Brayden clings to me, tears staining his face along with dried blood and dirt, but he's here, in my arms, and I'm never going to let him go.

"Brayden," I cry into his hair. "What happened? Tell me, baby. Are you all right? Where are you hurt?"

"I'm okay, Mom," he mumbles into my shoulder as I hold him tight.

I glance at Knox, standing close, watching us with an expression on his face I can't register. If I had to guess, I'd say it was a mixture of relief, surprise, and happiness, all rolled into one.

"I'm so glad you're okay," I whisper into his hair. "Did they hurt you?"

He shakes his head. "They said we were going for a ride to the pit…" He clings tighter as my heart breaks all over again. "Because that's where bad little boys go."

My eyes meet Knox's, and a cold shiver runs through me. He shakes his head once.

There is no need to put Brayden through any more trauma.

"You're not a bad little boy," I whisper, my voice close to breaking. "They were bad people, Bray, nothing about you is bad, baby."

"Why were they here, Mom?"

I don't want to lie to him, but I don't think he needs to hear the truth right now. He's been through enough.

"I'm still trying to work that out." I kiss the top of his head. "But nobody is ever going to hurt you again, do you hear me?"

He nods, wiping his face.

Knox places a hand on my shoulder as our eyes meet again.

"He's okay," I whisper.

Brayden turns to Knox. "Thanks... for getting me out."

Knox looks choked up as he says, "Anytime, bud."

The motorcycles all pull up two seconds later, Colt being the first one to reach us.

"Bekah? What the fuck?" He glances at me, and then reaches out to Brayden, cupping the side of his head. "Are you okay?"

"We're okay," I say, trying my hardest not to crack.

Then his eyes go wide as he peers over the side. "Guess

they got what they deserved."

Cop sirens sound. They're not far behind.

Colt wraps one arm around me, pulling me into his side.

"God, Colt, that was so scary." I'm still shaking, unable to really process the gravity of it all.

"You're both okay, that's all that matters." He kisses the top of my head, pulling Brayden into a hug as he holds us close.

Hutch, Bones, and two others, who I believe are Rubble and Gears walk towards us.

Hutch shakes his head as he processes the scene. "They got the fuckin' easy way out."

"The kid okay?" Bones gives me a chin lift.

I nod, unable to speak.

"Knox, what the hell happened?" Colt glares at him.

"They took the corner too fast as we chased them. Brayden only just got out before the car nose-dived off the cliff."

He winces. "You good?"

Knox nods, though he looks pale, and like he's only just registering what happened.

"It's over now," I interject. "I just want to go home."

"You okay, Knox?" Brayden waves his hand in front of Knox's face.

Everyone looks over to him as he takes a few deep breaths. "That was pretty intense."

"Do you need a hug?" Brayden asks him, and my heart swells.

Knox smiles. I know he wears his heart on his sleeve, which is one of the many things I love about him. He pulls Brayden into a one-armed hug and the sight of them embracing warms my heart even more. I could burst with how relieved I feel right at this moment. To have my child abducted, not knowing where he was.

He's here, I tell myself. We will get through this.

We can get through anything,

Thank you, I mouth to Knox. He has tears in his eyes when he smiles softly back at me.

Hutch comes to stand by me and Colt.

Looking down at me, he says, "Think we need to get Brayden checked out at the hospital."

I nod. "That's a good idea."

"Called Gunner. He's bringin' a cage so you can ride back together."

"A cage?"

"A car," Colt says. "I'll ride with you and Knox. What did Brayden say about the kidnappers? Who were they?"

I look over at my son as he and Knox talk, though I can't hear what they're saying.

"I don't know," I say softly. "But it had to do with my ex, I've no doubt about it. When he got arrested, I thought it was finally over." When he gives me a look, I realize I haven't told him the half of it. "Long story. I won't go into it now."

He nods. "All right."

"Did he… hurt Brayden?" Hutch presses. The concern on his face has me welling up again.

"Physically? He says they didn't. He wouldn't lie to me. The blood is from when the car crashed," I explain, my tone dropping. "They didn't come out here just for a joyride, though."

"I'll find out who did this," Colt tells me, his face grim. "And I'll cut anyone who was involved."

Hutch looks over my head to Colt. "We'll get to that, son. They're gonna pay, whoever they're associated with."

"A cult," I tell them. "I won't go into it here. Brayden knows nothing about his father, and I want to keep it that way, at least a while longer."

Hutch pats me on the shoulder. "You need anythin', sweetheart, you just gotta ask, you got me?"

I nod. "I'm… I'm afraid they'll try again."

"Over my dead body," Knox interrupts. "Nobody's gonna do nothin', Bekah, not anymore."

"He's got that right," Colt agrees. "You've got all of us now, Bekah, don't ever forget that."

I smile, trying not to lose it in front of them.

Being strong is something I've perfected over the years, but that eventually takes its toll.

"I appreciate that," I reply. "To all of you, for being here."

"Not like we did anythin'," Bones mutters, looking over the edge of the cliff. "Just glad they're down there and we're up here."

A few moments later, Steel and Brock arrive, followed by Gunner in a nice-looking SUV.

Knox cups my face as he moves toward me. "Let's go, baby."

They all watch me and Brayden, moving aside so we can pass. I've never been surrounded by people like this. Who care. Who want to protect us; it's foreign to me. I've also never felt the love I feel when Knox looks at me as I do right now.

Like we're his family.

What he did for Brayden... I shudder. Knox looks down at me, one arm around my shoulders, the other around Brayden.

"You okay to take my wheels back to the clubhouse?" Knox asks Gunner when he hands him the keys to the SUV.

"No problem."

Gunner gives me a chin lift. "You did good, Mama."

I shake my head. "It sure as heck doesn't feel like it," I admit.

"I'll let Angel and the girls know, they're beside themselves," he goes on. "Glad he's okay, Bekah."

"Thanks, Gunner."

Gunner gives him a brotherly pat on the back.

"We'll deal with the cops," Brock says. "They'll wanna speak to Brayden, but the priority is gettin' him checked out at the hospital. They can wait."

Knox drives, and Colt takes shotgun while me and Brayden sit in the back.

We pass the cop cars as I pull Brayden into my arms.

"I'm so sorry, baby," I whisper, kissing his head.

"It's okay, Mom," he whispers back.

I shake my head, a tear leaking from my eye. "It's not okay. None of this is okay, but I'm going to make it right. I promise."

To think what almost happened… Brayden was almost gone. I close my eyes.

When I open them again, Knox's eyes meet mine in the rear-view mirror.

I smile softly, unable to offer anything more. Without him, I don't know what I would have done, even though he won't see it that way. He thinks I'm brave, but next to him, I feel like a fraud. I should have been there. If I were a better mother…

No matter how I try, I keep coming back to that. When I glance at Knox again, he frowns and looks away. It's like he knows exactly what I'm thinking.

As we make our way down to the highway, I don't even absorb anything else, just Brayden in my arms and how grateful I am that he's here.

I wasn't lying to Hutch; I am worried about why they snatched my son and if they'll try again. Just because Peter is in custody doesn't mean he doesn't have connections. I know he does.

Exhibit A.

"What you thinkin', cuz?" Colt asks, snapping me out of my reverie.

I glance down at Brayden. He's fallen asleep in my arms. His soft breath is a warm comfort as I kiss his hair.

"All the things I shouldn't, like if I were a better mother…"

"Don't ever say that, Bekah," Knox bites back angrily. "Nobody loves their kid more than you do."

Colt turns to look at me. "You can't honestly believe that horseshit, Bek? None of this was your fault, don't you get that?"

I shrug. "I do to a degree, but I let my guard down. If I hadn't gone on that run…"

"Bekah, you've got to live your life, baby girl," Knox says. "Having one day of fun isn't letting your guard down. This is what normal people do; they don't live looking over their shoulder like you've been doing. All that changes now. All of it, you hear me? We'll make a plan."

I nod, feeling uncertain. I feel like this entire thing has just exasperated everything I've been working toward, including my mental health. I thought my son was dead.

It's such a helpless feeling, and I can't help but bathe in the guilt.

"Knox is right, Bek, you're used to doing everything yourself, not letting anyone help you out. I know what that feels like to a degree. I left my family too, remember, and I had nobody until I joined the club. I'm sorry this happened, but it doesn't mean that you have to feel unsafe. You have family here with me now, with Knox, with the club. You don't have to do this alone. We will protect you."

"Fucking right," Knox goes on. "One thing about being here with my brother and my sister and being around the club is that they've got your back, and so have I, baby. I know you think you can do this all alone, that you want to run because this scares you, hell, it scared the fuck out of me too, but understand my words when I say, nothing is ever gonna hurt you or Brayden again. I'll make sure of it."

"Thank you," I whisper. "It's a lot to get my head around. I just need some time."

"Take all the time you need," Knox replies. "But know we're here. A lot went on today, it's a lot to process. Just don't get lost in your own head when you don't need to."

I smile, knowing that the love and support I have all around me is what I've always wanted. A family of my own. A man to call my own, to make a life with and if it's in the plan; have more kids. I'm frightened of it, but also so happy that it seems it could be a possibility. I've always lived life on the run, never fully settling down, and I'm tired.

I don't have anything left in the tank.

The old me would run. Take off after Brayden gets the all-clear, look for another job in a new city, someplace nobody knows us. But there is always that fear he'd come find us again. And so, the cycle would begin.

No more.

That was the old me. I can't live in fear any longer. I have to trust in my faith and the people around me. I have to learn that not everybody wants something from me, that some of them actually want to help.

"I'll never be able to understand any of this," I say, my voice small. "But the only thing that matters right now is Brayden is safe. The rest we can deal with."

The next ten minutes that it takes to get to the emergency room, we travel in silence.

When we get inside and a doctor finally sees Brayden, he gives him the all-clear. Cleaning the cuts on his head and the grazing on his knees from the glass that shattered. Thank fuck he had his seat belt on, as it probably saved his life.

I turn away when he starts chatting to the doctor.

Knox is hovering in the doorway as I beckon him inside. He meets me halfway, folding me into a hug as I sigh.

"I'm so happy you're here," I tell him. "I don't want to run anymore, Knox."

He kisses the top of my head. "I know, baby, and you don't have to. The club is looking into who those guys were, as are the cops. Jenkins will need to still question Brayden shortly, get his statement, and we'll need to do the same."

I nod, looking up to him as he smiles down at me. "You're home, baby. I'm gonna protect you and Brayden. You're a strong and capable woman, Red, I can see that. But I want you to know that you can lean on me. I want to share the load. I'll be there for you and Brayden. I'll do whatever it takes to make you feel safe again."

I start to cry again. It's been one hell of an overwhelming day. "I thought I'd lost him," I whimper.

He kisses me on the forehead. "I know, but we didn't, he's here. He's safe. I'll keep saying it over and over until you understand. There's nothing I won't do." Then his lips twitch.

"What?" I frown.

"You with that fucking gun." He shakes his head.

"I have a license for it."

"Baby, that isn't the point. It cuts me to my very core to think that you've carried this around with you because you needed it for protection. I can't tell you what that does to me. As a man, it's my job to make you feel like you are safe, each and every day, that you have a home to go to where you can sleep at night and not feel like you have to lock all the doors and check security cameras and have a fucking gun under your pillow."

"Are you asking me to move in with you?"

His beautiful eyes stare down at me, giving me shivers that run all through my body. "Of course I want that. But if you think it's too soon…"

My lips meet his, and I kiss him with everything that I am. "I don't want to wait. I want you so damn much, Knox."

"I feel a 'but' coming on," he chuckles.

"Obviously, I want Brayden to feel comfortable, so if we have to take things slow… is that still okay, until he gets used to it?"

He smiles, his eyes crinkling at the sides in that way that I know and love so much.

He will always be the most handsome, gorgeous man I've ever laid eyes on. His heart is so big, and he has courage like I've never known.

"Of course it is, baby, anything you want." He kisses me softly again, muttering, "Anything you want."

They let Brayden out an hour or so later and we have to go give our statements to the police station. Aside from being extremely tired, Brayden seems in good spirits.

The rest of the motorcycle club showed up to make sure that Brayden was okay. Angel came with Rawlings, and we hugged. I told her that I didn't blame her; none of this was her fault, but I know that as a mother, it will probably haunt her for the rest of her life.

Knox brought Evie over to meet Brayden and to feed her, since it seems he won't leave my side so she'll be sleeping here.

"Oh, Mom, she's so cool!" Brayden cried when she licked his face and tried to curl up onto his lap.

"She's always been good with kids," Knox told us. "Very gentle with them, and she loves attention."

So that's what Brayden did for most of the night while he ate pizza on the couch, and I watched over him like a lioness.

Now she's taken up residence in Brayden's room, sprawled out on the floor near the bed as she makes cute little doggie noises in her sleep.

When I tuck Brayden into bed, he watches me as I move around the room, picking up his clothes and toys that he left from the day before.

"Mom?" He sounds so sleepy, yawning loudly when I turn.

"Yes, honey?"

"I'm gonna be okay," he says. "You don't have to worry."

I sit down on the side of his bed and stroke his hair. "I'm only worried about you, baby. If you want to talk about it…"

"I know those men had something to do with my dad, didn't they?"

I swallow hard. "Yes, baby, they did. He's not a good

man and neither were they. But I don't want you to feel unsafe or upset. I'm dealing with it and so is Knox. When you're better, I want you to tell me how you're really feeling. If we should stay here…"

"What?" he says, sitting up quickly as tears well in my eyes. "You mean, in Bracken Ridge?"

I nod. "Yes. I know this was a horrible ordeal for you, Bray, so if it's going to cause you to feel like you have to keep looking over your shoulder—"

"Mom, I don't feel like that. I promise. I love it here, and I really like Knox."

I smile down at him. "I'm glad, sweetie. How would you feel about Knox being around a little bit more?"

His eyes light up. "Like your boyfriend?"

I chuckle softly. "I guess so, though I think I'm a little old to be someone's girlfriend."

"You're not that old," he tells me. "And he really likes you."

"He does? You can tell?"

He nods. "Yup. It's so obvious. And he's kinda cool, in a badass kinda way."

"Don't say badass," I say, trying not to laugh. "He is a very kind man, and he cares a lot about us. He helped Mommy so much today…"

"Don't cry, Mom," he says, reaching for me when tears pool in my eyes again.

"It'll be okay."

I smile as I hold him tight. "You're always gonna be my strong little man, Bray. I love you so much."

"I love you too, Mom, but if it's okay…?" He pulls back as I look down at him. "I'd like to go to sleep now."

I laugh. "Of course it's okay." I kiss him again and he lies back down. I tuck him back in and switch out his lamp. "You know where I am if you need me."

He nods, closing his eyes as he falls asleep almost instantly. I don't know how long I lie there for, with him in my arms. But I see a shadow on the wall as Knox moves into the doorway.

"Baby?" he whispers. "Time to come to bed."

I turn my head and our eyes meet.

How long I've waited for this moment where I find the love of my life and he wants all the things that I do. I meant what I said, if we have to take things slow for Brayden's sake, then we will. But I want to be with Knox, now and forever.

I know it, like the air I breathe.

I stand and move toward him. His arm comes around me as we make our way to my room.

He keeps my bedroom door ajar as he starts to peel off his clothes. Turning to me, he nods down at my body. "Clothes off, time for a shower."

I nod, too exhausted to protest, even though I could just

climb into bed right now and sleep for a hundred years.

He moves past me, cupping my face softly as he does, kissing my lips chastely, and then I hear the taps in the shower turn on. When I shrug out of my clothes and make my way in after him, he's already in the shower, rubbing my fruity shower gel all over him.

I stand there, taking him in. His body is so beautiful. His muscles flexing as he moves his hands over his body. His abs are rippled and taut, his legs firm and strong, his cock hanging heavily between his legs is at half-mast.

"You gonna stand there and stare at it, or get in here with me?" He cocks a brow as my eyes meet his.

I smile, pushing my jeans and panties off as I step inside.

The warm spray feels so nice as we share the small space. "Turn around, I'll wash you," he says.

I do as he says, and he squirts my body wash into his hand as he starts to rub it all over my body.

"I love you so much, Bekah," he says. "I don't want you to ever doubt that."

"I know you do, Knox. I love you, too. I can't imagine my life without you in it."

His hands caress me, washing me as I let the warm water soothe away my aches and pains. His mouth comes to my neck, and I lean back into his body.

"I want you," I whisper.

He shakes his head. "Baby, I want you too, but I know how tired…"

"Shhh," I tell him. "I need to feel close to you."

He chuckles, shutting off the water and grabbing one of the towels slung over the shower door. He wraps me in it, pushing my wet hair off my face as he kisses me softly. "I want that too, but in your bed. I want to take my time and make love to you."

My heart fills with warmth as he lifts me out of the shower like I'm made of glass. He wraps a towel around his waist and sets about drying me as I let him.

I've never let a man take care of me and this feels nice.

When he's done, we move back into my room as he frees my towel, and when it drops to the ground, his towel follows. I climb into bed, my arms outstretched as he folds into them.

We kiss, tentatively at first, and then my hunger grows. I reach between his legs and cup his dick in my palm as he groans.

"Red," he murmurs. "Oh, baby."

"Make love to me, Knox," I whisper. "Make me come."

He moves over me, kissing my lips, my nose, my face, my neck. He moves his mouth down to my breasts and kisses those too. I spread my legs as he slips his hand down farther between my folds.

"So wet, baby."

"I always am for you."

He pushes his cock into my hand as I grasp him, needing him so much.

I move his tip to my entrance as his eyes don't leave mine.

When he sinks in slowly, we both groan.

"I'll never let you go, Bekah," he whispers, slowly pulling out as I wrap my legs around him, trying to get him deeper.

He pushes back in again, filling me so full that I sigh, relaxing into the soft pillows as he moves his hips and begins to pump me in and out, his rhythm slow, delicious and full of love.

"I love you, Knox," I whisper. "I'll love you forever."

He kisses me softly. "Right back at ya, baby."

Knox

BRACKEN RIDGE
REBELS
ARIZONA
M · C

EPILOGUE

REBEKAH

ONE YEAR LATER

I look up from the porch, smiling when I hear Brayden score a touchdown, and Knox lies flat on his back, holding his ribs. I laugh when Colt, Gunner, Rawlings, and three of Brayden's friends all high-five.

"How are we supposed to score at all with a useless line-backer?" Brock calls, clearly miffed he's on the losing team.

"Hey, who are you calling useless?" Angel yells back indignantly.

"You're not the line-backer, babe," Brock hollers back.

I'm used to these Sunday afternoon rituals on the back lawn, and Brayden's grown to love the club members, as well as make some new friends over the last year.

"He sure as heck idolizes Knox," Kirsty says beside me.

I give her a sideways glance. "Tell me about it, they have matching clothes."

She laughs, and I do too, shaking my head at the memory of them both wearing the same plaid shirts, jeans, and matching boots.

"He's good with him, all the kids love him," she goes on.

"He's a natural," I say, rubbing my swollen belly. I'm almost due. In a few weeks' time, I'll be giving birth, and I couldn't be happier.

"He sure is. My favorite thing about him is how he dotes on you." She smiles. Kirsty and I have gotten pretty close; she's like a mom to me. I've also grown quite close to Steel and Lily's mom, Helen. She and Knox met, and she was really amazing, considering all of the lies and betrayal involved in the making of the reunion.

"Oh, he's pretty good at that." As soon as I say it, Knox starts to jog over to us, giving Kirsty a wink as he drops down to his haunches and gives me a sweaty kiss.

"Brayden's killing it, baby girl. Did you see that last play?"

"Yes, I'm just waiting for someone to get hurt. Some of the boys don't understand it's supposed to be for the kids."

He kisses me chastely once more, placing his hands on my belly. "How is the little munchkin?"

"Active." I smile. "I think she's almost done cooking."

Knocking me up wasn't something we planned on right away, but Knox was thrilled when I announced that after three months of living together, I was pregnant.

The joy on his face is something I'll never forget. He and Brayden have been inseparable since we finally moved in.

I should have known the transition would be a smooth one, like everything involving Knox. He's everything I could ever want in a man and more.

When he said he'd protect us, he wasn't kidding.

After the kidnapping incident, Linc, Steel's informant, found out that the two guys who took Brayden were hired by Peter. The sickest thing of all is they were hit men.

Peter wanted to take the only thing in my life that gave me any joy. By taking Brayden, I can only assume he wanted to hurt me in a way that nothing else could.

That very notion kept me awake at night for a very long time.

He was charged and found guilty of several felonies and was sentenced to life in prison.

It took some time, but eventually, I had to let go. Of everything.

The past.

My ex and that whole situation.

The hold he had over me.

All of it.

When I came out from under the cloud, I saw more clearly.

Not everyone is out to get us. Not everyone is a bad person.

And it's taken me a long time to come to that understanding.

Now, with Knox by my side, I feel like nothing can touch us.

"She's feisty just like her mama," he goes on, rubbing my tummy in slow circles.

Knox hasn't been able to keep his hands off me. Up until recently, we've had a very active sex life while I've been pregnant.

He's obsessed with my body changing and growing. I couldn't have asked for a more attentive partner, and I know he's going to be a great dad.

We moved into a bigger house with a yard for Evie and Brayden to play in, leaving the apartment for the new management couple we hired six months ago. Kelsey helps out at the motel on the manager's days off.

It's been an amazing success. The rooms have been booked out and are turning over rapidly, especially with all the events like the Skywalk opening and the new monster truck speedway about ready to open for major events.

"I'm gonna grab a coffee, honey, do you want anything?" Kirsty asks, rising from the chair next to me.

"A peppermint tea would be great, thank you." I smile.

"You know," Knox says as soon as Kirsty is out of earshot, "I think we could cut this game short. Say you've got a headache, and I can make you forget all about your swollen feet and sore back."

I laugh. "I don't think even your oral skills could make me forget about that."

I haven't wanted sex this last month with being in too much pain, but that doesn't mean Knox hasn't been able to please me in other ways.

"Wanna bet?"

We kiss again as I wrap my arms around his neck. "So you know this kid is gonna give you hell right?"

He rubs his nose against mine. "One hundred percent. If she's anything like her Momma."

I shake my head. "That's not what I meant. I mean, men are always more protective over girls."

"No more than I will be over Brayden," he says, warming my heart. "But I get what you're saying, she's never gonna be allowed to date, if that's what you mean."

This man makes me laugh every day.

"Is that right?"

He nods. "But you're forgetting the best part."

I frown. "And that is?"

He leans to my ear. "I'll be able to put another one inside you pretty soon after."

I chuckle. "Yeah, no sex post-partum for four to six weeks," I remind him.

His eyes go wide. "You're fucking kidding me?"

I shake my head, though I know we've had this discussion before, he's living in denial. "But there is no downtime for those back and foot rubs, and for getting dinner and Brayden organized."

He smiles. "Whatever makes my baby happy."

"You make me happy."

We kiss again. He squeezes one breast softly. "These are so fuckin' huge," he murmurs. "Turns me rock hard seeing your body like this."

I bite down on my lip. "You mean fat?"

He shakes his head. "You're so beautiful, Red. I can't wait to be a father, and you've given that to me."

I pull him closer, so our foreheads are touching. "You've given me everything I ever wanted," I whisper. "It's only fair. Plus, you know I've always wanted more kids."

He smiles. "Plenty more where this one came from." He pats my stomach as his smile turns into a grin.

"I love you."

"I love you more."

"Not possible."

He lifts my chin. "Nothing will ever be more important than my family, baby. My compass points to wherever you are."

I cup his face. "My compass is you, Knox. It always will be."

Warmth fills me as his eyes shine in delight. He will always have the ability to send me to my knees with that one look. "Promise?"

"I promise."

The day I accepted that I had a family, that I didn't have to run, was the day I finally broke free.

My future is right now.

And I won't waste a single second.

HNOH
SIH MONTHS LATER

I cradle my daughter in my arms.

Harper Eve Steelman is six months old today, and she's absolutely perfect.

Nothing gave me greater joy than to witness her birth and every moment after that. The respect I have for Bekah could fly around the earth a hundred times. I can't believe what women go through. It's definitely given me a new perspective and a lot more appreciation for the female body and all that they endure.

Bekah is absolutely amazing. She's the rock of this family.

Every day I spend with her, the more I fall in love.

We were married in a private ceremony at the clubhouse just after the baby was born.

I wanted so much for Rebekah to have my name and be

my wife.

Nothing has brought me more joy than seeing her happy.

And she's such a great mom.

Brayden dotes on Harper too, it's so sweet. He loves having a little sister and I can see how protective he is of her already.

I got patched in a few months after Brayden's kidnapping. Steel and I get along well now, and I've even helped him restore a couple of cars, or rather, he grunts and tells me what to do. But we've bonded over the last year. He's a good guy. We're alike in so many ways, even if he still is the grumpiest son of a gun I've ever met.

Lily and I are close. She's a wonderful young woman, and I'm so proud of what she's achieved with her business and her life. She's good for Gunner, and I'm glad to see her happy.

As I look down the table, set up for Sunday dinner, I feel a sense of peace wash over me.

Kirsty, Angel, and Bekah are in the kitchen, and Brayden, Colt, and Cassidy sit to my left, followed by Steel, Sienna, and Helen. To my right are Hutch, Deanna, Brock, Rawlings, and Ethan Wolf, who is trying to climb on the table. Gunner and Lily, along with the kids table are at the end.

My family.

Earlier, when I caught up with Helen, she held Harper and had tears in her eyes.

"How can any of this be wrong?" She'd smiled up at me. "Everything is as it's supposed to be, Knox. I'm so happy for you and Bekah and Brayden."

I smiled, giving her a hug as I watched her rock my baby in her arms.

There's nothing but love here. She's always accepted me, even though she had every reason to not want me in her life period. I get that some things are just too hard to deal with.

But when I glance down the table, at everyone enjoying dinner in my house, it's everything I could have ever asked for and more.

"Dad?" Brayden says, throwing his arms around my neck from behind.

He asked if he could call me Dad when Harper was born, and I couldn't have been happier to hear him say it. I love him so much, like he's my own. We instantly connected, and I'm thankful for the opportunity to be a dad to him.

Nothing has given me greater pleasure than watching him grow and settle into his new school and make new friends. He's such an easy-going kid, which makes life a lot easier.

"Yeah, buddy?"

"Mom said she needs to feed Harper before she sits down."

I reach back and ruffle his hair. "Okay. Did you wash up?"

He nods. "Yup. Hey, can I sit in your seat until you get back?"

"Sure, but don't steal all the mash potatoes, you know those are my favorite."

He grins as we switch places and go toward the kitchen where all the women are making a fuss.

"Baby?" I say, as Bekah turns her head.

"Ooh, thanks, babe, I need to feed her before dinner's served."

I can do most things for the baby, but I can't do that.

I kiss Harper on the head as she starts to wake. She's a good baby. She sleeps well and has the most beautiful eyes, just like her mama.

I pass her over, and Kirsty gives my arm a squeeze as she passes me by. I follow Bekah out to the den.

I watch my wife and wonder how the fuck she does it all. All I do is show up.

Sure, I help around the house and do all the outside jobs as well as go to work, but Bekah brought a baby into the world. And she's never been more beautiful.

"Why are you looking at me like that?" she muses.

My eyes meet hers. "I'm just thinking about how

beautiful you are right now."

She smiles. "Someone's trying to get lucky tonight."

I shake my head. "The thought never occurred to me."

"Riiiiight."

I grin. "Bekah, it's not my fault your body drives me insane."

"You're the only one who thinks so. My boobs hurt all the time, my thighs are thicker than they were before, and I've got stretch marks all over me."

"You're so fucking sexy, too," I tell her, stroking Harper's face as she feeds. "I love every one of those stretch marks, baby. I'm gonna kiss every last one of them tonight, just to remind you."

"You are still the sweetest man I know," she says, her eyes sparkling at me.

I'm so lucky to have everything I want and to have it with her.

"Well, you're stuck with me now, sweetheart. For better or worse." I lean over and kiss her.

"I wouldn't want it any other way," she replies as I cup her face.

"Dinner is served…" Angel announces. When she sees us kissing, she adds, "You two keep that up, Bekah will be knocked up again in no time."

"That's the plan," I mutter as Bekah gasps and slaps me on the arm.

"If Brock had his way, I'd have five more kids by now."
She rolls her eyes as she takes off back into the kitchen.

"You hungry, babe?" Bekah asks, switching Harper to
the other side.

"For you? Always."

"Your mind is always in the gutter, isn't it?"

"I'm just making up for lost time, post-partum."

She laughs. "Well, watching you touch yourself and
come all over me was a sight I won't forget in a hurry."

"Couldn't help it, you turn me the fuck on."

"I love you. Did I tell you that today?"

"Not as much as I love you, Red."

"Oh, Red will come out tonight, when the kids are
asleep." She grins at me.

"I better be on my best behavior then, right?"

She shakes her head. "Nah, the badder the better."

She finishes up with Harper and I go to wash my hands.
When she comes back through the kitchen, I pinch her on
the ass as she squeals.

"Eww, Dad, gross," Brayden says, opening a can of
soda behind us.

"Didn't see you there, son," I reply as he rolls his
eyes at us. "I can't help it if your mama's ass is perfect for
grabbing hold of."

"Mom, Dad said ass!" Of course, his voice carries
across the room, making everyone laugh.

"You two are like a couple of teenagers," Kirsty says, giving me a sly grin.

"You've no idea," I reply, giving her a wink.

"I remember when Kirsty and I first met," Hutch begins. "And I can honestly say the drive I had back then is still alive and well, if not more."

"Oh God, no," Deanna moans. "Dad, nobody wants to hear about you and Mom's… adventures." She glances around to make sure the kids aren't listening.

"One day, you'll find a man who'll knock you off your feet," he tells her, giving her mom a wink. "And I'll pat the man on the back for takin' you off my hands."

She rolls her eyes. "Very funny."

I chuckle and turn to Bekah as she sits beside me, still holding Harper.

She's never looked more beautiful.

"Is this how you imagined family life would be?" I whisper to her as I glance down the table at everyone mingling, helping themselves to the amazing food the women prepared.

She smiles. "It's even better, Knox."

I smile back, leaning over as we kiss. "I think so too."

I've never felt anything more than I do right at this moment.

Family.

It can come in the most unconventional of ways, but at

the end of the day, all that matters is loyalty and love.

And I have that.

I have that and so much more.

It makes me the luckiest man on the planet.

THE END

ACKNOWLEDGMENTS

Thank you to my fabulous Alpha reader Michelle and Beta readers Alana and Kate for all that you do and for all your help making me a better writer.

Thank you, Kiki, for proofreading and making sure I don't sound dumb!

Hugs and so much appreciation for Alana @ thenovelassistant for being the best PA, listening to me cry, complain, jump up and down, keep me organized and do all that amazing stuff that I don't get time for like my newsletter, FB group posts, website management and plot ideas…we've got so much to look forward to!

To my sister D, thank you for reading and being in my corner.

Thank you to Savannah @ PeachyKeen author services for my blog tours and amazing graphics!

Hugs to my editor Mackenzie @nicegirlnaughtyedits for all that you do and for not getting cross at me when I use the same word fifty thousand times.

Kudos to Kelly Jean for naming Knox in my FB group poll – so thankful! I freaking love it!

Much appreciated to blogger ARC's who signed up to read and my existing ARC team who keep wanting more,

I'm so grateful!

Thanks once again for all my blogger friends, fellow authors, and all the amazing people on my journey. I'm so grateful for your support – I couldn't do this without you.

Thanks LJ from Mayhem Cover Creations for the cover design.

Thank you Eric Battershell Photography for this smokin' pic of John – he is the perfect Knox.

A huge, big hug to all my readers who continue to support me – I love you guys!

If you can spare the time to leave a review on GR and/or Amazon if you loved Knox or any of my books that would be greatly appreciated and helps me so much as an indie author. Links are on the following pages.

I can't wait to bring you the final book in the series – Hutch – the club Prez, book 11. This will be a shorter story and more of a novella but don't be worried, it will be filled with all the usual mayhem you are used to and a wrap up for the Bracken Ridge Rebels. And there will be an intro at the back to Cash and Deanna's story, which will be coming in June this year! I'm so pumped for their story!

Be sure to check out my private Facebook group (links below) as I update this page regularly before anything gets released on other social media channels.

Love from Australia, MF xx

FIND ME AT

Facebook: https://www.facebook.com/mackenzy.
foxauthor.5
Instagram: https://www.instagram.com/mackenzyfoxbooks/
Tiktok: https://www.tiktok.com/@mackenzyfoxauthor
Linktree: https://linktr.ee/mackenzyfox
Goodreads: https://bit.ly/2TKp7ck
https://books2read.com/Steel-BRR
Website: https://mackenzyfox.com

Join my private Facebook group for all the juicy gossip, giveaways and spicy reveals first at The Den - A Mackenzy Fox Reader Group - https://bit.ly/3dgQfKk

ABOUT THE AUTHOR

Mackenzy Fox is an author of contemporary, romantic and erotic themed romance novels. When she's not writing she loves vegan cooking, walking her beloved pooch's, reading books and is an expert on online shopping.

She's slightly obsessed with drinking tea, testing bubbly Moscato, watching home decorating shows and has a black belt in origami. She strives to live a quiet and introverted life in Western Australia's North West with her hubby, twin sister and her dogs.

ALSO BY MACKENZY FOX

Bracken Ridge Rebels MC:
Steel
Gunner
Brock
Colt
Rubble
Bones
Axton
Nitro
Gears
Knox

Medici Mafia:
Fortress of the King
Fortress of the Queen
Fortress of the Heart
Fortress of the Soul
Fortress of the Damned
Fortress of the Brave

Bad Boys of New York:
Jaxon

Standalone:
Broken Wings

www.ingramcontent.com/pod-product-compliance
Lightning Source LLC
Chambersburg PA
CBHW030950190726
48285CB00004BB/1291